Praise for Martin Cruz Smith

'Cruz Smith not only constructs grittily realistic plots, he also has a gift for characterisation of which most thriller writers can only dream'
Mail on Sunday

'Cruz Smith writes extraordinarily well in a genre not usually considered literature ... [He] is not merely our best writer of suspense, but one of our best writers, period'
New York Times

'When Cruz Smith is at his best, it is impossible to tell how much is research and how much imagination ... he moves into the realm of high adventure, alongside such writers as John Buchan, Hammond Innes, the great Lionel Davidson and Geoffrey Household'
Guardian

'Smith's strength is his ability to conjure atmosphere'
Daily Mirror

'Cruz Smith understands p........................g your research on your sleev.......................d virtues. In sl.........
Ind...

MARTIN CRUZ SMITH

AN ARKADY RENKO NOVEL

TATIANA

**SIMON &
SCHUSTER**

London · New York · Sydney · Toronto · New Delhi

A CBS COMPANY

First published in USA by Simon & Schuster, Inc., 2013
First published in Great Britain by Simon & Schuster UK Ltd, 2013
A CBS COMPANY

This paperback edition first published, 2014

1 3 5 7 9 10 8 6 4 2

Simon & Schuster UK Ltd
1st Floor
222 Gray's Inn Road
London WC1X 8HB

www.simonandschuster.co.uk

Simon & Schuster Australia, Sydney
Simon & Schuster India, New Delhi

A CIP catalogue record for this book
is available from the British Library

A FORMAT ISBN: 978-1-47113-254-4
B FORMAT ISBN: 978-1-84983-812-2
EBOOK ISBN: 978-1-84983-813-9

Typeset by M Rules
Printed and bound by CPI Group (UK) Ltd, Croydon, CR0 4YY

For Em Always

Acknowledgments

The sort of novel I write is populated by real people who lend their expertise and character to my slim story. Over and over I am amazed by their generosity. The interpreter Paolo Maria Noseda introduced me to the mysteries of his trade. In Moscow, no one could have been more generous than Dmitri Muratov and his staff at the *Novaya Gazeta*. The Moscow correspondents Ellen Barry and Sergei Loiko shared their valuable insights. The writer Yulia Latynina pointed me in the right direction and Yegor Tolstyakov was, once again, my thoughtful guide. In America Nelson Branco and Neil Benowitz led me to fast bikes, Drs. Kenneth Sack and Michael Weiner to a wandering bullet, and Jim and Martha Robinson to a burned-out houseboat. Ellen Irish Branco and Luisa Cruz Smith afforded important critical readings. Don Sanders and Sam Smith offered significant moral support, and my editor Jofie Ferrari-Adler offered only brilliant advice.

Then there is Andrew Nurnberg, who, book after book, has been agent, wizard and boon companion.

Prologue

It was the sort of day that didn't give a damn. Summer was over, the sky was low and drained of color, and dead leaves hung like crepe along the road. Into this stillness dashed a cyclist in red spandex, pumping furiously, taking advantage of the flat terrain.

Joseph spoke six languages. In restaurants he spoke French, with tradesmen he preferred Chinese and he dreamed in Thai. He was a one-man crowd. It meant that he could travel and find work anywhere in the world. The United Nations sent him one place and the European Union sent him somewhere else. Always, he took his black custom-made bike, his designer jersey and shorts, his molded saddle and tear-shaped helmet. He had started biking too late in life to be a competitive racer, but he could astonish the locals at most rallies. Anyway, winning didn't matter. It was the tension, the feeling of a drawn bow, that he found most satisfying. At this point he calculated he had ridden twice around the world. He'd never married. His schedule wouldn't allow it. He felt sorry for saps stuck on tandem bikes.

He loved word games. He had a photographic memory—an eidetic memory, to be exact. He could look at a crossword puzzle and play it out in his mind while he biked, teasing out those words that existed only in crossword puzzles: *ecru, ogee, amo, amas, amat*. A clue that was not in English was all the easier. A *tort* was a civil action; a *torte* was a piece of cake. A full-grown anagram could occupy his mind from Toulon to Aix-en-Provence. He had the afternoon off, and he needed it after interfacing in Russian and Chinese. When the two sides broke early, the interpreter seized the opportunity to ride.

He prided himself on finding routes out of the ordinary. His idea of hell was being in Tuscany or Provence stuck behind tourists wobbling on and off the road in rented bikes as they worked off a lunch of cheese and wine. Elastic pockets in the back of his jersey held water bottles, energy bars, a map and repair kit. He was willing to patch a tire or two if he could have a new vista to himself. Kaliningrad had a reputation of being ugly and crime ridden, a city that was an orphan or bastard or both. Escape the city, however, and, *voilà*, a pastoral delight.

He was born to translate; his father was Russian, his mother French, and both were Berlitz instructors. In boarding school he spread a rumor that they were dead, tragically killed in a car crash in Monte Carlo, and became the boy most invited for the holidays by wealthy classmates. He was ingratiating and sometimes he imagined ending his days as a guest in a villa not far from the sea. He still sent his parents a card at Christmastime, although he hadn't seen them for years.

He interpreted for film stars and heads of state, but the most lucrative work was corporate negotiations. They were usually carried out by small teams operating in strict confidentiality and an interpreter had to be omnipresent yet nearly invisible. Most of all, he had to be discreet, trusted to forget what he heard, to wipe the slate clean when the job was done.

As the road became a country lane he flew past occasional ruins of brick smothered by lilacs. Fortunately, there was almost no traffic. He navigated pothole after pothole and, at one point, rode through asphalt as humped as waves. A butcher's van with a plastic pig on the roof came the opposite way and seemed to aim straight at the bike until they passed like ships at sea.

In fact, the interpreter had not erased everything. There were his notes. Even if the notes were stolen, they would be safe, because nobody could read them but himself.

The road ended at a desolate parking area with a shuttered kiosk and a billboard of events past. An ice-cream cart lay on its side. Everything described postseason ennui. Nevertheless, when he heard the screech of gulls he got off his bike and carried it over the brow of a dune to a view of a beach that stretched in either direction as far as he could see and wavelets that advanced in regular order. Mist turned the sea and sky into luminous bands of blue. Sand skipped in the wind and nestled into beach grass that grew among the dunes. Rough wooden beach umbrellas, stripped of canvas, stood guard, but no one else was in view, which made it perfect.

He set the bicycle down on the sand and removed his helmet. This was a find. This was the sort of mini-adventure that would make for a good story around the fireplace with a glass of red wine and a captivated audience. A little derring-do to cap his career. To give it *significance*; that was the word.

Although the air was cool, Joseph was warm from cycling, and he removed his biking shoes and socks. The sand was fine, not like the loose stones of most resorts, and unspoiled, probably because Kaliningrad had been a closed city during the Cold War. Water rushed up, hissed around his feet, and drew back.

His reverie was interrupted by the approach of a vehicle rolling like a drunken sailor across the beach. It was the butcher van. The plastic piggy, pink and smiley, rocked from side to side until the van came to a stop and a man about thirty years old with a homburg and stringy hair climbed out. A dirty apron fluttered around him.

"Looking for amber?"

Joseph asked, "Why would I be looking for amber?"

"This is the place. But you have to wait for a storm. You have to wait for a storm to rile up all the amber."

Roil, not *rile*, Joseph thought, but let it pass. Joseph detected nothing in common with the man, no intellect to engage with. Sooner or later the character would demand money for vodka and they'd be done.

"I'm waiting for friends," Joseph said.

The tilt of the homburg lent the butcher an antic air. He seemed dizzy or drunk—in any case, so amused at a private joke that he stumbled into the bike.

"Idiot! Watch where you're going!" Joseph said.

"Sorry, real sorry. Say, is this Italian?" The butcher picked up the bicycle by its top rail. "S'fucking beautiful. You don't see many of these in Kaliningrad."

"I wouldn't know."

"You can take my word for it."

Joseph noticed that the butcher's hands were nicked and raw from handling frozen beef, and his apron was suitably daubed with liverish stains, although his sandals were hardly appropriate footwear for slippery ice lockers.

"Can you give me the bike, please? The last thing I want is sand in the gears."

"No problem." The butcher let the bike drop and brightly asked, "Holidays?"

"What?"

"It's a question. Are you here on holidays or business?"

"Holidays."

The butcher's face split into a grin. "Really? You came to Kaliningrad for a vacation? You deserve a medal." He pretended to pin a decoration to Joseph's chest. "Give me the highlights of Kaliningrad. Like, what did you see this morning?"

Joseph had worked all morning, not that it was anyone else's concern, but the butcher produced a nickel-plated pistol that he weighed in his hand like loose change. What had been to Joseph a cool breeze now gave him a chill, and grains of sand

5

stuck to the sweat on his skin. Maybe this was an ordinary shakedown. No problem. He would pay whatever was asked and be reimbursed by the client.

"Are you the police?"

"Do I look like the fucking police?"

"No." Joseph's heart sank. He had been trained to be calm and cooperative in hostage situations. The statistics were actually reassuring. People only got killed when someone tried to be a hero. "What do you want?"

"I saw you at the hotel with those people. They're surrounded by bodyguards and have a whole floor to themselves." The butcher became confidential. "Who are they?"

"Businessmen."

"International business or they wouldn't need an interpreter, right? Without you, everything comes to a halt. The machinery stops, doesn't it? The big wheel is stopped by the little wheel, isn't that so?"

Joseph was uneasy. This was Kaliningrad, after all. The pig glowed, happy to go to the abattoir. Joseph contemplated running from this madman. Even if he didn't get shot, he would have to abandon his bike; the sand was too deep and soft for the tires. The entire scene was demeaning.

"I just interpret," Joseph said. "I'm not responsible for content."

"And take notes of secret meetings."

"Totally legal. The notes simply aid my memory."

"Secret meetings or you wouldn't be in Kaliningrad; you'd be living it up in Paris."

"It's sensitive," Joseph conceded.

"I bet it is. You have a real skill. People run at the mouth and you translate it word for word. How do you remember it all?"

"That's where the notes come in."

"I'd like to see those."

"You wouldn't understand them."

"I can read."

Joseph was quick to say, "I wasn't suggesting that you couldn't, only that the material is highly technical. And they're confidential. We'd be breaking the law."

"Show me."

"I honestly can't." Joseph looked around and saw nothing but gulls patrolling the beach in case food appeared. No one had told the gulls that the season was over.

"You don't get it. I don't need to know the ins and outs. I'm a pirate like those Africans who hijack tankers. They don't know a dog's turd about oil. They're just a few black bastards with machine guns, but when they hijack a tanker they hold all the cards. Companies pay millions to get their ships back. The hijackers aren't going to war; they're just fucking up the system. Tankers are their targets of opportunity and that's what you are, my target of opportunity. All I'm asking is ten thousand dollars for a notebook. I'm not greedy."

"If you're just an errand boy that changes everything." Immediately, Joseph understood that it was the wrong thing to say and the wrong way to have said it. It was like poking a

7

cobra. "Let me . . . show . . ." Joseph reached around and wrestled with the pockets of his jersey, spilling a water bottle and energy bars until he found a notebook and pencils.

"Is this it?" the butcher asked.

"Yes, only it's not what you expect."

The butcher opened the notebook to the first page. Flipped to the second page, the third and fourth. Finally, he raced to the end.

"What the fuck is this? Pictures of cats? Doodles?"

"That's how I take notes." Joseph couldn't help a hint of pride.

"How do I know these are the notes?"

"I'll read them to you."

"You could say anything you fucking please. What am I supposed to show them?"

"Who is *them*?"

"Who do you think? These people, you fuck with them, they fuck with you."

His employers? If he could just explain.

"My notes—"

"Are a joke? I'll show you a joke." The butcher dragged Joseph to the back of the van and opened the rear door. Out of the interpreter's many languages, the only word that came to mind was *Jesu*. Inside the van, two skinned lambs hung upside down, looking cold and blue.

Joseph couldn't find more to say. He couldn't even find the air.

"Let the birds read it." The butcher cast the notebook into

the wind, then tossed Joseph into the back of the van and climbed in after.

From everywhere gulls materialized. They descended as a succession of thieves, each robbing the other. Every scrap from Joseph's pockets was snatched and inspected. A tug-of-war developed over a half-eaten energy bar. The birds were momentarily startled by a shot and a winner flew off, trailed by other gulls and screams of outrage. The rest settled into a sullen peace facing the wind. As the haze retreated, a horizon appeared and waves rolled in with the sound of beads spilled on a marble floor.

Chapter One

Time did not stand still at Vagankovo Cemetery, but it slowed. Leaves drifting from poplars and ash spread a sense of relief, informality and disrepair. Many sites were modest, a stone and bench in a wrought iron enclosure going to rust. A jar of flowers or a pack of cigarettes was evidence of care for ghosts that were at last allowed to indulge.

It could be said that Grisha Grigorenko had always indulged. He had lived in a grand manner and was going out the same way. For days, Senior Investigator Arkady Renko and Detective Sergeant Victor Orlov had trailed the dead man around Moscow. They started with an eviscerated Grisha at the morgue, followed by an herbal rinse and makeup at a spa. Finally, dressed and aromatic, the body was rolled out for view in a gold-plated coffin on a bed of roses in the basilica of the Cathedral of Christ the Redeemer. Everyone agreed that Grisha looked, considering the hole in the back of his head, pretty good.

For a senior investigator like Renko and a detective sergeant like Orlov, surveillance of this nature was fairly demeaning, a task that a ticket taker at a movie theater could have performed. The prosecutor had directed them to "note and photograph. Stay at a distance from the funeral cortege to watch only. Use discretion and make no contact."

They made a pair. Arkady was a thin man with lank dark hair who looked incomplete without a cigarette. Victor was a bloodshot wreck who substituted Fanta for vodka. Or tried. Because of his drinking no one dared work with him but Arkady. As long as he was working a case, he was sober and a good detective. He was like a hoop that stayed upright as long as it was moving, and fell when it stopped.

"'Make no contact,'" Victor said. "It's a funeral. What does he expect, arm wrestling? Hey, that's the weather girl from television." A blonde in black unfolded from a Maserati.

"If you wave, I'll shoot you."

"See, it's even getting to you. 'Use discretion.' For Grisha? He might have been a billionaire but he was still a glorified leg breaker."

There were two Grishas. There was the public benefactor, patron of charities and the arts, and a leading member of the Moscow Chamber of Commerce. Then there was the Grisha who had his thumb in drugs, arms and prostitution.

The funeral party was similarly mixed. Arkady spotted billionaires who had their arms around the nation's timber and natural gas, lawmakers who were sucking the state treasury dry, boxers who had become thugs, priests as round as beetles, models hobbling on stiletto heels and actors who only played assassins rubbing shoulders with the real thing. A green carpet of artificial grass was unrolled along the front row, where heads of the Moscow underworld surfaced in all their variety, from the old boys like Ape Beledon, a gnome in a coat and cap of Persian lamb, and his two burly sons; to Isaac and Valentina Shagelman, experts in insolvent banks; and Abdul, who had evolved from Chechen rebel to automobile smuggler and, in a dramatic career move, hip-hop artist. When Victor raised a camera, one of Beledon's sons blocked his view.

"This is fucked." It was Victor's favorite expression. This football game was fucked, this card game was fucked, this salad was fucked. He was constantly fucked. "You know what gets me?"

"What gets you?"

"We're going to go back with two hundred images in a digital camera of everyone at this fucked-up hole in the ground and the precinct commander is going to say, 'Thank you very much,' and then erase it right before my eyes."

"Feed it to a laptop first."

"That's not the point. The point is, you can't win. We're just playing it out. I could have spent a nice day in bed passed out and pissing drunk."

"And I interrupted that?"

"You did. I know you meant well."

A priest droned, "Blessed are those whose ways are blameless, who walk in the way of the Lord." A golden crucifix swayed at belly level; a golden Rolex shone on his wrist.

Arkady needed a break. He took a turn around the cemetery, browsing among the headstones. It could be said it was
his favorite statuary. In black marble, a grandmaster glowered
over a chessboard. In white marble, a ballerina floated
through the air. There was whimsy too. A woodland spirit rose
from a writer's grave. A comedian cast in bronze offered a
fresh carnation. On modest patches of grass, the living could
sit on a bench and carry on a conversation with someone long
departed.

Alexi Grigorenko stepped in Arkady's way. "My father can't
be buried in peace? You're going to hound him to his grave?"

"My condolences," Arkady said.

"You're interrupting a funeral."

"Alexi, it's a cemetery," Arkady said. "Everyone is welcome."

"This is harassment, and it's fucking sacrilegious."

"Is that how they speak in business school in America?"

Alexi said, "You weren't invited."

Alexi was a sleeker version of his father, stylishly unshaven,
his hair curled at the collar with gel. He was part of a new generation that attended business forums in Aspen and skied in
Chamonix and he let it be known that he expected to lead the
family to the next rung of legitimacy.

Meanwhile there was a genuine disturbance at the cemetery gate, where the grave diggers were turning away a group
bearing posters. Arkady didn't catch what the issue was, but he
did glimpse a photojournalist he knew. Anya Rudenko lived
across the hall from his flat and sometimes occupied his bed.
She was young and full of life and what she saw in Arkady was

a mystery to him. Why she was in the cemetery, he had no idea, and she shot him a look that warned him not to approach. No stylish celebrities or sleek Mafia here. Anya's friends were writers and intellectuals capable of folly but not of crime, and after a momentary fuss, they turned down the street and she stayed with them.

The priest cleared his throat and suggested to Alexi, "Maybe we should proceed to the eulogy before, you know, anything else happens."

It had to be more than a eulogy, Arkady thought. This was Alexi's introduction to many of the mourners, a tough audience. So far as they were concerned he was as likely to lose his head as wear a crown.

Victor said, "If he's smart this is the part where he waves good-bye and runs for his life."

Alexi began slowly. "My father, Grisha Ivanovich Grigorenko, was honest and fair, a visionary in business, a patron of the arts. Women knew what a gentleman he was. Still, he was a man's man. He never let down a friend or ran away from a fight, regardless of the attacks on his character and smears on his reputation. My father welcomed change. He understood that we are in a new era. He counseled a new generation of entrepreneurs and was a father to anyone in need. He was a spiritual man with a deep sense of community, intent on improving the quality of life in his adopted Kaliningrad as well as his native Moscow. I promised my father to fulfill his dream. I know that his true friends will follow me to make that dream come true."

"And maybe they'll open him like a zipper," Victor whispered.

Alexi added, "On a lighter note, I want to invite you all to enjoy the hospitality of the Grigorenko family on Grisha's boat, anchored at the Kremlin Pier."

Mourners filed by the open grave and dropped red roses on the coffin. No one lingered. The prospect of a banquet on a world-class yacht was irresistible and in a matter of minutes, the only ones left at the grave site were Arkady, Victor and diggers shoveling dirt. Grisha Grigorenko and his roses disappeared.

"Did you see this?" Victor pointed to the headstone.

Arkady focused on the stone. It must have been waiting only for a date, because a life-size portrait of Grisha was photo-engraved into polished granite. He wore a sea captain's cap, and his shirt was open at the neck to reveal a crucifix and chains. One foot rested on the bumper of a Jeep Cherokee. An actual car key was in his hand.

Victor said, "This stone cost more than I make in a year."

"Well, he got his head blown off, if that makes you feel any better."

"A little."

"But why shoot him?" Arkady asked.

"Why not? Gangsters have a limited life span. The story is that with Grisha out of the way, Kaliningrad is wide open. People don't think that Alexi has what it takes to keep it. These aren't schoolboys. If Alexi is smart, he'll go back to business school and stay away from business. Are you going to the yacht?"

"No, I don't think I can stifle envy any longer."

Victor looked around. "Calm, serenity, the whole bucolic bit. You do that. I'm going to go find the yacht and piss in the river."

As soon as Victor left, Arkady turned his attention to the grave diggers. They were still upset about the confrontation with Anya's friends.

"It was a demonstration. You can't have a demonstration without a permit."

Arkady was determined not to get involved in Anya's affairs but couldn't help asking, "A demonstration about what?"

"We told them, no matter how famous a person is, a suicide is a suicide and can't be buried in sanctified ground."

"Suicide?"

"Ask them. The whole group is walking toward Taganskaya. You can catch up."

"Whose suicide?"

"Tatiana."

The other said, "Tatiana Petrovna, a troublemaker to the end."

Outside the gates, Ape Beledon's two sons shared a joint.

"The old boy has us waiting around like he's the fucking Queen of England and we're the Prince of Wales. When is he going to let us take over? I'll tell you when. Never."

"Real authority."

"Real authority doesn't devolve on you."

"You take it. You exercise it."

"You demonstrate it, like, you know, 'Another great night here in Babylon.'"

"*Scarface*, Tony Montana. You call that a Cuban accent?"

"'You wanna fuck with me? You wanna play rough? Okay. Say hello to my little friend.' Then he blows them away."

"I must have seen that DVD a hundred times."

A cough.

"Don't let Ape catch you smoking that shit."

"He's such a fucking schoolmaster."

"Fuck Ape."

"Fuck Alexi too. Mr. Silver Platter."

Chapter Two

By the time Arkady caught up with the marchers, their numbers had swelled to more than one hundred and they had reached their destination, the cul-de-sac where the journalist Tatiana Petrovna had fallen to her death the week before. The buildings were all the same: six stories of drab cement, with dead saplings that had been plugged in and forgotten. A bench and seesaw were streaked with bird droppings, but the front steps where she had landed were newly scrubbed and bleached.

No one had been arrested, although a television reporter who stayed with the marchers breathlessly speculated that Petrovna's confrontational style of reporting had its risks. He couldn't dismiss the possibility that the journalist had taken her own life for publicity's sake. Officially, suicide was the call.

What had caught Arkady's attention was that a neighbor had heard her scream. Suicide usually took concentration.

People who committed suicide counted pills, stared in fascination at their pooling blood, took the high dive in silence. They rarely screamed. Besides, Arkady didn't see any neighbors. This was the sort of event that should have drawn gawkers to their windows.

The marchers lit candles and bore photographs that showed Tatiana as a negligently pretty woman at a desk, reading in a hammock, walking a dog, on the front line of a war zone. Her former editor, Sergei Obolensky, was in the forefront of the crowd. He was easy to spot because of his shaved skull, trim beard and wire-rimmed glasses. He and Arkady had met once and thoroughly despised each other. Through a bullhorn the editor demanded, "Where is Tatiana? What are they trying to hide?"

Anya and her camera seemed to be everywhere at once. Arkady had to snag her by the sleeve.

"You didn't tell me about this."

She said, "You would have told me not to come. This way we don't fight. The police claimed that she jumped from her balcony and took her life. We demanded an independent autopsy, and now they claim they can't produce her body. How can they lose a body?"

"They've lost bodies for years. It's one of their functions. More to the point, do you have a permit for this demonstration? Without a permit this could be regarded as a provocation."

"It is a provocation, Arkady. In the spirit of Tatiana Petrovna, that's exactly what it is. Why don't you join us?"

While Arkady hesitated, Obolensky appeared. "Anya, what are you doing back here? I need you up front to take pictures."

"A moment, Sergei. Remember Investigator Renko? He marched with us."

"Is that so? The one good apple among the rotten. We'll see if it's true or not." Obolensky gave Arkady a mocking salute before moving on to welcome a group of university students to the demonstration.

"We'll have two hundred marchers at least," Anya told Arkady.

"You should have told me."

"I knew what your answer would be and you didn't disappoint."

Everything was simple for her, he thought, so jet-black or snow-white. She held the advantage because he had never had that purity of conviction. If she was a spoiled child, he was a wet blanket, a spoilsport. As a journalist, Anya wanted to be close to the action, while Arkady was a man in retreat. She didn't pretend to be faithful and he didn't expect her to be. They were interim lovers. It simply happened that the margins of their lives overlapped. There were no expectations.

"Go home, Arkady," Anya said.

Obolensky returned to put a proprietary grip on her arm and led her to a bench where a man with a bullhorn was haranguing the wind. Arkady thought Tatiana Petrovna would have smiled to see who had come to pay their last respects. It was a middle-aged intellectual crowd. Publishers who abandoned their writers, writers who wrote for the drawer, artists who had become wealthy by turning Social Realism into kitsch.

He wondered what other accusations could be hurled at

them. That they once were a special generation that had over-thrown the dead weight of an empire? That they were romantics who lamented a rendezvous with history that never took place? That they had gone as soft as rotting pumpkins? That they had rallied around Tatiana when she was dead but stayed at arm's length when she was alive? That they were old?

It seemed to Arkady that Obolensky didn't need hundreds of marchers, he needed thousands. Where were the kids who Twittered and texted and organized a march of thousands with their iPhones? Where were the liberals, communists, anti-Putins, lesbians and gays? In comparison, Obolensky's march was a garden party. A geriatric ward.

If it had been up to Arkady, he would have sent everyone home at this point. Nothing that he could point to in particular, only an electric imbalance in the air waiting to be discharged. A protest was fitting because Tatiana was indeed a troublemaker. She attacked corruption among politicians and police. Her favorite targets were the former KGB who dwelled like bats in the Kremlin.

Arkady separated from the crowd and walked around the building. On one side was a row of derelict apartment houses, on the other, a chain-link fence and a construction site that had barely gotten off the ground. Stacks of rebar were covered with rust. Work trailers were abandoned, their windows punched in and swastikas spray-painted on the doors. A circle of men gathered around a cement mixer. They had shaved heads and wore red, the totemic color of the Spartak football club. At Spartak games they were often kept in a caged section of the stands. Arkady watched one pick up an iron rod and take a test swing.

By the time he returned to the demonstration it was well under way. There was no format. People shared the megaphone and poured out their guilt. Each had, at some point, advanced his or her career by pulling an article that Tatiana Petrovna had written at the risk of her neck. At the same time, they recalled, she knew what her end would be. She didn't own a car because, as she said, it would only be blown up, and what a waste of a perfectly good car. She could have moved to a larger flat—could have blackmailed her way to material luxury—but was content with her dead-end apartment, its rickety lift and insubstantial doors.

"Every snail prefers its own shell," Tatiana had said. But she knew. One way or another, it was just a matter of time.

Afternoon faded into twilight and the television news team had gone before the poet Maxim Dal stepped forward. Maxim was instantly recognizable, taller than anyone else, with a yellow-white ponytail and sheepskin coat and so heroically ugly that he was kind of beautiful. As soon as he got his hands on the megaphone, he condemned the investigation's lack of progress.

"Tolstoy wrote, 'God knows the truth, but waits.'" Maxim repeated, "God knows the truth, but waits to rectify the evil that men do. Tatiana Petrovna did not have that kind of patience. She did not have the patience of God. She wanted the evil that men do to be rectified now. Today. She was an impatient woman and for that reason she knew this day might come. She knew she was a marked woman. She was small but so dangerous to certain elements in the state that she had to be silenced, just as so many other Russian journalists have been intimidated, assaulted and murdered. She knew she was next on the list of martyrs and for that reason, too, she was an impatient woman."

One of the demonstrators fell to his knees. Arkady thought the man had tripped until a streetlight shattered. A general intake of breath was followed by cries of alarm.

From the edge of the crowd, Arkady had a clear view of the skinheads scaling the chain-link fence like Vikings boarding a ship. Just a handful, no more than twenty, wielding iron rods like broadswords.

Sedentary editors were no match for young thugs whose days were spent lifting weights and practicing karate blows to the kidney or the back of the knees. Professors backpedaled, taking their dignity with them, trying to fend off blows. Placards toppled into chaos as appeals were answered with kicks. A whack to the back took the air away. A brick to the head peeled back the scalp. Rescue seemed imminent when a police bus arrived and unloaded riot police. Arkady expected them to come to the aid of the demonstrators; instead, they waded into the marchers with batons.

Arkady was challenged by a mountainous policeman. Overmatched, he hit the man in the windpipe, more a cheap shot than a knockout blow, but the policeman staggered in circles searching for air. Anya was in the middle of the fray taking photographs while Maxim protected her, swinging the megaphone like a club. Arkady glimpsed the editor, Obolensky, also holding his own.

Arkady, however, went down. In a street fight the worst place to be was on the ground and that was where he was headed. Whose foot tripped him he did not know, but two riot police began dancing on his ribs. Well, he thought, in Victor's words, this was truly fucked.

He got to his feet, how he didn't know, and displayed his investigator's ID.

"He's with us?" A policeman dropped his fist. "He fooled me."

In minutes the battle was over. Skinheads slipped over the fence and disappeared. Police circulated among the casualties, gathering IDs. Arkady saw split lips and bloody noses, but the real damage had been to the spirits of the demonstrators. All afternoon they had relived and rekindled the passion of their youth, stood again with Yeltsin on a tank, again defied the apparatus of the KGB. Those heady days were gone, deflated, and all they had reaped was bruises.

Arkady's eye was swollen shut and from Anya's reaction he was glad he couldn't see himself. She, on the other hand, looked as if she had been on nothing more dangerous than a roller coaster. Obolensky had slipped away. The poet Maxim was also gone. Too bad. It had been like having a yeti fight on your side.

A police captain bellowed, "Assembly without a permit, spreading malicious rumors, obstructing officers of the law."

"Who were assaulting innocent civilians," Arkady said.

"Did they have a permit to assemble? Yes or no? See, that's where the trouble starts, with people who think they are special and above the law."

"People who were being beaten," Arkady said. Somehow, by virtue of his rank, he had become spokesman for the demonstrators.

"Troublemakers who viciously attacked police with bricks and stones. Who did you say your chief was?"

"Prosecutor Zurin."

"Good man."

"One in a million. I apologize, Captain. I haven't made myself clear. The people here are the victims and they need medical care."

"Once we have affairs sorted out. The first thing is to gather up all the cameras. All the cameras and cell phones."

"In a trash bag?"

"That way we'll be able to view and objectively evaluate any violations. Such as—"

Arkady winced because it hurt to laugh. "Do these people look as if they could assault anyone?"

"They're writers, artists, intellectual whores. Who knows what they'll get up to?"

The trash bag returned and the captain held it open for Anya. "Now yours."

Arkady knew that she wanted to drive a dagger into the captain's heart. At the same time, she was paralyzed by the threat of losing her camera.

"She's with me," Arkady said.

"Don't be ridiculous, she's not an investigator or militia."

"On special orders from Prosecutor Zurin."

"Really. I tell you what, Renko, let's call the prosecutor's office. Let's ask him."

"I doubt he's in his office now."

"I know his cell phone number."

"You're friends?"

"Yes."

Arkady had walked into a trap of his own devising. He was light-headed and heard a fluty wheeze in his chest. None of this was good.

A phone at the other end rang and rang until it finally produced a message. The captain clicked off. "The prosecutor is at his golf club and doesn't want to be disturbed."

The issue was still undecided when a massive sedan slid out of the dark. It was a dumbfounding sight, Maxim Dal in a silver ZIL, an armored Soviet-era limousine with double headlights, tail fins and whitewall tires. It had to be at least fifty years old. In an authoritative voice Dal ordered Anya and Arkady to get in.

It was like boarding a spaceship from the past.

Chapter Three

Anya made a terrible nurse. When she tried to cook, Arkady smelled food burning and heard her swearing at pots and pans. When she wrote in his apartment, he smelled her cigarettes and listened to her swear at her laptop. But he was surprised by Anya's patience. He would have expected her, like a cat, to move on. Although she had assignments—a fashion shoot, a photo essay on the Mafia—she dropped in several times a day to see how he was. "You'd miss me if I didn't. You're a secret romantic," she said.

"I'm a cynic. I believe in car wrecks, airline disasters, missing children, self-immolation, suffocation with pillows."

"What is it you don't believe in?"

"I don't believe in saints. They get people killed."

"It's no big deal," Victor said when he visited. "Seems to me that you're making a lot of fuss for a couple of busted ribs. What the devil is the matter with you anyway?"

"Punctured lung." A couple of days with a valve in his chest and the lung would reinflate itself on its own.

"It's like visiting Our Lady of the Camellias. Do you mind?" Victor held up a pack of cigarettes.

For once, Arkady didn't crave one.

"So it's suicide."

"Or murder," Arkady said.

"No, I heard it on the radio. The prosecutor determined that Tatiana Petrovna threw herself out her window. They say she was depressed. Of course she was depressed. Who isn't depressed? Anyone with eyes to see and ears to hear is depressed. The planet is depressed. That's what global warming is."

Arkady wished he had such insights. His mind was hung up on details. What of the neighbor? Who heard her screams? Screaming what?

Arkady felt painkillers lift him up to a dull euphoria. He could tell Zhenya had stopped by because a large chocolate chess piece wrapped in a bow sat on his nightstand. Arkady was a light sleeper but Zhenya was as elusive as a snow leopard.

A man confined to a few rooms becomes a meteorologist. Through the windowpane he charts clouds, tracks the stately passing of a thunderhead, notices the first streaks of rain. The bedroom wall becomes a screen on which he projects, "What if?" What if he had saved this woman? Or been saved? A person in this situation welcomes the clash and bang of a storm. Anything to interrupt a review of his life: Arkady Kyrilovich Renko, Senior Investigator for Very Important Cases, member of the Young Pioneers and a generation of "gilded youth" and, as luck would have it, an expert in self-destruction. His father, a military man, blew his head off. His mother, more genteel, weighted herself with stones and drowned. Arkady had dabbled in the act himself but been distracted at a critical moment and with that his suicide fever had passed. Still, with all this experience and expertise, he considered himself a fair judge of suicide. He defended the honor of people who killed themselves, the commitment that suicide demanded, the isolation and sweat, the willingness to follow through and open a second bottle of sleeping pills or make a deeper slice across the wrist. They had earned the title, and he was offended by the imposture of murder as something it was not. Tatiana Petrovna would no more have killed herself than flown to the moon.

When the tube was removed from Arkady's chest, the doctor had said, "We will put on a clean bandage every day and tape you up. The hole will heal itself. Your ribs will heal too, if you let them. No twisting, lifting, cigarettes or sudden moves. Think of yourself as a broken cup."

"I do."

Arkady had asked Victor to go through police files and make a list of Tatiana Petrovna's enemies.

"Incidentally, you look like hell," Victor said.

"Thank you."

The courtesies done, Victor sat by the bed and fanned a deck of index cards.

"Pick a card, any card."

"Is this a game?" Arkady asked.

"What else? Seven people with excellent reasons to kill Tatiana." He turned a card stapled to a color photo of a man with long bleached hair, evasive eyes and a tan. "Igor Mulovich threatened Tatiana in open court. He had recruited young women as models and sold them like meat in the Emirates."

Arkady said, "I remember him."

"You should. We arrested him, but it was Tatiana's articles that nailed him. He served one year in prison camp. He bought a judge on appeal, got out and gets run over by a truck, so the laugh's on him."

Victor turned over another card to another familiar face. Aza Baron, formerly Baranovsky, a broker whose clients had enjoyed phenomenal returns until Tatiana Petrovna exposed his pyramid scheme. "Baron is in Israel fighting extradition."

He turned over the third card.

"Tomsky. The big fish himself," Arkady said.

"Himself."

Kazimir Tomsky, deputy minister of defense. He had barely got his fingers in the pot when a Russian freighter limped into Malta. Its cargo had shifted in a storm and had to be reloaded. In the process, a dockside crane toppled and dropped crates labeled "Domestic Appliances." What spilled out, however, were rocket-propelled grenades. Everyone knew that the arms had been illegally sold by men high and low in the Defense Ministry. Tatiana named them.

Tomsky spent time in prison. He had been released ten days before Tatiana Petrovna was killed.

"Definitely a candidate," Arkady said.

"Except he went right to Brighton Beach to live with his mother. Too bad, he made a lovely candidate."

"Who's left?"

"The Shagelmans."

"Husband and wife."

Victor said, "I hear she's a terrific cook, if you don't mind picking fingers out of the stew. A sweet old lady who wants to transform Tatiana's neighborhood into a shopping mall and spa. Between one court and another, Tatiana was costing the project a fortune in bribes, loans and lawyers. She really knows the law. The Shagelmans want to raze and clear the site before winter sets in, whatever that takes. For them, it's a business decision, nothing personal."

"Then there's the joker." A blank card popped up on Victor's fingertips.

"Who is that?"

"I don't know. Someone she opened her door to. A trusted friend."

"What about Grisha? She did a piece on him a year ago that about took his hide off."

"Grisha was dead already."

"Don't you find it interesting that they died within a day of each other? That's quite a coincidence."

"Coincidence is relative. When I go to a bar, it's fate. If you're there too, that's coincidence." Victor went back to his cards. "It just gets better. There's Ape Beledon and Abdul, the Chechen superstar. I'll nose around."

"Give me a day and we'll do it together."

"As in, when I'm sober? Give me a little trust."

"All the faith in the world."

As for himself, Arkady knew he should quit the prosecutor's office. He should have years ago, but there was always a reason to stay and a semblance of control, as if a man falling with an anvil in his hands could be said to be in control.

Chapter Four

A dent in the ribs changed a person's perspective. A walk down the street became fraught with potential disaster. A boy on a skateboard was a runaway bull. Driving the Niva's manual shift demanded a stream of obscenities. His cell phone rang. Dr. Korsakova, a brain surgeon of his acquaintance. Another opinion he didn't need. Arkady didn't answer.

Tatiana's building and the grounds around it seemed even more empty than before, no one about but old women who tipped from side to side as they dragged their shopping carts behind. A true dead end.

Arkady mashed all the buzzers on the call box before a girl carrying a poncho came to the front door. She couldn't have been more than twenty, pretty in a street-urchin fashion, with a crust of mascara around the eyes and bleached hair as fine as chick's fluff.

She said, "Another investigator? If you're here about

Tatiana, you're a week too late. If you're here about the building, turn the power back on."

"I'm not here about the building."

The girl explained that developers had been trying to get rid of Tatiana Petrovna for months. "They turned off the elevator and heat. Look at this lobby. Nothing but trash and dirty words. Mailboxes ripped open. Disgusting. At least the cats keep the rats down."

"You mean there's no one else in the building?"

"No, now that Tatiana is gone."

"No staff?"

"No."

"What floor are you on?"

"The sixth, the top. Right across from her."

What else? Arkady thought.

"Your name is . . .?"

"Svetlana."

"You're not working today?"

"I don't know. We'll find out."

The stairs were tagged with suggestions of what people could do to themselves and declarations in red paint, "Spartak Rules!" and "Dynamo Sucks!" As he followed Svetlana he became aware that she was putting more sway into her steps than was absolutely necessary. You're stirring a cold pot, he thought. Thank you for trying.

"So it was the two of you against the world." As if Tatiana needed more enemies, he thought. The rubble outside could be cleared for a megamall or health club for members only. If

Svetlana could be believed, she and Tatiana must have been a maddening roadblock. "Were you here when she died?"

"The night she went out the window? I heard her come in around midnight. That wasn't unusual, she often worked late. She was famous, you know. She didn't have to live here. I asked her once, and she said she liked to mess with the system."

Arkady's ribs fought every step and he was sweating by the third floor.

"You okay?" Svetlana looked back.

"Perfect. Did you talk to her that night?"

"No, but I heard her come in."

"Alone?"

"I can't say for sure, I could only hear her in the hallway."

"And no one came after?"

"No."

"You were friends."

"Nobody would believe it, would they, her being who she was and all. She always brought milk for my cats. All she had to do was open her door and they'd start yowling."

"Were you alone?"

"Oh, yeah."

"How did you two meet?" Arkady asked. "At the fish market? On a tenants' committee?"

"Not quite. At a drop."

A "drop" was where men picked up prostitutes. It could be a traffic overpass, a pedestrian underpass, a children's playground.

"I had a fight with a guy and I wasn't in good shape. Tatiana saw me and took me in."

"Like that?"

"Like that. She owned two apartments and she set me up here across from hers."

"To protect you?"

"I dunno."

"When was the last time you talked to her?"

"The day of the accident, a week ago."

"How did she seem? Happy, normal, depressed?"

"Down. The cats sensed something was wrong. They mewed the whole day. Well, we're here."

He leaned against the wall and calculated how long it would take to roll down to the bottom. A police seal was plastered across the door and frame, and the door was locked. There were no signs of forced entry.

"So the police had a key?"

"I suppose. She always kept her door locked."

"Where would they get a key?"

"Why are you asking all these questions? Everyone says it was suicide."

"Can we talk in your apartment?"

Svetlana balked. "I dunno. Is this going to get me into trouble? Tatiana told me my rights. I don't have to let anybody in."

Arkady sneezed.

"How many cats?" he asked.

"Six. Do you like cats? I always feel they're a good judge of character. You have to let them come to you."

"Oh, they come."

In Arkady's experience, cats knew instantly who was allergic and gravitated to them. "You know, I'm like most people. Sometimes I forget my key or I can't find it, so I give a copy to a neighbor. Now, you're the only one here. You were doing Tatiana a favor."

No response.

"The police report said that a neighbor heard screaming. That was you, right?" He gave her time to answer before he added, "Did the screaming start inside or outside on the balcony?"

Svetlana wiped her nose.

"Did she scream or did she shout? There's a difference."

Tears blurred her eyes but she said nothing.

"Did she call your name? You were the only other person in the building. Didn't she know you were home?"

"I'll get you the key," Svetlana said.

There, he thought, not much crueler than carving out the answer with a knife. He needed the key. For an investigator, that excused everything, and when she opened her door, he stepped in after her.

A modest attempt had been made to turn the front room into a seraglio. Cheap Indian bedspreads hung in swags on the walls and over a narrow bed. A lava lamp stood on a nightstand, the lava limp on the bottom. Otherwise, Arkady saw nothing that couldn't be fit into a suitcase for a quick getaway. And cats. They swarmed over and around Arkady's feet, mewing piteously. While he was immobilized, Svetlana went to a connecting room and returned with a shiny, freshly cut key.

"A new copy?" Arkady asked.

"I'm so disorganized. I keep losing them."

Most of the cats were gray striped, one a tabby, and another white.

"They earn their keep. Every night I chase them out to catch rats, except Snowflake." She picked up the white cat. "Snowflake likes to hide and stay behind."

"You discovered her body?"

"Yes. There was no one else to hear her scream."

"Exactly what did you hear?"

Svetlana set the cat down. "Noises."

"Noises like . . . ?"

"I don't know. Furniture being moved."

"She was your friend. Did you go to her door to ask why she would be moving furniture at midnight?"

"No."

"Did she ever bring men to her apartment?"

"Of course. She was a very busy writer. That's the thing about being like me and a writer like her, you meet all types."

"All types?"

"She was involved in a lot of causes."

"Such as . . . ?"

"Chechens, criminals, veterans."

"Violent types?"

"Sure."

40

"Were they violent with her?"

"No. Anyway, the police said it was suicide."

"After moving her furniture."

"The police said her door was locked. She was alone."

"These officers, did you get their names?"

"Just police. They took my name in case there were questions."

"Were there?"

"No."

"But you identified her?"

"Yeah. What a mess."

"I'm sorry you had to see that."

"Thank you. You're the first one to say so."

His questions were repetitious, even confusing. It was like walking all around a horse before buying it. From the time Svetlana heard the scream until she found the body, how much time had elapsed? Five minutes? Ten?

"More like five."

"It took you five minutes to react?"

"I guess so."

It took a healthy young woman that long to descend six flights of stairs? If Svetlana was not an unreliable witness, her story had holes and ellipses.

"You're sure you were alone in your apartment?"

"Yes. I told you before."

"Right. How long are you going to stay here?"

"I don't know. It's day-to-day."

Or minute-to-minute, Arkady thought. He took her cell

phone number and gave her his card. "If you remember anything else, give me a call."

Svetlana asked, "Those five minutes, do you think she was
still alive?"

"From that fall? I think she died instantly. I doubt she felt a
thing."

"Who would do that?"

"I don't know, I think Tatiana Petrovna had so many enemies they were tripping over each other."

"Why do you care?"

"I don't. Just curious." An afterthought occurred to him.
"How did your cats get on with her dog? I saw a dog in pictures
of her."

"Her pug? Little Polo? What a coward. He didn't dare come
in here."

Arkady paused to pull on latex gloves before opening the door.
He had high hopes. He expected the apartment to be a reflec-
tion of a well-ordered mind, and clean surfaces meant good
fingerprints.

The balcony curtains were closed, allowing only chinks of
light. He threw a light switch to no effect and remembered
that the building's power had been turned off. The beam of his
penlight zigzagged to the dangling wires of a ceiling fixture.
He aimed down and found that he couldn't move without
stepping on open books or broken glass. He let the beam crawl
across the room to a sofa that was upended and gutted, spilling
foam. Next to it was a desk stripped of its drawers. Folders were

dumped out of file cabinets. Bookshelves were swept clear and loose papers strewn everywhere. Scattered shoe boxes held audiocassettes that went back twenty years according to their labels. The flotsam and jetsam of a professional reporter.

He took long, cautious steps to the kitchen. Everything that had been in a drawer or cabinet was on the floor. Knives glinted through a mélange of yogurt, melted ice cream and breakfast cereal. Both the refrigerator and the range had been moved aside. Two dog bowls, one upside down. In the bath-room, the medicine cabinet had been emptied into the sink. In the bedroom the mattress was filleted, her wardrobe tossed on the floor.

He crossed to the balcony and opened the doors. This was Tatiana's last view, bleaker than Arkady had anticipated, far from the glass towers of millionaires. Even with the doors folded, there was only room on the balcony for two people. A plaque on the rail said, PLEASE DO NOT PLACE OBJECTS ON LEDGE. Good idea, Arkady thought. In the corner of the bal-cony lay an ashtray and a shriveled geranium in a pot.

He returned to the living room, crushing a shoe box of tapes on the floor, and picked up a tape recorder. He expected dead batteries. Instead he heard the stutter of machine-gun fire and a woman's voice say, "Both sides have the same weapons. That's because our Soviet soldiers have traded their weapons for vodka. Here in Afghanistan, vodka is the great equalizer." Arkady tried another tape. "The sirens that you hear are ambu-lances taking children to a hospital already overflowing with casualties, over two hundred so far. It's now clear there was no rescue plan. The prime minister has yet to visit the scene." And a third. "The bomb went off during rush hour in the metro. Bodies and body parts are everywhere. We're trying to move closer but some tunnels are so filled with black smoke it's impossible to breathe or see." History rushed by.

He put in a new cassette. At first he thought it was blank and then he picked up her low, soft voice. "People ask me is it worth it."

A pause, but he knew that Tatiana was there on the other side of the tape. He could hear her breathing.

Chapter Five

The next morning, Arkady felt curiously well. Part of it was Vicodin and part a sense that he had come into direct contact with Tatiana Petrovna and had an idea where to begin. Sergei Obolensky had been one of the few men who put up a fight outside Tatiana's apartment building. He had been Tatiana's closest friend on the magazine *Now*.

"It's more like *Now and Then*," Obolensky said. "We pulled our latest issue so we could rethink our policy on investigative journalism. Maybe we'll have to put in a horoscope instead of investigation. Maybe we'll print only horoscopes. I'm not going to make the magazine's staff risk their lives. Personally, I've decided I'm too old to die. It's very simple when you're young and you don't have a family and financial obligations. At my age, it's a mess. No story is worth that." Obolensky rubbed the bruises on his shaved head. "Nothing compared to a punctured lung." He brought a bottle of vodka and two glasses from a desk drawer. "I normally don't drink in the middle of the day, but as we are two survivors of the Battle of the Bullhorn, I must salute you."

"A battle?" Arkady thought that was a little exaggerated.

One wall of Obolensky's office was covered with citations from news organizations and schools of journalism around the world. Two photographs were of Obolensky and Tatiana Petrovna accepting awards. A leather sofa was worn flat. A dead ficus haunted a corner. Obolensky's desk was half hidden by a computer and manuscripts and books that overflowed the shelves. All in all, pretty much the professional disorder that Arkady expected in an editor's office.

"What happened after Anya and I left?" he asked. "Did you get your cameras and cell phones back?"

"After the captain confiscated all the film and memory cards. The captain had his fun. He advised us not to make an issue of the beating because then they would really dish it out. 'Dish it out'? What does that mean? What's left after murder? For the meantime he cited us for unlawful assembly and libeling the office of the president. Not a word about the attack on us. I'm responsible for my people. I don't want their blood on my hands."

"Did you lodge a complaint with a prosecutor?"

"What would be the point? Prosecutors, investigators, militia, they're all thieves, present company excepted." Only two glasses of vodka, and Obolensky was becoming emotional. "Renko, you and I know that our demonstration was about more than Tatiana. It was about all journalists who have been attacked. There's a pattern. A journalist is murdered; an unlikely suspect is arrested, tried and found not guilty. And that's the end of it, except we get the message. Soon there will be no news but their news. They say it's better than a free press, it's a free but 'responsible' press." He poured a sloppy glass and raised it high. "So the nation moves on, blindfolded."

"What about Tatiana?"

"Tatiana was fearless. Independent. In other words, I couldn't stop her. She did what she wanted. She went to America once for a big humanitarian prize, and all she could talk about when she came back was bumper stickers. She said if she had a car, she'd have a sticker that said, 'So Much Corruption, So Little Time.' I think she knew her time was up. Why else would she live in a building next to skinheads?"

"Did they ever attack her?"

"No."

"Is it possible they respected her?"

"Why not? They're monsters but they're still human. She was always for the underdog." Obolensky hunched closer. "The official line is that Tatiana jumped and there will be no investigation. So, what are you doing? The war is over."

Arkady said, "People don't know about the demonstration."

"And they won't. The television news that night showed Putin petting a tiger cub and Medvedev arranging flowers. Anyway, Tatiana is missing again."

"Again?"

"First she was in the wrong drawer." Obolensky refilled the glasses. To the brim. "Now she's totally disappeared."

"What do you mean?"

"They can't find her. They say they've looked everywhere. They're just twisting our dicks. Apparently, the authorities are concerned that wherever our Tatiana is buried will become some sort of shrine. They're juggling her until they come up with an answer."

"Why not cremate her?"

"Maybe they have, who knows? But you're supposed to ask the family first."

"Did she have any family?"

"A sister in Kaliningrad that no one can locate. I tried. I went to Kaliningrad myself and knocked on her door, because if the sister doesn't claim her or they hide Tatiana long enough, she might end up in a grave for the unclaimed. A double disappearance."

"Was she secretive by nature?"

"She had a personal life. She would disappear for a week at a time and never say where she'd been. An unpredictable lady. I think it was her unpredictability that kept her alive. And she never revealed her sources, but we were watching the news and saw this body wash up on the beach in Kaliningrad. She insisted on going to the scene."

"What was his name?"

"She wouldn't tell me."

"How did she know him?"

"According to Tatiana, they met at a book event in Zurich. He was interpreting for one of the other authors. Of course, once he knew who she was, he tried to impress her and let her know that he had inside information about criminal activities in Moscow and Kaliningrad. The police didn't even make a pretense of an investigation of his death. They just hauled him off. It was local kids that found his notebook in the sea grass. The little ghouls sold it to Tatiana. Five hundred rubles for a notebook of puzzles. Only the joke's on us. It's completely useless." Obolensky unlocked a desk drawer and took out a reporter's spiral notebook.

"What is it?"

"Tatiana said they were the interpreter's notes."

"Notes about what?"

"You tell me. Tatiana kept it secret. It was going to be the capper of her career. She was headed for sainthood. Instead, here comes the Kremlin's smear campaign. She was a subverter of youth, an agent of the West, a wanton woman. They throw mud at you even as they kill you; that's the way they work."

"Who is 'they'?"

"'They' are those persons in the Kremlin who determine whether a journalist is digging too deep or reaching too high. The persons who like to say that only a coffin corrects a hunchback."

"Where is Tatiana's dog?"

"Polo? With Maxim, the last I heard. Renko, why is it you still sound like an investigator?"

"Habit." Arkady looked idly around the office. A cactus on the windowsill looked shriveled and defeated. "What happened to Tatiana's manuscript?"

"It disappeared. She was going to give me a rough draft the day she died. All I have is this notebook."

"May I see?"

Obolensky laughed. "Take a look."

Arkady turned to the first page. Second, third, and his confusion only grew. It was drawings. It was arrows, boxes, teardrops, fish, a cat and more, as if someone had poured out the contents of a typographer's box and tossed in gnostic symbols, dollar signs, stick figures and, most improbably, "Natalya Goncharova," the name of the unfaithful wife for whom the poet Pushkin lost his life.

"What does it mean?" Arkady asked.

"Who knows?" Obolensky took back the notebook and returned it to the drawer. "Sorry, I'm saving it for the writer I've assigned to do a follow-up article on Tatiana."

"After the attack on the demonstration I thought you stopped making waves."

"We did, we did. Nonetheless, we have a reporter who's eager to try. How can I deny her?"

"Who?"

"Anya. It's her big chance, don't you think?"

Arkady's car was just out of the repair shop, and now that he had it back, he was as edgy as a parent. Every vehicle was within a millimeter of another's skin. Other drivers made no eye contact and gave no quarter.

Victor gloated. "It's like the running of the bulls in Pamplona, but in slow motion. It's good to see your car again. A bit macho for my taste, if you know what I mean."

"I can only guess."

"The problem is the precinct commander says that since Tatiana Petrovna's death was clearly a suicide, there is no basis for further investigation. That means no depositions, no subpoenas and no lawyers. The body's disappeared. The commander has turned me down. So we have overfulfilled our quota of nothing. Where are we going?"

"To see our witness."

"The neighbor? Svetlana?"

"I told you, she heard screams."

"Okay, let's say you have approval for an investigation—which you don't, but never mind—did she actually see anything? Was she under the influence of any drugs? Could she swear to the time? Was she with a customer? This is some witness."

"We'll need more, I agree."

"More?"

"We should talk to all Tatiana's colleagues and friends to understand her state of mind. Also, she was investigating a death in Kaliningrad. She had a dozen battles going on."

"Arkady—"

"And she seems to have held up an expensive real estate development."

"Arkady, I hate to say this, but the case is closed. The investigation is over. Not only that, it does look like suicide. She came home alone, locked the door, and jumped off the balcony. Alone. She trusted no one, and under the circumstances, that made a lot of sense. It's as if the whole city was out to get her. They drove her to it."

"She entrusted her apartment key to her neighbor."

"Unfortunately, a mental case. It's time for you to get back on your feet, but on a real homicide. Without a body there is no case. We'll start slowly with aggravated assault and work our way up. Or, on a personal level, why not find out who stomped you? I made some calls about the demonstration while you were lazing about in bed."

"And?"

"Half the people you say were in the demonstration deny that they were ever there. The only two who really support the accusation are Anya and Obolensky, but that sells magazines, doesn't it?"

"What about Maxim Dal? He rescued us."

"Gone to ground. To hear anyone but Anya, Obolensky and you, there was no demonstration. It's like that old adage about a tree falling in the forest; if nobody hears it, was there a sound?"

"What if it falls on you?"

As they slogged up the six stories to Svetlana's apartment, Victor wheezed and said, "You know, I really missed you while you were laid up. Now I'm not so sure."

Taped to Tatiana's door was a receipt for the "occupant" from the Curonian Renaissance Corporation for the contents of the apartment, which could be retrieved within a month upon payment of a storage fee. After thirty days, the contents would be disposed of.

The door opened at a touch.

Tatiana's apartment had been swept clean. Furniture, electronics, even carpets had been removed. Books, photographs, music were gone. Every footfall echoed in rooms that were pools of late-afternoon light and motes in motion.

"A Renaissance Corporation? That sounds nice," Arkady said. "I think of Leonardo, Michelangelo, Bernini."

Victor said, "I think of the Borgias. So, we've got no witness, no corpse and now no scene of the crime."

"That's right."

"I'll tell you what we do have." Victor sniffed the air as they stepped back into the hall. "Cats."

There were five cats in Svetlana's apartment. They hadn't been fed or had their box changed for at least a day, and they swarmed around Victor while he poured milk into a saucer. Victor, oddly enough, was a cat person. An admirer not of fluffy Persian cats or exotic Siamese, but of feral survivors of the street. Did they eat songbirds? Let them. Victor's favorite birds were crows.

Svetlana was gone. As Arkady remembered, she more camped in the apartment than lived in it. It wouldn't have taken her more than ten minutes to stuff all her personal possessions into a suitcase. The cats mewed and purred around the bowl, dots of milk on their whiskers.

There had been six cats on his first visit. Snowflake, Svetlana's favorite, was gone. It occurred to Arkady that a woman who took her pet hadn't been grabbed. She was on the run.

"Let me remind you," Victor said, "that even if the walls

were splattered with blood, you have no authority to do any-thing, not until the prosecutor has assigned the case to you. You haven't seen him for weeks."

"Well, I've neglected him," Arkady admitted.

Since Arkady did not play golf, he didn't know how many swings a player was allowed to knock a ball off a tee. Prosecutor Zurin's swings only became more erratic with each effort.

"You don't have to stand there like a vulture, Renko. I was doing perfectly well before you showed up."

"Isn't that the way it goes?"

So this was the prosecutor's famous golf club. The operation was simple, an open cage and pads of artificial grass between a car dealership and a paintball course. The range was illu-minated and signs marked distance from the tee: "100 meters," "150," "200." For Zurin they might as well have said, "Mars," "Saturn," "Jupiter." The problem was he looked like a real golfer: tall, tan and silver haired. Just like he looked like a real prosecutor.

"Have you tried paintball?" Arkady asked.

"Get to the point. What do you want?"

"I wanted to inform you that I'm back on duty."

"You've got one more week on medical leave."

"I've rested enough. I tried to reach you by phone. I left messages."

Zurin glanced in the direction of Victor and the Niva. "You could come by the office and pick up your mail, but I have no case for you to work on. Everyone else is on a team. I can't break up teams. There's really nothing for you to do at the moment."

"I'll find something."

"Like what?"

"A dead body from the morgue. They seem to have misplaced her."

"Homicide?"

"Suicide," Arkady assured him.

He could see Zurin turn the news over in his mind, unsure whether this was a windfall or a trap.

"You know, when you get involved in radical demonstrations and street brawls, it reflects on the entire office. We are hostages to you. Your colleagues are fed up with the melodrama of your life. Finding the body of a suicide isn't going to make any difference, is it? Dead is dead." The prosecutor's attention wavered as the tee beckoned. Half a pail of balls to go. "If you want to chase a dead body, go ahead. It's your style, a totally pointless gesture. But, please, at least sign in at the office as if you work there."

Only bad things happen when you go to the office, Arkady thought. He had been Pluto, a lump of ice in outer space, content in his obscurity. One step into his office, however, and he encountered the full force of gravity. Memos, notes and reminders were stacked on his desk and Dr. Korsakova was waiting in an armchair with X ray films on her lap.

"What a pleasure," Arkady said.

"A surprise too, I'm sure. Apparently, you're a phantom or you have been avoiding me."

"Never."

He wanted to offer her tea but his electric teapot was missing. Korsakova had treated Arkady for a gunshot wound, a bullet to the brain that should have killed him and would have if the round had not been a relic degraded by time. Instead of plowing a causeway through Arkady's head, bits had lodged between the skull and the covering of the brain, and caused bleeding enough to justify drilling drain holes and lifting the lid of his head. Ever since, she had taken a proprietary interest in his health.

"Well, here we are. I would offer you tea and something to eat but the cupboard seems to be bare."

"Not everyone who is shot in the head gets a second chance. You should be appreciative of that. Remember your headaches?"

The medical term was "thunderclap headache," a sudden howl in the black of the night that was the marker of a bleeding brain. Arkady remembered.

Dr. Korsakova said, "Exercising caution, there might be nothing to be alarmed about. Are you paying attention?"

"I'm glued. You told me not to worry, that probably nothing would happen."

She stood to slide out the films and rearranged Arkady's desk so that his lamp lay on its back and faced upward. "You don't mind?"

"Not a bit."

"Six months ago." She held an X ray above the light and then a second X ray over the first. "A week ago."

The X rays merged into a single luminous skull, similar in every detail except for a white speck circled in each plate.

"Something has ..."

"Moved," Dr. Korsakova said. "We never know when such a particle will stop or move or in what direction. Shrapnel emerges from war veterans after fifty years. We do know that violence doesn't help. Did you consider that when you joined the demonstration for Tatiana Petrovna?"

"It was a public gathering."

"It was a demonstration, and for you it could have been fatal. Who knows what direction this particle may take? Right now pieces are aimed at the frontal lobe. You may experience confusion, nausea, personality changes."

"I could live with that. Who knows, it may be for the better." He opened desk drawers rapid-fire until he found an ashtray and a pack of cigarettes.

Dr. Korsakova, at once, was on her feet. "You're going to smoke too?"

"While I can, like a chimney."

Chapter Six

When Arkady and Anya sat down for breakfast, the bread was fresh, the coffee was hot and she wanted to know why he was spoiling a perfectly good morning by going to meet Maxim Dal at a church of all places.

"Hoping for a confession? And after, are the two of you going to sit down with a comforter and a pot of tea and reminisce about being clubbed by the riot police?"

"No, that's what vodka is for. The church was Maxim's idea. Besides, he might know something about Tatiana's death that would help us."

"Exactly what are you after? What is the case?"

"Tatiana's body is missing. I'm looking for it."

"A senior investigator searching closets at the morgue? Do you know how pathetic that sounds?"

Arkady's cell phone rang.

"Who is that?"

"Zhenya." He looked at the phone and turned it off. He had to gird himself for a conversation with the most truculent boy on earth, so he stalled as usual. Between Anya and Zhenya, he didn't think he could fight on two fronts at the same time.

Anya asked, "Are there any witnesses besides the girl with the cats? As I remember the buildings around Tatiana's apartment were empty."

"Nearly. You never know when someone will turn up, but you have to knock on doors. I don't have enough men to do that and even if I did . . ."

"No one will talk to the police. After last week, who can blame them? Have you seen the editor, Obolensky? I thought he was pretty brave when the riot police attacked. Didn't you think he was brave?"

"Very. Is he going to keep the journal going?"

"Of course."

"As long as he has writers."

"Yes. Why this sudden interest in Sergei Obolensky?"

Arkady rushed a bit, like a skater approaching thin ice. "I went to see him."

"At his office?"

"I know he gave you Tatiana's final notes for a glorious, going-down-in-flames sort of article. They also may be the notes that got her killed."

"When were you going to tell me about this visit?"

"When were you going to tell me about the article?"

Arkady thought that the two demands had equal weight but she ignored logic. Instantly the bread was stale and the coffee cold.

He never had been good at arguing with women; they tapped into pools of resentment over slights that had steeped for years.

She asked, "Do you have any idea how disrespectful that is? Do you have any idea how long it's taken me to be accepted as a reporter? Or how humiliating it is to be 'saved' by a hero from the Prosecutor's Office? And now you want me to turn down the most important article of my life?"

"I only meant that Tatiana's notes might contain information that got her killed and it might be wise to let Victor and me go over them first."

"Sergei gave me the notes on the condition that I share them with no one."

"At least tell me, was there any mention of Grisha Grigorenko?"

"I can't tell you."

"Or Kaliningrad?"

"Why Kaliningrad?"

"It just keeps popping up. I have no doubt that Sergei Obolensky is a great editor but there's the possibility that he is also, let's say, creative at the expense of his writers."

Anya pushed herself away from the table. "I can take care of myself."

"Like at the demonstration?"

"Maybe, but that's my choice. It has nothing to do with you. You know, Arkady, if you wanted to be more involved in my life, you had your chance."

That, Arkady thought, would silence any man.

*

The Cathedral of Christ the Redeemer was a copy of a church demolished by Stalin to make room for a statue of Lenin pointing to the future, only the statue was never erected and the Soviet future never arrived. The new cathedral was a white confection with golden onion domes. Grisha Grigorenko had contributed the cost of a dome and cashed in his investment with a funeral service fit for royalty.

Arkady preferred a smoky hole-in-the-wall sort of church with stooped priests whose beards touched the floor. Babushkas visited the chapels of their favorite saints, standing on tiptoe to kiss beloved books and icons. They bought thin candles for one, five or ten rubles depending on their length. Arkady thought if he lit a candle for everyone Grisha had wronged, the cathedral would burn down.

He could see why Maxim chose to meet at the cathedral; it was one of the few places that commanded a 360-degree view of the city. In other words, a person could see who was coming. Gypsies suckled babies at the door. Beggars demanded charity. Tourists were immobilized by their guidebooks while babushkas glided by on polishing rags wrapped around their feet. Icons of saints, prophets and apostles covered the walls, even the poorest in gold frames. Most of the figures offered a languid blessing and their flatness gave the impression of being inside a house of cards.

"Saint Pelagia. One of my favorite martyrs," said Maxim. The poet nodded to the icon of a girl stoically on fire. "Martyred by being roasted in a bronze bull. Patron saint of chefs, or ought to be."

"It sounds as if you know the saints intimately," Arkady said.

"And sinners. I knew your father. What a son of a bitch he was."

Arkady couldn't disagree. His father had been an army officer who had never adjusted to peacetime. The last person Arkady wanted to talk about was his father.

Maxim moved along the wall. "Here is another favorite, Saint Phanourios. First beaten with stones, then stretched and flogged and put on the rack, crushed and burned with coals. Sounds like you."

"I hope not."

"You should take a good look at yourself sometime."

Maxim himself deserved more than a glance. As a boy Arkady had devoured adventure stories set in the Wild West. That the authors had never been to America bothered him not in the least, and Maxim, with his narrow eyes, buckskin jacket and ponytail, had a wolfish charm. Two of the floor polishers stared at him and whispered behind their hands as if they were teenage girls.

"This is a little public," Arkady said.

"Oh, nobody pays attention. They're all in their own world, thinking deep religious thoughts. The church is a dead telephone; even though people know better, they pick it up and listen. Have you been listening?"

Arkady wondered whether Maxim was referring to the cassettes of Tatiana that he had been listening to late into the night, until Maxim added, "The acoustics of a church like this can carry whispers through the air."

"That's very poetic. What did you want to talk about?"

"Look at the murals here. All that swirling; Botticelli with a beach towel. I understand you were at Grisha Grigorenko's funeral service."

"Yes."

"That was the same day as the rally for Tatiana Petrovna."

"It was a busy day."

"Where I rescued you, remember?"

"I remember and I thank you again."

Chinese tourists streamed into the church and set off rounds of echoes. Men and women, they all had the same enthusiasm and all wore the same crushable hats.

"Have they located her body?" Maxim asked.

"Not that I know of."

"Obolensky called and asked if I would write a poem about the police and the rally. Since I was there, perfectly placed. Serendipity, you could say."

"For his magazine?"

"For a special Tatiana Petrovna issue of *Now*. I understand that your friend Anya will contribute an article based on notes that Tatiana acquired."

"Who else did Obolensky tell?"

"No one. What do the notes say?"

"I don't know."

"But you saw them."

"For a moment. And even if I knew, why would I tell you?"

"You owe me."

"What possible interest can you have in Tatiana's notes?"

"I'm interested in everything about Tatiana."

"Why?"

"Because once upon a time I loved her."

The ZIL was superannuated, but it had style. A silver chassis lashed with chrome, lots of chrome. Twin headlights that signified alertness, leather upholstery that offered comfort, tail fins that promised speed. A futuristic touch was a push-button transmission.

"They manufactured a total of ten ZILs in 1958. Of course, it swallows gas like a drunk, but a man who lets guilt ruin pleasure is the pincushion of fate. Go ahead, you drive."

It was a rare experience. As Arkady edged into traffic on the Boulevard Ring, other cars—Mercedes, Porsches and especially Ladas—parted.

"You certainly make an impression in a car like this," Arkady said.

"That's the idea."

The ZIL also afforded privacy. With the windows rolled up, all Arkady heard was the whisper of air-conditioning.

"You and Tatiana? No offense, but that seems, in terms of personality, a bit of a mismatch. Not to mention the fact that you're thirty years older."

"I know. No one knows better than me."

"Where?"

"Sochi. The Black Sea Cultural Festival. I was doing readings. Tatiana was a student on holiday with friends. When they left early, she stayed. Some guys who were high on drugs tried to mug her. I chased them off. I bought her a drink, and she bought me a drink, and one thing led to another. By the time the festival ended, we were totally in love. Forever.

"In Moscow everything changed. Everybody needed her. She was involved in every cause. Palestinians, Africans, Cubans. Russians too, can't forget reform in Russia. I was drowning and she was in her element. We both knew it. At the end, I didn't think she even noticed I was gone. As a philosopher once said, 'There's no fool like an old fool.'"

They cruised by the art galleries and florist shops on the Boulevard Ring. Maxim rolled a cigarette. Arkady declined. More and more, the poet put Arkady in mind of a mountain man checking his line of traps.

"Why do you want the notes? Do you think you're in them? It sounds like it's been years since you and Tatiana saw each other. Why would she be writing about you now?"

"It was years, then I ran into her a month ago. And a couple of times after that. There's just a chance that I would be mentioned."

"If you were, so what?"

"Personal reasons."

"That's not good enough."

"Okay. I'm up for an award in America. A lifetime achievement award."

"What does that mean?"

"Basically, that you're still alive. The dead do not qualify. Standards in the United States are low."

"Then why do it?"

"The prize comes with money."

"Even so."

"Fifty thousand dollars."

"Ah."

"If the Americans hear that I'm involved somehow in a murder case, I can kiss the prize good-bye."

"The person you should talk to is Obolensky. He's the man with the notes."

"Obolensky? When shrimp whistle. No, I'm talking about your friend Anya. I understand she has the notes. She'd let you see."

"I doubt that. I don't know that she's even talking to me."

"I've seen you two together. She was born to talk to you, like drops of water drilling through a stone. Drip, drip, drip. Drilling until there's space for dynamite."

They had made a circle back to Arkady's Niva, which became smaller with the approach of the ZIL.

"A fantastic car," Arkady said.

"And bulletproof. You're in the illustrious company of presidents, despots and hero cosmonauts who have led parades." Maxim handed Arkady a business card with the address and telephone number crossed out and a new phone number penciled in. "It would be even better to get a copy of the notes."

"With Anya's consent."

Maxim said, "Any way you want to do it."

When Arkady first met Zhenya, the boy was standing in the cold outside a children's shelter. He was eight years old,

stunted like a boy who pushed tubs in a coal mine and virtually mute. At seventeen, Zhenya seemed simply a larger
version of himself. He was the ugly duckling that did not
change into a swan and was self-effacing to the point of disappearing. Except in chess. In the confines of a chessboard he
ruled and humiliated players whose ratings were far higher
than his because he preferred cash to tournament trophies.

Arkady found Zhenya at a computer repair shop a block off
the Arbat. Three technicians were at work, each surrounded by
plastic trays of candy-colored diodes, miniature tools and flex-
ible lights. Each also wore earphones connected to his separate
world. Zhenya's specialty was audio enhancement. Not music,
just sound. A hookah bliss hung in the air.

The first man to notice Arkady was startled.

Zhenya pulled his earphones off. "It's okay. He's with me."
To Arkady he said, "What are you doing here?"

"Here? You called and left a message." Arkady always felt on
the defensive with Zhenya. "Besides, I wanted to thank you for
the chocolate chess piece you brought when I was laid up. I
should have thanked you before."

"I didn't have a card."

"That's okay. Since it was a chess piece, I took a wild
guess."

"Yeah." Zhenya cleared his throat. "Speaking of chess, I
made some decisions. I don't think hustling chess is going to
do it for me. There's no money, not real money."

"What about computers?"

"Hacking?"

"Try something legal."

"Not a desk job. I've been sitting all my life. I've been playing chess since I was five years old. I mean, I've got to find a different route. Not this place."

"So?" This was hopeful, a real conversation.

"I need your help."

Arkady was way ahead. He was already figuring which university or technical institute Zhenya should apply to. How to use what influence he had. "Whatever you need, just tell me."

"Great." Zhenya dug into his backpack and presented Arkady with a folded letter.

"What is this?"

"Read it."

Arkady skimmed the letter. He knew what it was.

"Parental permission," Zhenya said. "I'm underage and you're the closest thing to a father I have. I'm enlisting in the army."

"No, you're not."

"I can wait seven months and do it by myself, but I'm ready now."

"No."

"You don't think I would make a good soldier?"

Arkady thought Zhenya would make a good punching bag for soldiers.

"It's not that."

"You were in the army. Your father was a general. I read about him. He was a killer."

"It's a different army now."

"You don't think I can take the hazing?"

It was more than hazing, Arkady thought. It was a system of brutalization at the hands of drunken noncoms and officers. It was daily beatings with fists and chairs, standing naked in freezing weather and the least sign of intelligence stamped out. It was a system that produced soldiers who went AWOL, strung themselves up by their belts or traded their weapons for vodka.

"In seven months—"

"I wish your father was here," Zhenya said. "He'd let me sign up."

"Well he's not here. He's shoveling coals in hell. I'm not going to sign anything."

Arkady tried to be calm and reasonable but he didn't sound that way, even to himself. He sounded angry and frustrated. To hear his father invoked as a model was the last straw.

Zhenya said, "I've never asked you for anything. You always claim you want to help, but the first time I actually ask you to, you say no."

Arkady looked for something to hit even though any dramatics would make him look ridiculous. He wasn't Zhenya's father, and that was the point, wasn't it, to play him a fool for caring. For what, Arkady thought? If you put a snake in a jar, nine years later he will still be a snake. Zhenya deserved to be in the army. All the same, Arkady balled up the letter and dropped it in the basket.

"You can do better for yourself."

Zhenya said, "Like you're an example. At least the general was somebody."

Memory was a loop of film that played over and over, each time a little different until frames overlapped. Furious at Zhenya, Arkady remembered a story about his own father sitting at a chessboard, joking, pretending that a glass of vodka was a piece in play. The general's opponent was a captured German SS officer, not a bad player, but unfamiliar with the effects of vodka. He was incoherent by the time he lost and the general left him hanging from the gallows until his neck stretched like taffy.

Chapter Seven

Taking Victor to Tatiana's apartment, Arkady drove by blocks of empty, toothless housing projects.

"Maybe you need backup?"

Victor said, "Nonsense. I'm looking for my pussy cat, Snowflake, last seen in the company of a woman about twenty years old, with short hair dyed yellow, possibly carrying a red suitcase."

"That's very sentimental."

"It's human nature," Victor said. "People who wouldn't give up Jack the Ripper are still suckers for pets. Cat people, especially."

"Don't you have cats?"

"Three, but they're outdoor cats."

"Feral?"

"Free range."

Arkady looked around as they approached Tatiana's building.

This was the first time he'd seen the cul-de-sac in daylight, and he realized that once it must have been a pleasant neighborhood with benches for the elderly, monkey bars for kids, families instead of ghosts.

"On the other side of the back fence is a construction site where skinheads like to camp."

"Good to know," Victor said.

"Svetlana is the closest thing we have to a witness."

"I know, I know. I'll meet you at the Den." The Den was a restaurant in back of police headquarters.

"Are you going to be okay?"

"I'm set," Victor said, and shook his raincoat so that Arkady could hear the soda he carried in his pockets to cope with his thirst.

The clouds were spiked with lightning, much like Arkady's personal life. He kept busy rather than think about Anya or Zhenya. He tried to reach Tatiana's sister by phone. Her number had a 4012 area code. Kaliningrad. There was no answer and no message machine.

He cruised by "drops"—the underpasses, bus shelters and truck stops where prostitutes congregated. These were not the exotic models that crossed their legs in the plush lobbies of fine hotels and made assignations by cell phone. These were girls who were underage and underfed, wrapped in flimsy coats against the cold. At every drop he visited, they approached his car, inquiring as to his needs while a pimp hovered anxiously by. Little wonder that capitalism took so long to come to Russia. No one remembered a skinny girl and a white cat.

On the chance that Tatiana's body had been moved, Arkady searched different morgues, rolling out the deceased, checking their toe tag and appearance, which was generally not good. There were fourteen morgues in Moscow, some as clean as model kitchens, others abattoirs with carts of bloody saws and chisels. Arkady fell into a kind of fugue state, seeing with a cold professional eye, being there and not there.

At the end, he found himself in a mourning room with a few folding chairs and a vase of artificial lilies. One body was on view, a man in the uniform of an army general. His uniform had stayed the same size, but the general had shrunk. His face, sallow and peaked, was nearly hidden between his cap and a chest full of honors: Order of Lenin, campaigns at Stalingrad and Bessarabia, a ribbon for the fall of Berlin. His only mourner was a teenage girl listening to her iPod, oblivious to death, which was probably the way it should be, Arkady thought.

Crossing the river by the Kremlin Pier, Arkady saw Grisha Grigorenko's superyacht, the *Natalya Goncharova*, anchored in the middle of the water. The *Natalya* was white as a swan, a vessel that inspired envy and ambition, with three decks, wraparound windows, sunning deck, dance floor and Jet Skis docked on the stern. Figures moved around doing whatever the crew on a superyacht did, polishing the brass, fine-tuning the radar, shuttling passengers back and forth. Still there was,

Arkady thought, an air of indecision. The king was dead and the new king had yet to be anointed.

Sometimes it was hard to say where crime ended and punishment began. Police headquarters was a town house on Petrovka Street with a bust of Dzerzhinsky, the vulpine founder of revolutionary terror, watching over beds of petunias. In the heady days of democracy this symbol of terror had been pulled down from his pedestal. After years in exile he had been returned to his perch.

Behind headquarters spread a complex of holding cells, laboratories and ballistics. Blue and white police cars, mainly Skodas and Fords, were parked haphazardly. Next to the district prosecutor's office, witnesses gathered for a smoke. In a basement directly across the street was the Den, a restaurant favored by both sides of the law as they drifted back and forth from the courtroom door for a drink, a cigarette, a word with a lawyer or a confederate. From time to time, patrons noticed thunderheads piling up and moved inside the restaurant, where the atmosphere was blue with smoke. Autographed photos of hockey and soccer stars, snapshots of catered affairs and postcards of belly dancers decorated the walls. Grilled kebabs and Middle Eastern music played in an absentminded way. Victor had yet to arrive but through the haze Arkady saw Anya at a corner table drinking Champagne with Alexi Grigorenko. He would have taken odds that Grisha's son would not survive a week in Moscow and here he was practically a celebrity hobnobbing with the press. Arkady knew he should wait outside for Victor, just avoid the whole scene, but he was drawn irresistibly to Alexi's table, and when a bodyguard moved to intercept Arkady, Alexi waved the man back.

"It's all right," Alexi said. "I know Investigator Renko. He even attended my father's funeral."

"What's the happy occasion today?" Arkady asked.

"Two of Alexi's friends were found innocent of murder," Anya said.

"Innocent as a baby or innocent as a bought judge?"

"The judge ruled there was insufficient evidence to hold them," Alexi said.

"Judges can be expensive," Arkady told Anya. "They should put an ATM in the courtroom and eliminate the middleman."

Alexi allowed Arkady a smile. "That, of course, would be the lawyer."

Alexi was not a typical gangster. He had a healthy tan, sculpted hair, a tailored suit casually worn. The kind of man, Arkady thought, who belonged to an athletic club and could swim more than fifty meters without sinking. He leaned forward confidentially.

"What are you after, Renko? I heard you're looking for missing bodies now. Do you expect one to pop up here?"

"You never know. Last month a man was gunned down at this very table. Was he a friend of yours?"

"I knew him."

"Was he also from Kaliningrad?"

"I think so."

"All these people from Kaliningrad. Maybe it's a matter of

perspective. I read a story once about a man who fell in love with a one-legged redhead, and from then on he saw one-legged redheads everywhere."

Anya said, "We would ask you to join us but we know how busy you are chasing ghosts."

Arkady pulled up a chair. "No, no, I've all the time in the world; that's the thing about ghosts. They'll always be there."

At a nod from Alexi, a waiter brought another glass. Such service! Arkady thought it was good to be a Mafia chief, until you were shot.

He was interested in how Anya would play this encounter. He noticed a necklace of amber the color of honey that hung around her neck.

"Very nice."

"A gift from Alexi."

"Take a closer look," Alexi said. "In the centerpiece, you'll see a mosquito trapped sixty thousand years ago."

"Even longer than you've been an investigator." Anya blew smoke Arkady's way.

The serious journalist Anya seemed to have been replaced by Anya the gun moll. What Arkady did not understand was why Anya was wasting time with a would-be Mafia chief like Alexi when she was supposed to be writing an earthshaking article about Tatiana.

"You and Anya are old friends," Alexi said.

"Our paths have crossed."

"So Anya told me." Alexi's smile was like a hook in the mouth. "Is it true that you don't carry a firearm? For what reason?"

"I'm lazy."

"No, really."

"Well, when I did carry one I hardly ever used it. And it makes you stupid. You stop thinking of options. The gun doesn't want options."

"But you've been shot."

"There's the downside."

"Cheers!" Anya said.

They drank, listened to thunder and poured some more, as if they were old friends gathering before a storm. A waiter coasted by with menus.

"You know, I've never actually eaten here. Recommendations?" Alexi asked Arkady.

"Wait for my partner Detective Orlov. He's an epicure. So, Alexi, who do you think killed your father?"

"You're very rude for a man without a gun."

"I'm simply wondering how you expect to take over your father's varied business interests."

"I will put things on a genuine business setting. This country is run like an Arab bazaar. There have to be rules and norms. How can there be investment when there is no future, and how can there be a future when there is no honesty?"

"Alexi has plans," Anya said.

"My father was a great man, make no mistake, but he lacked a business strategy, an overall plan. I'll correct that."

"But first a little revenge?"

Alexi softly drummed his fingers on the table.

"Your friend is joking," he told Anya.

"I'm joking," Arkady said.

"Because you're jealous," Alexi said. "You see your beautiful woman with me and you're jealous. *Cherchez la femme*, right?"

"He's after a different *femme*. Someone he lost," Anya said.

"Anyone I know?"

"Tatiana Petrovna."

"The journalist? I heard she jumped out a window."

"Arkady has dark suspicions," Anya said. "Did you ever meet Tatiana?"

"All I know is that she wrote a good deal of lies about my father. She probably got what she deserved."

"Then you don't think it was suicide, either," Arkady said.

"I didn't say that."

"Of course not."

"Don't put words in my mouth."

"Wouldn't dream of it." Arkady got to his feet. He decided he didn't want to be a spoilsport any longer. Anya had her own game to play. Perhaps it had something to do with marrying a millionaire.

Besides, Victor had arrived with a recommendation.

"Try the soup. I think they stir it with a mop."

Victor's car was parked half over the curb outside the courtroom door. In the backseat was a cardboard box that rocked and howled. ·

"Don't open it," Victor said, and showed Arkady the bloody scratches on his hands.

"Snowflake?"

"Snowflake."

The box was open just enough for a maddened green eye to peer out.

"It's white?" Arkady asked.

"Take my word for it."

"You found it in the care of some sweet old lady?"

Victor leaned on the car. "Not quite. I found Snowflake in the arms of a skinhead called Conan at the construction site next to Svetlana's. Apparently, they had a relationship. A skinhead and a prostitute; could love be far behind? She left Snowflake in his keeping because she was going home."

In the box, the green eye retreated, replaced by a swipe of claws.

"Where is home?"

"Kaliningrad. Nothing more specific."

"Did you get a true ID on him?"

"No."

"What does he look like?"

"Like a Conan. Lots of time in the weight room, leather vest, abs you could crack clams on. Plenty of tattoos, but Nazi, not Mafia. I promised him I would find Snowflake a home with ample mice."

"Why would he give you the cat?"

"He was going on a bike ride. He left there and then on a black Harley. I wasn't close enough to catch the license."

"Did he say where he was going?"

"He mentioned Central Asia."

"Look on the bright side, you did find Snowflake."

"Now all I need is a suit of armor to open the fucking box." Victor looked at the Den. "What is Anya up to with Alexi Grigorenko?"

"Research."

"His father's not around to protect him anymore, so I hope she works fast."

Night and day, Arkady thought.

When Victor got in the car, Snowflake produced a genuine growl. Victor rolled down the window to say, "One other thing. Conan liked Tatiana for helping Svetlana. He thought she was a saint."

Arkady's apartment was a battlement against the storm. Sometimes it sounded as if nature was laying siege against the city, as if black furies and Irish banshees were tearing up and down the streets. It was two in the morning and he was wide awake. For dinner he had eaten something greasy with bread and vodka. It occurred to him that quite possibly this might be his last case, that he might close his so called career chasing the anonymous dead. Which served him right. He picked up a shoe box of audiocassettes he had taken from Tatiana Petrovna's apartment and fed one into his own recorder. What did a saint sound like?

He pushed "Play."

"The bastards won't let me through. They did before. This time they won't. There are more than three hundred children in the school and this is the second day of the siege. I've

brought food and medical supplies and the chance to negotiate. The FSB doesn't want negotiations. In fact, the federal
troops, the FSB, GRU and OMON sharpshooters, have been
ordered further back from the school, further away from any
communication. It's not as if they have any plan apart from 'no
negotiation with terrorists.' If not negotiations, what? Without
negotiations, there will be a slaughter of horrific dimensions,
but is anyone from the Kremlin here? The Chechen leaders
are no better. They could intercede with their brothers in the
building. Instead, they remain silent. They all remain silent as
the slaughter of three hundred children draws closer."

By the end of the tape, his throat was constricted and he discovered that his face was wet with tears. An unlit, forgotten
cigarette was still in his hand. He screwed the cap back on the
vodka bottle and tried another tape.

"Am I a dupe? They've asked me to be part of the negotiat-
ing team. We walk into the theater with food and messages, we
walk out with hostages that have been freed, mainly women,
children, and Muslims. So far, two hundred of them have
been released, leaving an estimated seven hundred hostages in
the hands of Chechen rebels. A musical revue was taking
place when the rebels appeared so suddenly onstage that
people thought they were part of the entertainment. The body
in the aisle brings us back to reality. I suppose I'm one of the
few Russians the Chechens have any trust in, but their
demands are impossible. And for a negotiator in a hostage situation, it's difficult to bargain with someone who wants to die.

"Ten hours into the siege. For the hostages this must be like finding yourself a passenger on an airplane flight of unknown destination. The orchestra pit is their toilet. It's no time for heroism. A man broke through the police barrier to bring out his son. A courageous soul. The rebels threw his dead body out like trash."

Outside, the storm slapped a door shut and seemed to echo a shot fired ages ago.

"Twenty-eight hours. The Black Widows wear long black burkas with eye panels to see through. The burkas are loose, to hide the belts of high explosives strapped around their waists. I wonder about these young women and their suicidal mission. True, they have lost their husbands, but most of their own lives lie before them. I think each must live in the stultifying confines of her husband's coffin, until her own death will release her. I know the feeling."

Arkady heard voices and footsteps on the landing as Anya slipped into her apartment. It was three in the morning, an hour shared by insomniacs.

"It's over," Tatiana said. "Fifty-seven hours into the siege, a sleeping gas was introduced by Special Operations into the ventilation system and when Russian troops entered thirty minutes later, there was virtually no resistance. Fifty Chechen rebels—including Black Widows—were executed where they were found. Seven hundred hostages were freed and not a single one of our soldiers lost in what clearly should have been a triumph in the war against terrorism. However, the gas also killed one hundred thirty hostages; families without a breath between them still occupy their theater seats. Hundreds more need hospitalization. There is an antidote, but we are informed that the nature of the gas is a state secret and cannot be divulged. The man from Special Operations says, 'When you chop wood, chips fly.'"

The rest of the cassette was so faint it was virtually blank, a heartbeat in the dark.

Chapter Eight

Arkady squinted in a morning light so bright that crumbs cast shadows on the kitchen table. Anya was in dark glasses, her fingernails painted scarlet red, black hair brushed to a shine. Uncertainty was in the air. She had spent the evening and half the night with Alexi, and Arkady didn't know whether to be angry or feign nonchalance. He hadn't expected her to show up on his doorstep the morning after, looking fresh as a daisy, although she held his gaze a little too long and lit a cigarette with movements that were a little too quick.

"Have some caffeine with that." He poured her a cup. "You were out late."

"Alexi and I went to a club."

"That sounds like fun."

"He says you're jealous."

"He told me." Since there was nothing he could say now

that wouldn't sound jealous, he plunged ahead. "How is the writing going?"

"I'm still doing research."

"With Alexi?"

"What have you got against him?"

"Nothing, except that he's a slicked-back version of a real Mafia boss. Someone is going to put a bullet through his empty head any day now." That didn't sound fair, he thought. "I just hope you're not in the way." That didn't sound any better.

"So you were up late too."

"Listening to Tatiana. I found some old tapes in her apartment."

"Sometimes I think you'd rather listen to ghosts than to someone alive."

"It depends."

"And now, on top of ghosts, you have a Saint Tatiana. Maybe you should pray."

"What would help more than prayers is the notebook Tatiana brought back from Kaliningrad."

"It's funny. Everybody wants it and no one can read it."

"I'd like to try."

She opened her tote bag and produced the spiral notebook that Obolensky had shown him. "Just for you, the Holy Grail."

"You've read it?"

"Over and over."

"May I?"

"Be my guest."

The pages were covered with enigmatic symbols. Inside the back cover were geometric shapes, a list of numbers and sketches of a cat.

Anya gathered up her coat. "I myself prefer a hothead to an ice cube."

He heard the decisive slap of her shoes and perhaps the word *idiot* as she shut the door.

Whenever Arkady visited the university, he could not help but measure his progress in life against the precocious student he had been. What promise! A golden youth, son of an infamous general, he had floated easily to the top. By now, he should have been a deputy minister or, at the very least, a prosecutor, ruler of his own precinct and feasting at the public trough. Somehow, he had wandered. Almost all the cases that came his way were fueled by vodka and capped by a drunken confession. Crimes that displayed planning and intelligence were all too often followed by a phone call from above, with advice to "go easy" or not "make waves." Instead of bending, he pushed back, and so guaranteed his descent from early promise to pariah.

One exception to the general disappointment was Professor Emeritus Kunin, an elderly iconoclast who dragged an oxygen tank and breathing tube around his office. A linguistics expert, he had once been arrested for speaking Esperanto, considered in Soviet times a language of conspiracy. Arkady convinced the judge that the professor was speaking Portuguese.

"I apologize, my dear Renko, that my office is such a mess.

There is a system, I promise you. With all these . . . charts and chalkboards . . . I can't even see the windows. I know there's a bottle of cherry liqueur here somewhere." He waved his arms futilely at charts, at audio equipment, at photographs of small brown people with oversize bows and arrows. Two blue macaws in separate cages cocked their heads skeptically at Arkady and blinked their sapphire eyes.

"Do they have names?" Arkady asked.

"Fuck off," said one bird.

"Piss off," said the other.

"Don't get them started," Kunin said. "It's bad enough that the tropical forest they came from has been despoiled . . . by international corporations . . . logging in the Amazon, paradise lost. My charts are virtual tombstones . . . Thank God for DNA . . . For example, who the devil are the Lapps? Really."

"A good question. Do you have five minutes to look at this?" Arkady produced the notebook.

"Ah, as you mentioned on the telephone; your piece of evidence." The professor pushed books off his desk to make room. "You're in luck. I have been making a study of 'interpretation' to see whether it tells us something about the foundations of language. The basic words. *Mother. Father.*"

"*Murder?*"

"You get the drift. Because each interpreter creates his own language."

"Ah."

"You'll see." Kunin sipped oxygen and studied the pages. "I can tell you, to begin with, one thing that's odd. Usually the first thing a professional interpreter does is write on the cover of his notebook the name of the event, the parties involved, and the place and date the notes were taken. Also his name, mobile phone and an email address in case the notebook is lost or stolen. Perhaps promise of a reward if found. This notebook has no identification. There is the name Natalya Goncharova, Pushkin's wife, but of course she was a historical figure and a slut to boot." The professor emeritus stopped for air and returned to the first page. "It's hard to say with so few pages actually written on but it seems to be a notebook commonly used by journalists or consecutive interpreters. I would say that by the use of some commonly used symbols this was the notebook of a consecutive interpreter. Party A speaks in one language, which the interpreter relays in a second language to Party B. So it goes back and forth. If he keeps good notes, he can deliver a complete and accurate translation whether the parties speak for one minute or ten. It's an amazing mental feat."

Arkady was more confused than ever. Each page was blocked into four panels with a dizzying solar system of hieroglyphs, half words and diagrams. He felt like a fisherman who had hooked a creature far below the surface of the water with no idea of what he had caught.

"From these pages an interpreter can reconstruct an entire conversation?"

"Yes. And aren't they lovely? Beyond arrows signifying 'up' or 'down.' A bumpy line for 'difficulties.' A loop and an arrow meaning 'as a consequence.' Genius. A ball and line for 'before'; a line through the ball for 'now.' An interpreter creates a new symbol and other interpreters follow. It's the creation of language before your eyes. A ball in a three-sided box? 'A goal,' naturally. Crossed swords? 'War.' A cross? 'Death.'"

"Then we should be able to read it too."

"No." Kunin was just as definite.

"Why?"

"These are just the commonly accepted symbols. I can write them in for you. The rest are his. We don't know the context."

"If we knew, could we read the notes?"

"Probably not. It's not a language and it's not shorthand. Interpretation is a system of personal cues. No two interpreters are alike and no two systems are the same. For one interpreter, the symbol for 'death' might be a gravestone, for another a skull, for another a cross like this one. Symbols for 'mother' run the gamut. Cats can be sinister or cozy."

"They don't look warm and fuzzy to me."

"See, the double triangles could be a map, or a constellation, or a route with four stops."

Arkady had seen the shape before; it danced just beyond his grasp. He tried not to try too hard to remember because answers came when the mind wandered. Stalin used to draw wolves over and over.

"Or a bicycle frame," Arkady said. He remembered going into a bike shop with Zhenya. Hanging from the shop ceiling had been a row of bicycle frames in different colors. "Someone was building a bike." He walked the idea through. "An expensive bike for a serious biker."

"You don't know that for a fact."

"This was custom-made. Not like adding a bell to the handlebars."

"Renko, I'm dragging around an oxygen tank. Do I look like I know from bicycles?"

And that was it. Abruptly, Arkady was dry. He had gone as far as this slender branch of guesswork could support him.

"Is this Lieutenant Stasov?"

"I'll put you on hold."

"Tell the lieutenant that Senior Investigator Renko is on his cell phone from Moscow and wants to talk to him."

"You're first in line."

Arkady was first in line for twenty minutes, time enough to return to his apartment and heat a cup of stale coffee.

Finally, a voice as deep as a barrel answered.

"Lieutenant Stasov."

"Lieutenant, I need just a minute of your time."

"If you're calling from Moscow, it must be important," Stasov said. Arkady could picture him winking to his pals in the squad room, taking the piss out of the big shot from Moscow. "What can I do for you?"

"I understand that you are the lead detective in the case of a dead body found ten days ago on one of your beaches."

"A male homicide, about forty. That's correct, at the spit."

"The spit?"

"Where the land narrows. Beautiful beach."

"Is the victim still unidentified?"

"No ID and no address, I'm afraid. If he had a wallet, it's gone. I'm just glad it didn't happen in the summertime when the beach is full of families. Anyway, we dug a bullet out of his head. Low caliber, but sometimes that's what professional killers use."

"A contract killer?"

"In my opinion. We will conduct a thorough investigation. Just keep in mind, we don't have the technical gear that you have in Moscow. Or money, after Moscow drains the coffers. Moscow is the center and we are the stepchild. I'm not complaining, only putting you in the picture. Don't worry, we'll get to the bottom of this."

"What did he look like?"

"We had some photos. I'll find them."

"Besides photographs, what was your general impression of the victim?"

"Skinny. Short and skinny."

"His clothes?"

"Tight and shiny."

The lieutenant was going to drag it out, Arkady thought.

"Tight and shiny as in biking gear?"

"Could be."

"Shoes? There's no mention of them in your report."

"Is that so? I guess he took them off to walk in the sand. Or one of the local boys stole them."

"That makes sense. Did you find anything else?"

"Such as?"

"Well, if he were an artist he might have brushes and an

easel. Or if he collected butterflies, he'd have a net. If he was a biker, he had a bike. He was found on the beach. There was no bike?"

"Who bikes in the sand?" Stasov asked.

"That's what I'm asking you."

"I'm really sorry I can't help you out. The guy was a fruit."

Now, what could make the lieutenant say that about a dead man he had never met? Arkady wondered.

"Did he shave his legs?"

"Weird, huh?"

"What kind of public transportation is there from the city of Kaliningrad to this place you call the spit?"

"During the off-season, none."

"A person would have to drive or walk?"

"I suppose so." The lieutenant was wary now.

"Were any cars reported stolen or abandoned near the beach?"

"No."

"Bicycles?"

"No."

"Helmets?"

"Shit, Renko, relax. I'll let you know when we find something."

"Tell me again exactly where the body was discovered?"

Lieutenant Stasov hung up, leaving Arkady staring out the kitchen window. The coffee was vile. It had been made the night before and warmed up at least twice. He had heard that in Japan restaurants were rated according to how many times the same cooking oil was used. Naturally, the first time was the best. The oil was then used by one restaurant after another, steadily degrading into brown sludge. He contemplated his cup and wondered what the record was. Always a thrill for the heart. He drank it in one go.

Professional cyclists shaved their legs for an infinitesimal edge in aerodynamics. An amateur might too if he was serious enough—serious enough to have a custom bike built just for him. What sort of personality would that demand? Athletic. Competitive. Older than twenty-five, younger than forty-five. Willing to invest much of his life in cycling. Well ordered, not Russian. Obsessive. Swiss? German? Comfortable traveling alone and on business; no one went to Kaliningrad for pleasure. For that matter, no one had reported him missing. An invisible man.

Arkady was startled to find Zhenya behind him.

"In a trance?" Zhenya asked.

"Just thinking."

"Well, it looks strange."

"No doubt," Arkady said.

"I came to pick up some clothes. That's all."

It was clear now that Zhenya would never kick a winning goal at Dynamo Stadium or inspire supermodels to sigh in his direction. A camouflage jacket overwhelmed his shoulders; his hair was twisted and his features pinched, redeemed only by the vibrancy in his gray eyes.

What to Arkady was really odd was how Zhenya managed to enter the apartment and get to the kitchen without being heard. The parquet floor squeaked under anyone else.

"How are you?"

Zhenya reacted as if Arkady had uttered the stupidest question ever formed by the mouth of man. "What's this?"

"A notebook of interpretation."

"Whatever that is." Zhenya flipped the cover back and forth.

"Code. A personal code written by a dead man."

"Oh. What's it about?"

"I don't know."

"Is this what got him killed?"

"Maybe. Are you hungry?"

"There's nothing in the refrigerator. I checked it out. Hey, you never told me how famous your father was. The army guys were real excited."

"They can stay excited until you're eighteen."

"This is such bullshit. Who gave you the authority to boss me around?"

"The court did, so you could register for school."

"I quit school."

"I noticed."

"No, I mean I really quit school. I went to the registrar's office and told them, so there's nothing for me to do but enlist early."

"Not without my signature. Seven months. You'll just have to wait to be crazy."

"You're just putting it off."

"That's right."

"Do you know how old Alexander the Great was when he conquered the world? Nineteen."

"A precocious lad."

"Do you know who his teacher was?"

"Who?"

"Aristotle. Aristotle told him to go conquer the world."

"Maybe he just meant travel."

"You're impossible." This was the point when Zhenya usually turned around and went out the door. This time he slumped into a chair and let his backpack fall. He always carried a folded chessboard, pieces and a game clock, but he was becoming too well-known as a hustler. He no longer looked innocent. Maybe he never looked innocent, Arkady thought. Perhaps that was his fantasy.

"What do you know about bikes?"

"Bikes?" As if Arkady had asked him about Shetland ponies. "I know you'd have to be an idiot to ride one in Moscow traffic. Why, were you thinking of getting one?"

"Finding one."

Zhenya reached out for the notebook and idly turned the pages. "So what's the story on this code?"

"It's a code, hieroglyphics, anagram, riddle and worse because it's not meant to be solved. There's no Rosetta stone, no context. It might be about the price of bananas but if we don't know his symbol for 'banana,' we're lost. In this case, the only context, maybe, is bicycles."

"It doesn't sound like you got very far."

"You never know."

"Profound. Is there any milk?" Zhenya launched himself in the direction of the refrigerator.

"See for yourself." A psychologist had once told Arkady that Zhenya was finding it difficult to separate. Arkady was finding that harder and harder to buy. "So, what do you know about expensive, custom-made bikes?"

"About as much as you do."

"That's too bad, because I know nothing."

"Then you're fucked, aren't you? Well ... I only came to pick up some clothes."

That served Zhenya as hello and good-bye.

Chapter Nine

Whenever Arkady opened the laptop on his desk, he felt like a pianist who, as he sat at the keyboard, realized he had no idea which keys to hit. He felt the audience stir, caught the panicky eye of the conductor, heard whispers from the string section. Fraud!

Arkady searched for "Kaliningrad interpreter." It turned out that Kaliningrad interpreters doubled as romantic escorts, which was a bit too general. He tried "Kaliningrad conference interpreter" and learned that various conferences would soon be held: "Immanuel Kant Today," "Endangered Mollusks of the Baltic Sea," "Friendship with North Korea," "Amity with Poland," "Welcome to BMW," etc., all of which demanded interpreters but gave not a hint of who they were. "Kaliningrad hotels" prompted a list that offered a fitness center, indoor pools and views of Old Town and Victory Square. More specifically, "Kaliningrad conference hotels" offered Wi Fi, business centers, meeting rooms and authentic Russian banyas. Arkady pictured foreign businessmen, red as boiled lobsters, whipping each other with birch twigs.

Arkady felt reasonably sure that an international interpreter was well paid and well traveled. He discounted the possibility that the dead man had been staying with friends. Why sleep on a couch when he could enjoy the attentions of a luxury hotel where his employers presumably paid the bills? They wouldn't want their interpreter out of reach, not when he was vital to any business they carried on. Anyway, there was something solitary about the interpreter. Arkady could not imagine two people with less in common than himself and Tatiana Petrovna.

How long could they keep the interpreter's body if he went unclaimed? That depended on shelf space at the morgue and the medical school's demand for cadavers, in which case he would be whittled away, slice after slice, like a Spanish ham.

Arkady called Kaliningrad's small clutch of four- and five-star hotels; the replies were humiliating.

"You want to know if we have lost a guest. You don't know his name or nationality. When he checked in or checked out. Whether he was at a conference or alone. You think he rode a bike. That's all?"

"Yes."

"Is this a joke?"

"So far."

One hotel advised Arkady that "all inquiries concerning criminal or suspicious activity should be reported immediately to Lieutenant Stasov." A plum assignment, Arkady thought, to have passports, credit cards and luggage pass through his hands.

Arkady moved on to "bicycle rentals." He doubted that anyone would risk bringing his own custom bike to a city that was famous for the theft of anything on wheels. The problem was that thieves did not advertise and few shops could afford a website.

Noon. After four hours at the computer, he couldn't stand one more cup of bitter coffee and went to an Irish pub around the corner. The bartender was a genuine Irishman surrounded by faux atmosphere: crossed hurley sticks, a ladder of Irish football teams, a song wailed by the Chieftains. A flat-screen monitor showed of all things a bicycle race in progress. Arkady watched the wheels hypnotically go round and round and round. The chalkboard offered ten beers on tap. A food board offered, among other items, soda bread, barmbrack, goody and crubeens.

Arkady was intrigued. "What is barmbrack?"

"Fooked if I know."

"What is a goody?"

"Beats me."

"Crubeens?"

"Pig trotters. A man could starve to death from the fookin' ambiance here. Come back tonight. We have waitresses in short skirts who step-dance on the bar."

Arkady didn't feel up to that. "Just a beer and soda bread."

"With gluten or without?"

"Just a beer."

The bartender sneaked a look at the television. "It's the Irish Ultra Marathon World Cup. Want a thrill?" He picked up the remote control and froze the picture. "That's me in the emerald-green jersey, right behind the asshole in the Union Jack who's about to crash. I can't stand this." He turned the monitor off. "It gives me a chill every time I see it. Like a goose flew over my grave. What was your order?"

"Just the beer." Arkady squinted to read the bartender's name tag. Mick. Mick sounded authentic enough. "So you know about bikes?"

"I hope so. Where are you going?"

"I'll be back."

By the time Arkady was nine years old, General Renko had largely retreated to his library, into an aura of red velvet drapes. The room was forbidden to Arkady. Occasionally, the general called for him to bring vodka or tea and he glimpsed irresistible photographs of a gutted city, and a collection of German helmets and tattered battle standards. The room's single light was a desk lamp, and there the general conjured up his enemies.

Arkady waited for his chance, and when the door was left ajar, he sneaked in. He raced around the room taking inventory, until he came to standards topped by swastikas and eagles. He was fascinated most by an SS standard of a skull and bones. The fabric was silk, stiff with blood. He didn't hear the general return until he was almost in the room.

Arkady dove behind the drapes as the old man came in with a bottle of vodka and a water glass that he stopped to wipe clean with his nightshirt. Every move was solemn and ceremonial, like a priest's at communion; he sat and drank half a glass of the vodka in one go. On the desk were a typewriter and three phones, white, black and red, in ascending importance. Arkady was silent. The general was so quiet Arkady thought he must have fallen asleep. He waited for an opportunity to creep out but then the general twitched or muttered or refilled his glass. He laughed. Waved his hand in a vague manner. Shook his fist as if addressing a crowd. Perhaps he had not been given the field marshal's baton that was his due, but people who knew, knew!

The red telephone, the line to the Kremlin, hadn't rung for a year. Nevertheless, he was ready. Just a matter of getting into his uniform and shaving.

"Who's there?"

Arkady wasn't aware of having made a sound. He did hear the general's chair roll back and desk drawers rapidly open and slam shut. He heard the cylinder of a revolver swing open and bullets roll across the desk. "Is that you, Fritz?"

Arkady dug deeper into the curtain.

"I'm going to give you a hint, Fritz," the general whispered. "If you want to kill a man, if you want to be sure, get close."

The general succeeded in loading only one bullet. Five hit the floor. Nevertheless, he pulled the trigger. The chamber was empty but the cylinder advanced and he squeezed the trigger three more times hard with no result. Arkady's calls for help were smothered by the heavy drapes while the general held the drape across his face and clicked on another empty cylinder.

Arkady slipped free and cried, "It's me!"

As they stood face-to-face, the general raised his gun to Arkady's forehead.

For a moment they were locked. Then the general blinked in the manner of someone coming awake and a deep groan escaped his chest. He turned the gun on himself and pulled the trigger.

The world came to a stop. The general's eyes screwed shut and his face turned chalk white as he squeezed the trigger again and again, until, exhausted, he let the gun hang.

Arkady took the revolver away and swung the cylinder open. "It's jammed."

The bullet was stuck between chambers, which sometimes happened to revolvers when the trigger was pulled in too much of a rush.

Mick the bartender was serving other customers when Arkady returned to the pub. He watched the traffic pass. This was what much of life was all about, doing nothing but counting cars as they went by. Boomer, Boomer, Merc, Lada, Volvo, Lada, Boomer. Russian cars were as scarce as natives struck by a plague.

"You forgot something." The bartender brought Arkady a beer and pointed to his head for its keenness. "As I remember, the subject was bikes."

"One bike in particular."

"Which one?"

"I don't know because I don't know what I'm looking at. You tell me." This time Arkady had brought the notebook. He turned to the rear inside cover with the list of numbers, silhouettes of a cat drawn over and over and a double triangle. "It's a bicycle frame?"

"Sure."

"And cats."

"Those aren't cats. They're panthers."

"How can you tell?"

"It's the logo of an Ercolo Pantera, except it should be red. It's like the Ferrari of bicycles."

"Is it expensive?"

The bartender smiled at such ignorance. "A Pantera costs thirty thousand dollars and up. Every bike is custom-made in Milan like an Italian suit and there's a waiting list as long as your arm."

On the way back to his apartment, Arkady passed the still-warm scene of a traffic accident: police cars and paramedics shoving their way through stalled traffic, broken glass and a bike leaning on a car like a mere observer.

Chapter Ten

The website for Bicicletta Ercolo was a single screen in gothic red on black, with its name, phone number, fax and email address. Its severity suggested that it did not welcome casual visitors.

"Excuse me, do you speak Russian?"

Click.

"English?"

Click.

"German?"

Click.

"Is Mr. Ercolo there? I'll only keep calling."

"Mr. Ercolo is not here. Ercolo is Hercules, sometimes Heracles. He is a mythical character. Good-bye."

A good start. The man spoke English. In the background Arkady heard the clanging of a workshop.

He called again. "That was stupid of me. I should have known about Ercolo."

"That was stupid."

"But I have your bike."

"What do you mean, you have my bike? Who are you?"

"I am Senior Investigator Renko calling from Moscow. I think one of your bikes was stolen."

"From Moscow? You're crazy."

"We think it may have been involved in a homicide."

"*Sei pazzo.*"

"I have just faxed you a copy of my identification card and phone number."

"I'm hanging up."

Arkady thought microwave ovens were the greatest boon to the single man. Men were meant to warm things up. To take blocks of ice and change them into peas or enchiladas and have time to stand in the kitchen and ponder the digital seconds as they ticked by. The bicycle makers at Ercolo had not called or faxed. They were probably sitting down to a platter of spaghetti.

One angle he had not pursued was the shooting of Grisha Grigorenko. There was a bumper crop of suspects for that deed, and the prospect of more to come as long as Alexi Grigorenko stayed in Moscow. It mystified Arkady why Anya wanted to be so close to a likely target. Maybe it was for the sake of the article, for a proper climax. He remembered what she said was the secret of better photographs: "Get closer."

The phone rang. Arkady picked up and caught the whine of a saw. It was Milan.

"Senior Investigator Renko, in Italy a senior investigator is a man with a broom."

"The same here. May I ask who I'm talking to?"

"Lorenzo, chief designer."

Arkady got the impression of a Vulcan smeared with charcoal and sweat.

"What about the bicycle?" Lorenzo asked.

"We have a dead man here with no identification other than his connection to an Ercolo Pantera."

"So?"

"I'm hoping you can help us."

"Why? If someone is shot in an American car, do you question Mr. Ford? Let me warn you, many of the Panteras out there are imitations. Each authentic Ercolo is unique. That's why the high and mighty come to Milan to be measured and fitted. We don't sell to just anyone. Bicycle and buyer must be a match."

"Absolutely."

"So each Pantera is numbered on the underside of the top tube. Can you read the number to me?"

"I'm afraid not."

"You don't have the bicycle."

"No."

"And you don't have the rider."

"No."

"You don't have anything."

"That is, more or less, correct."

"This must be difficult work."

"It takes perseverance. You say that each Pantera is unique."

"Yes."

Arkady read from the notebook's back cover. "Who was this? 'Sixty centimeters, fifty-six point five centimeters, nineteen-ninety grams'?"

Lorenzo took over. "Sixty-centimeter frame, fifty-six-point-five-centimeter top tube, nineteen-ninety-gram weight, for someone with long legs and a short torso. We call it high hipped. It's a funny thing; I remember bikes better than the people who buy them. I'll find you the order form or the receipt. Signor Bonnafos, I remember. I told him he didn't need ten gears, eight would do, but he thinks he's in the Tour de France."

"A steel frame, not carbon?"

Lorenzo made a noise as if sharing a joke. "Carbon is fine unless it breaks. We have built with steel for over a hundred years."

"Your help is vital. Would you call me if you find the number of the bike? Do you happen to remember his first name?"

Joseph Bonnafos, thirty-eight, was a Swiss national, interpreter and translator, single, income two hundred thousand euros. No arrests. Received Russian tourist visa, entered Russia at Moscow Domededovo Airport, continued to Kaliningrad the same day, information gathered from data programs at the

Ministry of the Interior that watched and cataloged people the way astronomers ceaselessly scanned the night sky.

There was a footnote. Before the Kaliningrad flight, the ground staff had refused to load his bicycle in its hard case on the grounds that it was too large and too heavy. Bonnafos called somebody, who must have called *somebody*, because in a minute the crew loaded the bike with special care.

Arkady wasn't superstitious but he did believe that momentum only existed if used. He called the same Kaliningrad hotels he had before, this time asking for a guest named Bonnafos. All but one hotel receptionist took a moment to search the guest list before saying no. The exception was Hydro Park, which said no at once. Arkady wondered whether she was just as quick at alerting Lieutenant Stasov. Just a thought.

Arkady tried calling Tatiana's sister. Ludmila Petrovna was not home but a neighbor who happened to be in the apartment said she would be back in an hour.

And he tried calling Victor in his car.

"Any luck with Svetlana?"

"She's on the night train to Kaliningrad, arriving in the morning at oh nine-fifty."

"Amazing. Who told you?"

"Conan. He may have been headed to Central Asia, but he only got as far as the drunk tank. They know me there. He had my card and I got him out."

"Nicely done."

"So now you can fly to Kaliningrad and bring her back. That

113

way we keep the investigation contained. Just us, just Moscow, right?"

"Actually, it's getting a little complicated. The scope of the investigation has broadened."

Victor said, "I don't like *broadened* and I hate *complicated*."

"Two days before she was killed, Tatiana went to Kaliningrad and came back with a notebook. So far, nobody can read it because the notes are written by a professional interpreter in a kind of personal code. He could help us but he's dead, shot on the same beach where the notebook was found. We have his name: Joseph Bonnafos, Swiss, an interpreter. Who knows, the notebook may tell us everything we need to know."

"Where is it now?"

"It's locked in a drawer of my desk."

"You don't know what the notes are for?"

"Some sort of international event, I assume, since they needed the services of an interpreter."

"Can't the local police take care of business there?"

"The case is being torpedoed by a Lieutenant Stasov, who seems to regard the hotels in Kaliningrad as his slice of the pie. There hasn't been any real investigation into Bonnafos's death."

Victor said, "Wait, all we signed on for was to find Tatiana's body. Just find her, not who killed her, if she was killed. Now you're phoning people in Kaliningrad? She wasn't killed in Kaliningrad and her body isn't in Kaliningrad. I'm saying this as a sober man: we should stay with what we know."

"There's also a missing Italian custom bicycle," Arkady said. By then, Victor had hung up.

How does a man know when he becomes obsessive? Who can tell him except a friend? More specifically, how could two men cover one city, let alone two cities, hundreds of miles apart? He would need a dozen detectives and police dogs, none of which the prosecutor would authorize. All Zurin would support was a game of musical chairs in the morgue. At this point, if Tatiana had been moved from drawer to drawer, her body would be light blue with a film of crystals. Perhaps the person hiding her was waiting for the first mantle of snow to lay her down properly, when outrage was spent and she was just one saint out of many. The strange thing was Arkady looked forward to listening to the other tapes, not because Tatiana's voice was especially mellifluous, but because it was clear, and not because the events she described were dramatic but because she underplayed her part. And because, listening to the tapes, he thought he knew her and that they had met before. Was that obsessive?

Chapter Eleven

"The moon will float up in the sky, / Dropping the oars into the water. / As ever, Russia will get by, / And dance and weep in every quarter."

"So nothing changes," Tatiana said. "The poet Yesenin knew it a hundred years ago. Russia is a drunken bear, sometimes an entertainment, sometimes a threat, often a genius, but as night falls, always a drunken bear curled up in the corner. Sometimes, in another corner lies a journalist whose arms and hands have systematically been broken. The thugs who do such work are meticulous. We don't have to go to Chechnya to find such men. We recruit them and train them and call them patriots. And when they find an honest journalist, they let the bear loose.

"Is it worth it? The problem with martyrdom is the waiting. Sooner or later, I will be poisoned or nudged off a cliff or shot by a stranger, but first I will put a torpedo under their waterline, so to speak.

"Also, why does heaven seem so dull? There's love in heaven but is there passion? Do we really have to go barefoot and wear those robes? Are we allowed high heels? I have always envied women in high heels. I would like to spend my first thousand years in heaven learning to tango. In the meantime, I'll stay ahead of the bear as long as I can."

It wasn't so much that he was listening to her, it was more a sense of being alone with her, and if they were alone, he would have been so bold as to offer her a cigarette.

When Arkady heard a key in the door, his first impulse was to gather the tapes and recorder and put them in a kitchen cabinet. He didn't. Then wished he had.

Anya came in and Alexi Grigorenko piled in after. They were flushed with pre-party hysteria and the first bottle of Champagne. If it was bad taste for him to celebrate so soon after a father's death, there also was a message to men of his father's generation that old manners, even between thieves, were out of date. He seemed to think he was a prince. In fact, he was a sitting duck. They made a handsome pair of boutique darlings, Arkady had to admit. In comparison, he looked as if he had dressed from a stranger's clothesline.

Anya said, "Alexi said he wanted to see my apartment, then I thought I heard Tatiana in yours."

"She's an interesting woman," Arkady said.

"She's seductive even dead, apparently." Anya walked back and forth, almost sniffing the air.

"I hope we're not disturbing you," Alexi said.

Anya said, "Arkady is always up, like a monk at his prayers."

"Is that how you solve your cases?" Alexi asked. "Prayer?"

"A good deal of the time."

Alexi's eyes were slightly hooded. Hands quick and delicate as a croupier's. Under his jacket the hitch of a gun.

"Can I offer you a drink? Something to eat?" Arkady asked, as if there were any food in the refrigerator.

"No thanks," Anya said. "He's going to show me his new apartment. It's a penthouse."

"Penthouse?" That was a word Arkady never expected to hear on Russian lips. "You're moving to Moscow?"

"Why not?" Alexi said. "Grisha left a number of properties and investments here and in Kaliningrad."

"He left the makings of a war. Things were quiet until your father was killed. Quiet like a jungle, but quiet. Why don't you cash out and live peacefully on some tropical island?"

"Perhaps I have more faith and less negativity than you do." Alexi's gaze lit on Tatiana's cassette tapes, still on the table. "For instance, how can you stand to listen to this garbage?"

Alexi reached for the cassettes and Arkady seized his wrist. "Don't."

"Okay, relax." Alexi straightened up and rubbed his arm. "I had no idea they meant that much to you. My mistake."

Arkady knew it was a moment that distilled the day. Alexi's ambition compared to his own isolation. He didn't dare look at Anya.

One in the morning was a territory as much as a time, and Victor Orlov and Arkady were long-term residents. Victor

119

dropped into a chair and contemplated the recorder and cassettes on the kitchen table.

"Is this what you've been listening to?"

"Tatiana."

"Huh. She's the one who's been fucking you over."

"Victor, she's dead."

"Doesn't matter. She has you ready to make a swan dive into a bucket of shit. Just because you got authority to go to Kaliningrad doesn't mean you have to do it. This is not exactly hot pursuit. She's been dead for ten days and my only hope is that whoever got her has her on ice."

"There's a connection—"

"There's no connection. Tatiana Petrovna jumped off her apartment balcony in Moscow, was autopsied in Moscow, and if the fuck-ups in the morgue lost her, they did it in Moscow."

"I visited her apartment twice," Arkady said. "The first time, it was turned upside down by someone searching for something, maybe the notebook. The second time, it was absolutely bare, to take no chances."

Victor said, "I asked around. The first time was skinheads trashing the place just for the fun of it. The second time the apartment was bare because the developer wants to build a shopping mall. Those are the facts. I have to ask, Arkady, are you feeling okay?"

"I talked to the prosecutor. He agreed that I could search in Kaliningrad."

"Of course he did. Kaliningrad is like Siberia. He'd like it if you spent the rest of your life searching for bodies in Kaliningrad."

"Just a day trip."

"To Kaliningrad? No such thing, you'll see. Chasing a body from town to town, calling a bicycle maker in Milan? That's too crazy even for me."

Too crazy for Victor? That was worrisome, Arkady thought.

He said, "The bicycle maker led us to Bonnafos, who, I believe, was a source for Tatiana. We can't question him because, unfortunately, he was shot and killed on the same beach where the notebook was found. It was important enough for Tatiana to make a special trip to Kaliningrad. I don't know what she was after, but the notebook is the key."

"Only you can't read it."

"That's right. We'll have to call in some experts."

"Didn't you try with Professor Kunin?"

"We'll try again."

Victor said, "I just don't get it. Why are you so hooked by a notebook no one can read? I'm with you, but I want you to know how I feel."

"Now I know."

"That we're covering two cities. This should be interesting."

"Do you want to see the notebook? See what the fuss is all about? It's in the desk."

Victor dug his hands into his coat pockets. "I'll pass. It's late and I can already feel the blade of the guillotine. We're so fucked."

It was a shameful thing for Arkady to admit, but he couldn't wait for Victor to leave so he could return to the tapes and listen to the voice within the words. He had read that auditory hallucinations were more subtle and more powerful than their visual counterparts. He still occasionally heard his wife, Irina. Which was crazy, since she was dead.

On the last cassettes, Tatiana sounded tired, her guard down.

"I am supposed to be so grave but I am sick of gravity. Of being Our Lady of the Sorrows. Of being Tatiana Petrovna. In fact, I'd rather steal away with the Gypsies. Perhaps I'm insane. I ache for a man I haven't met."

That said enough, Arkady thought. Yet there was the last cassette with a metallic tapping so faint it was hardly worth recording. Arkady dug into Zhenya's box of castaway computer gear, USB connections, tapes, headphones, disks, electrical chessboards. Monkey see, monkey do. He had seen Zhenya attach the sound-enhancer system to his earphones a hundred times. Arkady plugged them into the recorder and listened.

Silence. Vacuum. An amplified three taps of metal on metal. Then three scrapes. Silence. Tap, tap, tap.

Arkady's father had taught him a number of useful skills. How to field-strip a gun, signal with flags, send Morse code.

The tapping and scraping was in Morse code and said over and over, "We are alive."

Who was alive? For how long? Why would Tatiana keep such a faint recording? The realization came with a cold sweat. How could he not know?

The nuclear submarine *Kursk* had been carrying one hundred and eighteen officers and sailors to war games in Arctic waters when, for unexplained reasons, its forward torpedoes exploded, setting off fires the length of the ship. The crew had operated in the highest tradition of the Russian navy and were posthumously awarded Orders of Courage. Families were reassured that the entire crew died almost instantaneously.

Tap. Tap. Scrape.

The chief of rescue operations reported that he heard knocking in the submarine's Compartment 9 at the rear of the hull.

"Everything is being done. People should remain calm and stay at their position," the prime minister said, and hosted a barbecue at a Black Sea villa.

Tap ... Tap ...

At a press conference, the mother of a crewman demanded the truth. She was forcibly sedated and dragged from the hall. The chief of operations decided that he must have misinterpreted signs of life from Compartment 9.

The tapping came to an end.

Finally, ten days after the accident, Norwegian divers breached the hatch and found a scribbled note wrapped in plastic on the body of a seaman dredged from Compartment 9. He had marked his note 15:15, four hours after the explosion. Some experts thought that the twenty-three submariners may have lived another three to four days.

The label on the cassette said "Grisha," although the connection to the *Kursk* escaped Arkady like a fish between his hands.

Chapter Twelve

His wife, Irina, had died years ago. Still, whenever Arkady heard a voice like hers in the hubbub of the metro or saw a beautiful woman in full stride, he remembered her. While she was alive, the mystery had been why a woman as intelligent as Irina would cast her lot with a man as lacking in prospects as Arkady. Later, he didn't talk about her for fear of turning her death into a "story" inevitably altered by the telling, the way a gold coin handled year after year is rubbed smooth and effaced.

Arkady remembered every detail.

They were going out for dinner and a film. Irina had a minor infection and it was Arkady's inspiration to stop at the local polyclinic for an antibiotic. The waiting room was full of skaters, drunks and grandmothers with sniffling children in hand. Irina asked Arkady to step out and find a newsstand. She was a journalist, and for her, going without a newspaper was like going without oxygen.

He remembered a balmy evening, cottonwood fluff gathering in the air and, stapled to trees, notices that offered medicines for sale.

Meanwhile the waiting room emptied and Irina was taken in to see the doctor, who prescribed Bactrim. On the books, the polyclinic had an ample supply. In reality, the cupboard was bare, the drugs having vanished out the back door.

Was Irina allergic to penicillin? So much so that she underlined the words on her chart. But the nurse's mind was on a letter she had received that day informing her that her son had sold her apartment and she had a week to pack. The only word she heard was *penicillin*. Since the polyclinic was out of oral doses, she gave Irina an injection and left the room. By the time Arkady returned with a newspaper and a magazine, Irina was dead.

Wrapped in a damp sheet, she looked as if she had washed up on shore. Apparently, as her windpipe began to close in anaphylactic shock, Irina recognized the nurse's error and came out of the examining room with the vial in her hand. A counterinjection of adrenaline would have saved her. In a panic, the doctor snapped off the key to the pharmacy cabinet, sealing her fate. She saw. She knew.

When Arkady closed her eyes the doctor warned him not to touch the "corpus." Arkady's face went dark, his hands became grappling hooks and he threw the doctor against a wall. The rest of the staff retreated to the hallway and called the militia to deal with the madman. In the meantime, Arkady sat and held her hand as if they were going someplace together.

Tatiana reminded him of Irina. They were both fearless and idealistic. And, Arkady conceded, they were both dead.

The phone jarred him. It was Maxim Dal, the poet.

"Do you call everyone in the middle of the night?" Arkady asked.

"Only night people. I rarely make a mistake. The pallor, silence, malnutrition—you have all the signs. Do you have a microwave?"

"Of course."

"I will bet you fifty-fifty that there is some forgotten food in that microwave."

Arkady opened the microwave. Inside was a shriveled enchilada. "What do you want?"

"Do you remember our conversation about Tatiana's notebook?"

"You were up for some sort of American prize for lifetime achievement?"

"For being alive, yes. Do you remember that I asked you about Tatiana's notebook and whether I'm mentioned in it?"

"What does it matter? You told me you had a short-lived romantic liaison with her twenty years ago."

"That's the problem. Once upon a time I was a professor and Tatiana was a young student. American universities do not approve of such liaisons. They're Puritans. If there's a hint of scandal my prize becomes a spitball."

"Haven't you had enough honors in your career?"

"I've had a dry spell. Fuck the honor. The difference is fifty thousand dollars as a visiting poet in America or a beggar's bowl in Kaliningrad. Have you ever been in Kaliningrad?"

"No."

"There's no security anymore. It's not like the old days when a member of the Writers' Union could compose an ode to rutabagas and be paid. It's not like Moscow either. It's a separate world. Really, if you ever go there, you have to let me take you around."

Arkady yawned. His eyes felt as though they were sinking into his head. "I don't think so. How would they even hear about the notebook?"

"Other poets. I'm not the only candidate."

"I didn't know that poetry was such a cutthroat occupation. I don't think you have anything to worry about. There's only a few pages and I didn't see your name."

"Do you have the notebook?"

"Yes, under lock and key."

"Have you read it?"

"No one has. No one can. Relax. Good night."

Arkady was about to go to bed when Victor called to apologize for some of his earlier comments.

"You're entitled to an opinion. We'll talk in the morning."

"Wait, I was out of line. It's the focus on Kaliningrad. Remember, I was stationed there when I was in the navy. It was a top-secret piss hole. You couldn't even find it on the map."

"Thanks." Arkady took it as a vote of confidence.

"One other thing I forgot to mention. I saw Zhenya on your street today. Did you talk to him?"

"No. Where was he?"

"Outside the building."

"Did he see you?"

"I think so, because he ducked out of sight like a squirrel."

"Typical."

"I just thought I'd let you know."

Arkady was asleep as soon as his head hit the pillow. He had the sensation of being wrapped in a spiderweb, but comfortably. Snug. Tucked in. Then plunging into a black depth, a cold wind on his face. Still, no complaints. If this was sleep, so be it. Above, a fading dot of light. Below, an invisible city.

The city spread and turned to liquid. Arkady made a splash and became a torpedo speeding toward the outline of a ship. It was odd that Tatiana had fixed on a submarine accident that occurred twelve years before. *Squirrel* described Zhenya perfectly.

Zhenya.

Arkady's eyes were wide open. He swung out of bed and went to his office, turning on lights along the way. The desk was mahogany with brass hardware, and on the right bottom drawer, there was a false front and a dial safe that only he knew the combination to. Nevertheless, he held his breath while he tried the handle and found it closed and locked.

Perhaps Zhenya had simply been in the neighborhood or happened to come by while Arkady was out. There were any number of explanations. Arkady didn't believe any of them.

As he turned the dial, he could feel the tumblers fall: two turns to the right, two left, one right. With a soft pop the door eased open.

His gun, a presentation Makarov, lay on the bottom of the safe, but the notebook was gone. In its place was the form for parental permission for early enlistment in the army waiting to be signed.

Chapter Thirteen

Zhenya lived out of train station lockers and hustled chess. Not tedious four-hour games with locked antlers but Blitz: forty moves in five minutes. He took $50 from a ship's cook waiting for the train to Archangel and as much from an oilman headed to the rigs of Samarkand. Zhenya's fingers moved pizzicato, plucking pieces off the board. Boarding in ten minutes? Zhenya could fit in two games, maybe three.

His favorite site was a small park called Patriarch's Ponds, in a neighborhood of embassies, town houses and sidewalk cafés. He sat on a bench and set out his chessboard and pieces as if musing over a difficult position. Sooner or later, someone would stop to give him advice.

In the meantime, he enjoyed the pond's collection of swans and ducks—mallard, goldeneye, teal—dressed in iridescent feathers. He knew the names of all the waterfowl and the trees. When a boy skipped bottle caps at the swans and was led away by the ear, Zhenya heartily approved. A breeze drove cotton-wood fluff to a corner of the pond. The papery seeds of elms were slow enough to catch.

The architecture school of the university was close by, and students on a midday break congregated around benches. Although they were only two years older than Zhenya, they were infinitely more sophisticated. All the students, male and female, held open bottles of beer, casually posing like models in a glossy magazine. Their jeans were torn at the knee as a fashion statement. His jeans were simply worn through. It wasn't as if they snubbed him. They didn't see him at all. And what kind of conversation would they have if they did notice him? Snorkeling off the coast of Mexico? Skiing in France? There were half a dozen girls in the group, including a redhead with milk-white skin who was so beautiful that all Zhenya could do was stare. She whispered behind her hand and Zhenya watched the whisper travel through the group.

"Excuse me."

"What?" Zhenya was startled when a boy spoke to him. He was the largest in the group and wore a Stanford sweatshirt.

"I'm sorry, I didn't mean to surprise you, but aren't you the Chess Creep?"

"I'm what?"

Other conversations died down.

"We've seen you at different train stations hustling games. You're doing the same thing here. What's the deal?"

Zhenya felt like an insect under a microscope.

"I don't know what you're talking about."

"Sure you do. You're doing it now. That's why we call you the Chess Creep."

Zhenya stood, his face burning. Even so, the Stanford boy loomed over him and said, "Relax, I'm not picking on you. I just want to know, are you the Chess Creep? From your lips. No?" Mr. Stanford turned toward the redhead. "Lotte, is this the Creep or not?"

She said, "The word I used was—"

At that moment a swan came out of the water, hissing, wings spread, neck stretched like a snake, to chase the same brat who had bedeviled him before. As the architecture students bolted, the chessboard was knocked off the bench, scattering pieces in all directions.

Zhenya found himself alone, searching the path and grass and fallen leaves for kings and queens. He found all the pieces except a black pawn that bobbed in the pond out of reach.

Creep rang in Zhenya's head.

He stuffed everything into his backpack, pushing aside the notebook he had taken from Arkady's desk. It was a puzzle without a clue but it served a purpose if it forced Arkady to sign the forms for early enlistment in the army. Zhenya had been truant so long he was off the books and going nowhere. How long could he survive by cadging games with weary travelers? Most young people coming through the stations were connected to iPhones. Some didn't even know basic openings in chess, the most Russian of intellectual tests. Without a diploma, Zhenya would be vying with Tajiks and Uzbeks to push a broom. His other options were the army or the police. He certainly wouldn't do the latter. The solution rate for professional murders was 4 percent. How could they even call themselves police?

Chapter Fourteen

A pathologist was no respecter of men. To him, heroes, tyrants, holy men were all meat on a slab. Alive, they may have been draped in military decorations or a professor's robes. Dead, their secrets poured out as cheesy rolls of fat, blackened liver, the tender brain exposed in its bowl. Nothing more.

That Willy Polenko was still alive was a relief to the other pathologists, because nobody wanted to carve up a colleague. He had done his part, lost a hundred pounds, huffed and puffed around the dim halls of the morgue for exercise, a half-deflated balloon moving in slow motion. Tatiana's body had been found—not only found, but burned, and her ashes resided in a cardboard box labeled "Unknown Female #13312."

Willy told Arkady, "You can upgrade to an urn of ceramic or wood. Most people choose the wood."

"I told you there was to be no cremation."

"I know, I know, it happened when I wasn't here. Half the assistants are Tajiks. If you give them orders and they nod their heads, it means they haven't understood a word you said. On the other hand, they don't drink the disinfectant. Anyway, with this and that, she was two weeks unclaimed and you know how it is, the lowest fruit is picked first."

"But cremated?"

Willy consulted a folder. "She was identified by her sister, her only sibling. She made the request."

"Her sister was here in Moscow?"

"No. She wasn't well enough to travel from Kaliningrad, so she performed the identification by phone from her home."

"On a cell phone? We're in a tunnel here and the reception is impossible."

"We took the picture here and went up to the street and transmitted it."

"Who took the picture?"

"Someone."

"Was it saved?"

"Unfortunately not."

"Teeth?"

"You might find some pulverized in the bottom of the box."

"Enough for DNA?"

"Not after cremation. What can I tell you, I'm surrounded by incompetents."

"Did they, at least, get any corroborating identification?"

"By a Detective Lieutenant Stasov of the Kaliningrad police." Willy patted the folder. "It's all in here."

"One last question. If this is Tatiana Petrovna, why is the box labeled 'Unknown Female'?"

"It could mean we're running out of boxes. Do you want it? Her sister said we should dispose of it any way we want."

"You're not serious."

"It's you or the trash bin."

"Have you tried her magazine or her friends?"

"I can't dash around scattering ashes like salt and pepper. You know these people."

"And the folder?"

"All yours." He handed everything over and gave Arkady a critical opinion. "I really think you should go with wood."

In his car, Arkady tried calling Ludmila Petrovna again, and got no answer. The same with Detective Stasov. The operator at *Now* said that Obolensky had not come in. The dead were dead. The living marched on.

Arkady visited the computer repair shop where Zhenya sometimes worked. The technicians said that he had been in earlier to borrow a laptop.

As Arkady drove away, he kept an eye out for the boy's skulking figure. Zhenya had not picked up any of Arkady's calls, in itself a form of negotiation.

Victor had called and left a message to meet at the cemetery where Grisha Grigorenko was buried. Two men had been shot execution-style and dumped like offerings at Grisha's headstone. The War of Succession had begun.

Detectives Slovo and Blok had partnered so long they had come to look like each other, with similar steel glasses and jowls of white stubble. They had plans to retire together and live in a dacha and garden in Sochi, and they were not about to be dragged into a shooting war. They had produced the outer semblance of an investigation—the immediate site was cordoned off—but the forensic van had not arrived.

Victor led Arkady through the cemetery gate. "Blok and Slovo are old-school. As far as they're concerned, if two gangs want to fight it out, fuck 'em, let them kill each other. Two dead is a good start."

"Welcome, gentlemen," Slovo said. "Do you know how much I'm going to miss your two ugly mugs? Zero. We're having a good-bye party. You're not invited. And neither are these two."

The victims had bloody hair and a Nordic pallor. Arkady recognized them from the Den as Alexi's men; they had swaggered then, released from a murder charge for lack of evidence. Arkady wanted to see if they were armed but didn't dare move the bodies before the forensic van arrived. Slovo and Blok were happy to do nothing. Their attention had moved on to their next life. Blok's clipboard carried an article on "planning a subtropical garden." "Did you know that there are two hundred sixty-four days of sunshine annually in Sochi?" he asked Victor.

"Amazing."

Slovo indicated a grave digger who stood at attention with a shovel. "Here's the man who found them."

It was one of the grave diggers that Arkady had talked to two weeks before, on the night of the demonstration. It occurred to Arkady that there was no one else in sight.

"Where is everybody?"

Slovo said, "The workers are celebrating Sanitary Internment Day."

"What does that mean? 'Sanitize' what? It's a cemetery."

"It means they're taking the day off," Victor said. "That's why it took so long for the bodies to be discovered."

The angles of the entry wounds suggested that the men had died on their feet. In both cases the bullet entered through the right rear quadrant of the skull and exited through the opposite eye. Been executed, not died. The lack of blood on the headstone and on the ground around them indicated that the victims had been shot somewhere else and brought to Grisha's headstone to add insult to injury.

"Like bookends," Blok said.

"Like a gang war," Slovo said. "Well, we'll be out of it soon."

"Counting the days."

"Peace and quiet."

Arkady played the beam of his penlight on one body and then the other. Revolvers were reliable and Glocks were in style, but real artistes used a pistol with a .22 slug that would carom like a billiard ball within the cranium and even stay inside. Nothing was so tidy about the dead men themselves. Bloodstains and gray matter speckled them from head to toe, as if they had shared one last, enormous sneeze.

Arkady said, "It makes no sense. Who would want to start a gang war now? The pot is always simmering, but there's a rough understanding now. A parity. Everyone is making money."

"That doesn't change the fact they're killers," said Slovo.

"They'd shoot their mother if she was standing on a dollar bill," said Blok.

"It looks like a gang war to me," said Victor. "Now Alexi has to do something."

Arkady took in Grisha's headstone and its life-size portrait etched in granite. Was this a gangster's pyramid, his landmark for the ages? Or a biography with just the good parts: the civic leader, bon vivant, generous donor, rugged sportsman, family man standing with one foot up on the bumper of a Jeep Cherokee, a ski slope in the background, with a yachtsman's cap cocked on his head and on his face the grin of a man who had it all. Yet something was missing or out of place.

"The car key is gone," Victor said.

It was snapped off at the surface of the headstone, a message that anyone could understand.

"That reminds me," Slovo told Arkady, "Abdul Khan wants to see you."

"*The* Abdul Khan?"

"Actually, he wants to talk to whoever is handling the Tatiana Petrovna case. I told him there was no case anymore but he refused to take no for an answer. I said you'd be in touch."

"Abdul is one of your players in the Tatiana case," Victor said.

"So far as I can see, there is no Grigorenko case or Tatiana case," Arkady said.

"I couldn't agree more," said Blok.

"It's a double negative," said Slovo.

Victor said, "It's a dog chasing his fucking tail."

140

Chapter Fifteen

Millions of Russians are terrified by a few Chechens.
Why?
Because when they are brutal, we are ten times as brutal.
For every blow delivered to us, ten blows will rain down
    on them.
You say, I don't know whom to strike.
I say, strike them all.
You say, I don't know whom to strike.
I say, strike them all.

Abdul wore a black T shirt with his name written in white across the chest and he delivered his video rap on a burned-out Russian tank, a rocket-propelled grenade launcher on his shoulder. Next, Abdul was in an iron cage, beating another man's face to a pulp. Then he raced a BMW, a "Boomer" as they were known, in and out of high-speed traffic. Next, he carried the limp figure of a woman to a four-poster bed. Abdul had thick black hair and yellow eyes and Arkady would not have been surprised to see him lean back and howl like a wolf.

> *You say you don't know whom to fuck,*
> *I say fuck them all,*
> *Fuck them all,*
> *Fuck them all.*

The screening room went dark and when the lights came up, Abdul was bent over a video console scribbling notes. An entourage of beefed-up guards stood with arms crossed. Beautiful women as listless as mannequins sprawled in leather chairs. They all wore black "Abdul" T shirts. Arkady planned to interview major Mafia chiefs about Tatiana. Admittedly, there was no case, but maybe this was the best time.

"What do you think?" Abdul asked.

"Of the video? I'm really not a critic." Arkady hoped he seemed impressed. The soundproofed walls, minibar, audio mixer and video console the size of a spaceship bridge were symbols of success. They were also subtle reminders of Abdul's enterprises: the demolition business in Grozny, the cars he stole in Germany, the prostitutes he ran in Moscow's finest hotels, all advertised to the insistent beat of rap.

"Your honest opinion?"

"Well, a bit . . ."

"Yeah?"

"Over-the-top."

"Over-the-top?"

"A touch."

"Fuck you. My last DVD sold five hundred thousand copies worldwide. I get a thousand hits on my website in a day. Does that sound over-the-top?"

"It sounds frightening." It seemed to Arkady that they were getting off track. "You told Detectives Slovo and Blok that you knew Tatiana Petrovna?" It still seemed unlikely to Arkady.

"Yeah."

"On a friendly basis?"

"You find that unbelievable. A policeman should know that no one is one hundred percent saint or sinner."

"And now you're a good citizen?"

"Why not?"

Victor had selected Abdul, "Ape" Beledon and Valentina Shagelman as the Mafia heads most likely to order a bullet for Grisha Grigorenko. Otherwise, they were all good citizens.

"During the war Tatiana was a friend to the Chechen people and tried to make peace. Every time there was an atrocity—and, believe me, there were atrocities on a daily basis—she would show up, unbidden as it were." He heard a snicker run through his entourage. "Get out. What the fuck are you sitting around for? All of you. Out!"

The men appeared used to their leader's mercurial changes in attitude. They sighed and left and the women stumbled after. Abdul paused to let the dust settle.

"Cretins."

143

"No problem. It sounds as if you and Tatiana got along."

"Got along? You could say so. Twice in Chechnya I had my sights on her. The first time I noticed she was carrying a child covered in blood. The next time I had her in my sights, she was carrying a grandmother to safety. I decided that before I pulled the trigger I should try to discover who this person was."

Was the story true? Abdul was an expert at creating his own legend.

Abdul dug into his minibar. "Would you like some water, beer, brandy?"

"No, thanks."

"So I sought her out."

"And?"

"Well, I learned she was a woman."

"What does that mean?"

"You figure it out, you're the investigator. I'll only say this: Tatiana Petrovna was a fighter. She never jumped from any balcony."

"It doesn't matter. There's no case and no body."

"I know. People say you're crazy." Abdul threw punches in the air. "They really do. They say you're nuts. I saw you at Grisha's funeral giving his son, Alexi, a tough time. And you don't carry a gun? That's lunatic."

"There's no case."

"If you care, there's always a case. Hey, I want your opinion. I have a second DVD."

"Another?"

"Tatiana thought the video needed, maybe, a little balance.

144

To expand my base, you know." He nodded toward the door. "My friends are my friends but artistically, they're bricks."

"Go ahead." Why not another bath of testosterone? Arkady thought. So far as he could tell, the only information that Abdul had provided was an insinuation that he had slept with Tatiana, a boast she was too dead to deny.

It was the same DVD with the same combination of vanity and gore. Identical, except for a closing shot of Abdul looking directly at the camera as a tear coursed down his cheek.

"Empathy," Abdul said.

"By the ton."

Shagelman did a good imitation of a cretin. His shirt and suit were a size too small, so that his tattoos seemed to creep out of his cuffs. His smile was a simpleton's grin, lit by two gold teeth. He said virtually nothing. At Mafia councils, he was mute. Later, he would go home to the kitchen of his apartment and report every word to his wife, Valentina, while she sharpened her knives and sliced meat, peppers and onions for shish kebab. Shagelman always cried when she cut the onions.

Valentina did not approve of Tatiana. "A woman's place is in the home, listening to a husband, helping him, guiding him, not drawing attention to herself."

Without drawing attention to herself, Valentina had built a fortune out of public construction done in her husband's name.

She insisted on serving Arkady and her husband black tea and cookies in the living room that was a nest of tapestries and

Persian rugs. With her hair drawn in a bun she looked like a tea cozy herself.

"I can't say I'm sorry that Tatiana Petrovna has passed. She always had good things to say about the Chechens and bad things to say about Russia. It's a terrible thing to say, but good riddance."

"Do you think someone might have actually felt the same and harmed her?"

"I'm only saying that Tatiana Petrovna was a traitor and a whore."

Isaac Shagelman kept his gaze down and out of trouble.

Valentina stirred strawberry jam into her tea. "Don't you think Grisha Grigorenko had a dignified funeral service?"

Well, yes, Arkady thought. Except for the bullet hole in the back of his head. "Were Grisha and Tatiana friends?"

The question took Valentina by surprise.

"People said so. I don't pay attention to such rumors. Grisha liked to take chances. He took up waterskiing. I told him, waterskiing is for grandchildren. Him and his boat!"

"What was it called?"

"*Natalya Goncharova*. Such a boat."

On a side table, Arkady noticed a short stack of glossy calendars from something called the Curonian Bank. He had never heard of it but the Shagelmans were known for setting up banks that were little more than slick catalogs and shell games. The cover photo was of a pelican swallowing a fish.

"A pretty picture." He picked up a calendar.

"Take one, please."

"Is there any connection to Curonian Renaissance, the real estate developer?"

"Hmm." Valentina found something at the bottom of her cup to stir.

"Wasn't Curonian Renaissance trying to develop the building where Tatiana Petrovna lived?"

"I suppose so."

"Wasn't she holding up the project?"

"You know, people like Tatiana Petrovna act as if gentrification is a dirty word. We are going to build a beautiful shopping mall with over a hundred stores. Chips fly when you're chopping wood."

"That's what everybody tells me," Arkady said.

Ivan "Ape" Beledon was proud of living in a dacha that had once been a country residence of the KGB. No rustic cabin this, instead a spa with a pool, tennis court, masseur, mud bath, billiard table, cigar humidor and bodyguards indoors and out.

Ape Beledon and Arkady sat by the tennis court. The Mafia chief had stripped to swim trunks and showed off spindly arms and a back of thick hairs that wafted in the breeze. No one called him Ape in his presence, and although he specialized in the trafficking of drugs, he dismissed anyone in his organization who "tasted the goods," as he put it.

His two sons were playing on the court and Ape looked benignly in their direction from time to time. "They have it so easy, they don't know. Respect is dead."

"Do you ever play them?"

"Do I look crazy? They hang out a lot with Grisha's son, Alexi. Ambitious kids. I once saw Yeltsin play Pavarotti on this tennis court. Now, that was a game." Beledon sorted through an array of vitamins and fruit on a silver tray. "Boris hit every ball hard, no matter what. Pavarotti's weight was misleading. He could have been a professional soccer player. The look on Yeltsin's face when Pavarotti played a drop shot. I wiped away tears. The question is, what was the look on Grisha's face when someone put a pistol to his head? Was it surprise or resignation? To die is one thing; to be betrayed is another. It all depends on who the 'someone' is, right? The relationship." Ape stopped to applaud an ace. "Don't you love kids? Not a care in the world. Remember Brando in *The Godfather*? Has a heart attack playing with his grandson. That's the way to go. Family. Of course, it helps if the kid's an earner. Develops business. Shows a little ambition. Although there's such a thing as too much ambition too soon. That can create conflicts. Take you, for example. So far as I can tell, the only thing you were supposed to be doing was finding the body of Tatiana Petrovna, who, by the way, I always held in high regard despite the fact we were on opposite sides of the fence, so to speak. Okay. But she's been found, at least her ashes. What are you after now? You tell me."

"I'm after whoever killed her," Arkady said.

"See? An honest answer. I like that. No official authority, no waiting for a prosecutor to find his dick, just stubborn determination. Whose ox is gored? That's what to look for. Who benefits. Here, take some pills with you. You look like you could use a little vitamin C. And D." Ape got to his feet. "The boys will show you out."

"I thought we were going to talk about Tatiana Petrovna."

"We did."

Victor still hadn't answered his phone. He wasn't at the Den or any of the half dozen bars or stand-up cafeterias with steamy windows that he frequented. Finally, Arkady tried the Armory, a watering hole for frontier guards. Victor was in a rear booth, ashamed at being found but—as if his legs had been sawed off—unable to leave his new comrades.

"Wait, these are very educated gentlemen."

"Let's go," Arkady said.

"Their words are few but profound."

Two faces with lopsided grins looked up at Arkady.

"He's our buddy."

"He's going to join us on Frontier Guards Day."

That was a rash promise. On their day, the Frontier Guards were famous for drinking and mobbing Red Square.

"One more glass," Victor begged Arkady.

"Stand up."

"I can do it. I don't need any help. For God's sake, leave a man a little dignity." Victor bowed theatrically and slid off the bench in a heap.

Arkady managed to get him to the car.

As they drove, Arkady noticed that the *Natalya Goncharova*, Grisha's superyacht, was no longer anchored off the Kremlin

Pier. In which case, where was Alexi staying? He had boasted to Anya about having a penthouse. Either way he was out of Arkady's reach.

Victor hung his head out the window and sniffed like a connoisseur. "Fresh air."

Chapter Sixteen

Whose ox was gored?

The question had a biblical resonance. Arkady imagined an ancient Sumerian standing in a field of trampled grain and asking the same question. Who suffered? Who gained?

Beledon and Valentina were established organizations, doing very nicely, thank you, and not likely to see any benefit in upsetting the apple cart. Or the ox.

Abdul observed no such niceties. *You say, I don't know whom to strike. I say, strike them all.* But was a Chechen organization going to take on every Russian gang? Abdul seemed more involved with the sales of his DVDs than he was with revolution.

Alexi Grigorenko thought that he could inherit his father's enterprises by making a public claim on them. Just by his ignorance, he was dangerous.

Whose ox was gored?

*

At night, Arkady drove along the halo of car dealerships and gentlemen's clubs that stretched along the Ring Road. Zhenya called on Arkady's cell phone and was even more maddening than usual.

"What is the notebook about?"

Arkady said, "It's nothing. It's just a notebook. The main thing is that you stole it and I want it back."

"You said it was in code."

"I don't know what it is. It has no value."

"Is that why you locked it in a safe? Maybe I should tear it up."

"Don't."

"Maybe I should be asking for money too. But I'll be generous. All I want is the parental form signed so I can enlist. I can join the army, and you can keep a notebook that nobody can read."

"It's for a dead case."

"It's not dead if you're working it."

"It's for Tatiana Petrovna."

"I know that."

"How do you know that?" There were no names on or in the notebook as far as Arkady remembered.

An edge developed in Zhenya's voice. "Just sign the permission."

"Are you breaking the code?"

"I'll give you an hour, and then I'll start tearing up the notebook."

"Have you been reading it? What else have you learned?"

"Sign the slip," Zhenya said, and hung up.

"Shit," Arkady said. No other word would do.

As soon as he reached his apartment, Arkady dropped onto his bed. He had heard not a sound from Anya's flat and was not about to knock on her door. Perhaps she and Alexi were enjoying a pre-party party. Arkady didn't care. All he craved was sleep, and he was still dressed when he pulled up his coverlet.

Fatigue conjured up the strangest dreams. He found himself following a tapping sound down a dark hallway, rapid claw taps on a wooden floor. As he caught up, it became evident that he was following a white rabbit that slipped in and out of red velvet drapes. Arkady was nearly within reach when the rabbit bolted into a room that was full of men in Nazi SS uniforms who bore horrible wounds.

Arkady's father sat at a table with a revolver and three telephones, white, red and black. What the colors signified, Arkady didn't know. Although the top of the general's head was shaved off, he smoked a cigarette with aplomb and when the white cat jumped onto his lap, he let it nestle like a favored pet. Anticipation was building. Although Arkady didn't understand a word, he was aware of hands pushing him toward the table. The pug turned his face up to Arkady.

The red telephone rang. It rang and rang until he woke in a sweat. The Germans and his father were gone. The revolver was gone and the nightmare was incomplete. The telephone, however, was ringing off its cradle.

"Hello."

"Hello, Investigator Renko. It's Lorenzo."

Arkady found his watch. It was three in the morning.

"Lorenzo . . ."

"From Ercolo Bicycles in Milan."

"What time is it there?"

"Midnight."

"I thought so." Arkady rubbed sleep out of his eyes.

"You told me to call if I found the receipt or number of the bike we made for a Signor Bonnafos. You have a pen and paper?"

Arkady fumbled in the drawer of his night table. "Yes."

"This will take just a second," Lorenzo promised.

"I'm ready."

"A bicycle is fitted like a custom suit, only more so."

"I understand."

"After all, a bicycle has to be not only a thing of beauty but durable enough to withstand the rigors of the road."

"I'm sure. What is the number?"

"This took hours of research. Are you ready?" Lorenzo asked. He called out the identification numbers like a bingo master: "JB-10-25-12-81. JB 10-25-12-81."

"Can you remember anything else about Bonnafos?"

"Cast bottom bracket and exposed cables."

"I meant personally."

"A fitness fanatic, but otherwise, I would have to say he had no personality."

"Women?"

"No."

"Politics?"

"No."

"Sports?"

"Aside from biking, no."

Arkady thought that Joseph Bonnafos sounded more and more a perfect cipher; perhaps that was an advantage for an interpreter.

"Anything else?" Lorenzo asked. "It's getting late."

"It is. Thank you. You've been very patient."

Arkady expected some polite disengagement. Lorenzo simply said, "Find the bike."

Arkady thought that even if Bonnafos was a cipher, his brain had to be phenomenal. According to studies, each human brain was different according to age, gender, consumption of vodka and disease. Was there a difference according to language? Around the world, people mimicked the sound of cats differently. If they heard cats differently, how could they ever understand each other? Eternal questions, Arkady thought. Obviously he was asleep on his feet.

But he heard the horn of a car alarm and from the bedroom window looked down on the garages across the street where the car alarm of his Niva blared. Arkady pressed his remote control to no effect, which only put him in more of a mood to shoot the car and be done with it.

Finally, for the sake of the neighbors, he took the elevator down and opened the garage. It was a tight little shack with just enough room for his car, a work counter and jerry cans. The garage light was out and when the car alarm quit he was in complete darkness.

He smelled ether.

When Arkady awoke, he was on his back between slabs of concrete covered in slime. He could raise his head halfway and cross one knee over the other. He had nothing but peripheral vision, black on one side and, on the other, the blinding headlights of a car.

He touched a knob that sat in the middle of his forehead from his first attempt to sit up.

"Where am I?"

"I'll give you a clue," Alexi said. "You're not on a yacht."

"A houseboat?"

"Close enough. A barge. Barge ballast, to be exact."

It was suspended on straps over another concrete pad where he was laid out like a canapé. Arkady twisted from side to side. He was, in effect, entombed with less room than a coffin.

"What do you want?"

"Very good. Under control. Because we want your full concentration."

Arkady felt his eyes open wide and found that he was on a level with the other man's shoes, not the best level to negotiate from. What he needed was a rabbit hole and a white rabbit to lead the way.

"What do you want?" Arkady repeated.

"I want the notebook that Anya gave you."

"I don't have it."

"Who does?"

"I don't know."

The ballast came to life and dropped enough to make a point. Totally without effect, Arkady tried to raise his knees and push back. He didn't shout. It seemed understood that any call for help would swiftly terminate the conversation. It wasn't the sort of situation that would end any other way. Only right away or a little later.

Alexi asked, "Do you think this will make an impression on Ape Beledon or Abdul? Maybe they'll take me more seriously. Make them suck up their balls. No opinion? Very well, I'll try again. Who has the notebook? I know it's not Anya. So, who can it be?"

"I told you, I don't know."

Alexi lowered the ballast again, so that Arkady breathed directly into it. The question was, what would be crushed first, rib cage or skull?

Thinking rationally in this situation demanded discipline. Nevertheless, Arkady was almost positive he was at the Moscow Marina. In the day some poor deckhand would have to scrape him off the pad. Meanwhile, Alexi had a remote-control wand and would go spotless.

"Tell me about Kaliningrad," Alexi said.

"Kaliningrad?" Arkady was taken by surprise.

"Kaliningrad. What's happening there?"

"I didn't know anything was happening there."

"It's all in the notebook."

"No one can read the notebook."

"Then give it back."

"I don't have the notebook, I can't read the notebook and I have no idea what's happening in Kaliningrad."

"Then there's no point in keeping you alive."

"I have a lot of other notebooks."

"You're stalling."

"No." Not literally, Arkady thought. Stalling involved the hope of rescue. He was only playing the game out.

The remote clicked and the ballast resumed its slow descent.

Alexi said, "I think it's a sin to kill yourself over a notebook you can't even read. It's not even wasteful, it's immoral."

"As soon as I tell you, you'll kill me."

"That's a pessimistic point of view. What have you got to lose?"

"I'll take you there."

"No expeditions. You tell me where the notebook is here and now."

"Wait."

"Too bad. Last chance. Good-bye."

A small something ran across the headlights. Not a white rabbit with pink eyes, long ears and a watch, but a dog with short ears and expressive eyes. The ballast stopped abruptly as the dog sniffed along its edge. A pug. Once it discovered Arkady, it squirmed with delight and crawled up his chest to lick his face.

Pugs were rare in Moscow. Arkady knew of only one.

Shouts and whistles tried to lure the dog out of his reach, but Arkady called, "Polo," and the dog came back.

When Alexi reached in, Arkady seized his arm and gave it a counterclockwise twist hard enough to dislocate the shoulder. This posed a dilemma for Alexi. He had the remote, but in a struggle, he could press the wrong button and crush half of himself as well because he was in the ferocious grip of someone who had decided to live.

The two men backed out from under the ballast like crabs locked in combat. Arkady was aware of fetid air lifting, of boats hauled out under the stars, of the dog running off and headlights retreating. For Alexi the pain of a dislocated shoulder left little time for decision making. He broke free but his gun was holstered under his left arm and his right arm hung uselessly.

Alexi said, "This never happened."

Arkady hit him in the face.

"That happened."

Hit him again on the same cheek.

"And that happened. Show yourself to Ape Beledon or Abdul now. Tell them any story you want."

Chapter Seventeen

The rain was miserable. The mud was miserable. Tomorrow would probably be miserable.

"Kaliningrad." Maxim spread his arms to welcome Arkady. "A fantasy gone wrong."

Starting with its Third World airport, Arkady thought. Construction and aspirations had each halted midway. Much of the roof had collapsed and what remained revealed twisted rebar and streaks of rust. Road barriers forced traffic to approach in a zigzag manner. Black BMW sedans queued to pick up officialdom, but Maxim trumped them all with his majestic ZIL.

"You drove from Moscow?" Arkady asked.

"Do you think I would leave my most valuable possession behind?"

"How did you know I would be on the plane?"

"Anya told me. I decided that like Dante in the inferno, you

would need a guide. 'All hope abandon, ye who enter here.'"
Maxim loaded Arkady's bag. He actually seemed cheery.
"Remember, I taught here for years. If anyone can lead you
safely through the dangers in this land of contradiction, it's
me." He showed Arkady a bottle of twelve-year-old Hennessy
in a paper bag. "For special parking privileges. In fact, I'm
showcasing the ZIL to promote a classic car rally from Moscow
to Kaliningrad. Get in and I'll be back in a minute."

Maxim bounded through the rain, bag and cognac tucked
under one arm.

Arkady understood that, basically, Maxim Dal had volun-
teered in order to protect his Ancient Poet's Prize and its
windfall of $50,000. So why would he endanger the prize by
going to a demonstration? The prize was American, but the
relevant authorities in Moscow might take away his passport.
Hard to say. Maxim was skilled at playing both sides. The old
boy also had flair, as did the ZIL with its push-button controls,
leather interior and swing-out ashtrays. Arkady lit a cigarette
and immediately twisted it out. Ever since he had escaped
being crushed, he was giving in to good habits.

"You look like hell," Maxim said on return. "Just an obser-
vation."

"Many have made it."

Bleak fields lay on either side of the highway but the surface
of the road was as smooth as the felt of a billiard table, and the
streetlights sported fanciful galleon designs.

"We are now riding on the most expensive highway in
Europe. In other words, the mayor's wife has a road construction

company. That's the way things are done here. See, you need somebody to show you what's what." Maxim looked over. "You're not happy. You don't think we can work together?"

"You're not a detective or an investigator."

"I'm a poet. Same thing. Even more, I'm a Koenig."

"What's a Koenig?"

"A Koenig is a native of Kaliningrad. I can help you. We'll be partners, as close as pickles in a jar."

Kaliningrad had none of the sweep and power of Moscow or the elegance of Petersburg. Pickles sounded right.

"How can you help me?"

"Show you around."

"Why?"

"I loved Tatiana," Maxim said. "At least tell me what you came here for. If there's no body and no case, what's left?"

"A ghost. As a poet you should know that much."

That was an arrow that found its mark; Maxim was always accused of being a one-song poet, just as Arkady was becoming a one-note investigator. If Ludmila Petrovna didn't have any new information about her sister, Arkady could have saved himself the trip.

"Is it true what they say, that you're finished?" Maxim asked. "Some people say you have a little piece of lead rattling around inside your skull, a time bomb that surgeons can't remove."

"Are you finished?" Arkady asked.

"Poets aren't finished. They just babble on."

"Well, there is an element of risk. I couldn't let you help me if I wanted to."

"That's my problem."

"No, it's mine. Russia can't afford to lose another beloved poet."

Arkady glanced over. Maxim's face was red as if slapped. As they approached the city, the architecture changed from the cement five-story horrors of the Khrushchev era to the cement eight-story horrors of the Brezhnev era.

"You visited my school," Arkady said.

"Did I?"

"I was in third grade. It was a cultural outreach by members of the Writers' Union to boys with runny noses."

"Yes, yes, I'm sure it had a great effect."

"I remember one poem in particular, 'All Horses Are Aristocrats.'"

Rain settled into a pace of steady drumming. Pedestrians gathered on the corners and crossed in opposite tides of umbrellas. Maxim allowed himself a smile.

"So you liked that poem?"

Zhenya hadn't played chess for weeks, but he was low on money, and an outdoor tournament at Moscow State University promised easy pickings. One or two club members recognized Zhenya and tried to escape his draw, but in general, confidence reigned among the students. Online gamers who usually tracked flashing lights sat at outdoor tables and chairs. The fashion among graduate students was torn denim and sweaters from Milan. Zhenya arrived in rumpled camo looking like a prisoner of war.

The university embodied everything he hated, which was what he didn't have. Access, money, a future. He had no future and no past, only a circle. His father had shot Arkady and Victor had killed his father. Who knew what Arkady might have become without a bullet in his brain? A great pianist? A profound philosopher? At least prosecutor general. Zhenya imagined that nine grams of lead had lit up his brain like a Catherine wheel. The man had his limits. What was he chasing in Kaliningrad? Tatiana was dead and gone. The magazine, *Now*, was promoting a new cast of heroes. The prosecutor was targeting new agents of social disruption.

Zhenya recognized Stanford, the graduate student who had beleaguered him at Patriarch's Ponds, and almost went dizzy trying to keep his head low. There were twenty contestants, including the girl with red hair who had been part of his humiliation. She probably screwed Mr. Stanford, Zhenya thought. They made a pair.

Stanford was Zhenya's first opponent. Most of the students had kept their game sharp by playing electronic chess. Suckers. Taking away a face from the other side of the board eliminated tempo, psychology and the threat of violence.

A clinking of beer bottles drew his attention. Stanford stood opposite Zhenya and made an announcement. "It's the Chess Creep. He's back among us. '*Beware the Jabberwock, my son! The jaws that bite, the claws that catch!*'"

It was his last laugh. Zhenya feigned the Dutch Opening, sucked in Stanford's pieces and spat them out to dry. Zhenya had to inform him it was "mate in three."

The rest of Zhenya's matches went much the same way. He didn't realize the girl had maintained the same pace until she sat across the board from him for the final match.

"We've played before," she said.

"I doubt it. I remember good matches."

"Years ago at a casino. We were kids."

Zhenya remembered now. It was an exhibition. He had barely escaped with his skin.

"Why do you and your friend call me a creep?"

"That was his word, not mine. I said genius."

The faint down on her cheek was illuminated by the afternoon sun. Her brows were thoughtful wisps of hair, her eyes a crystal green, and Zhenya was a dozen moves into the game before he realized that he was about to lose a pawn.

Chapter Eighteen

The cottage of Ludmila Petrovna had, perhaps, been a carriage house before the war. Although bricks had half disintegrated to rust-colored sand and tape crisscrossed the windows, the house preserved a faint imprint of Koenigsberg style in a neighborhood of grim architecture and small shops selling CDs and cut-rate travel. Arkady and Maxim opened the gate to a vegetable garden where sunflowers peered over the wall, fat tomatoes drooped from wooden stakes and eggplants lay fat and lazy on the ground.

When Ludmila didn't answer her doorbell, Maxim tossed pebbles up against a window. Arkady saw no lights inside but the window creaked open and a woman hung a cage with a canary. She wore a scarf babushka style, gardening gloves and wraparound dark glasses, and she teased the bird for fluffing up in the cold.

"Always complaining, always looking for sympathy. Just like our old friend Maxim. Always the center of attention."

"Hello, Ludmila," Maxim said.

"And with a disreputable friend," she added when Arkady introduced himself.

"I'm sorry about your sister."

"Then I'm sure you have some scheme to make money out of her death. You and Obolensky, so ready to make her a martyr."

"Did you identify Tatiana Petrovna's body?" Arkady asked.

"From a photograph. There was no use going to Moscow."

Maxim said, "Ludmila is sensitive to light. It makes traveling difficult."

"Didn't you want to identify her body?"

"The picture was enough."

"Weren't you concerned with what happened to her body?"

"Frankly, I'm more concerned about my body."

"Did you ask to have her cremated?"

A minute before the rain had almost stopped; now it was drumming. Arkady heard the bustle of the market beyond the garden wall as racks were pulled under cover. Anyone else would have invited Arkady and Maxim in.

"Poor Juliet is getting wet." She stroked the canary under its beak. "They don't sing, you know, after they've lost their mate."

"You don't remember whether you asked to have your own sister cremated?"

"I have my own life to live."

A circumspect one between the vegetables and the bird, Arkady thought.

"What other animals do you have?"

"Well, we can't have any cats. That would make Juliet too nervous." She pulled in the cage.

Arkady asked, "Didn't Tatiana have a dog?"

"Yes, a nasty little thing. You know what my favorite pets are? Vegetables." She closed the window, only to reopen it a second later. "Don't steal any either," she added, and shut the window for good.

"Sorry," said Maxim. "Like I told you, Ludmila is hard."

Arkady lingered between tomato plants. He had counted on Ludmila Petrovna's outrage or, at least, curiosity about the death and ill handling of her sister.

"You can catch the evening flight to Moscow," Maxim said. "Too bad you came all this way for nothing. What's that?"

Arkady waved him over, and the two of them stood over a small dog turd that was liquefying in the rain. Headlines raced through his mind. SHIT BRIGADE CALLED OUT. TURD DISCOVERED IN VEGETABLE GARDEN. EVIDENCE LOST IN DOWNPOUR.

It was not nothing, but laughably close.

Chapter Nineteen

Her name was Lotte. This time she didn't let Zhenya off the hook. Being a pawn down to her was a slow descent into the grave. He knew what she was going to do; he simply couldn't stop her. By the end of the match, her cheeks were flushed and Zhenya was as sweaty as a wrestler. Mr. Stanford was gone. Almost all the onlookers were gone because they had expected a quick victory for Lotte, and the match had run into class time. It was the first game Zhenya had lost in weeks, yet he was strangely exhilarated.

She lived in an artistic household across from the conservatory, where music drifted from floor to floor. Her grandfather was Vladimir Sternberg, the most famous portrait artist of his time. Sternberg had cannily decided to paint only one subject: Stalin. Stalin addressing the Sixteenth Congress of the Soviets, Stalin addressing the Seventeenth Congress of the Soviets, and on and on, painting a Stalin a little taller, a bit more substantial, without a withered arm and never, ever with another Party leader, those fatuous demi-tyrants who sooner or later were erased from pictures and marched to a cell. Sternberg avoided them as if they were contagious, while the stature of the Beloved Leader only grew until all that surrounded him were silvery clouds and the beams of a radiant sun.

Sternberg was little more than bones and blue veins dressed in a lounge robe and slippers, but he maneuvered his rattan wheelchair around easels draped with cloths. Smaller works of art, also covered, hung on the wall.

"Lotte, sweetheart, get this young man some tea. You've put him through the wringer."

Zhenya took his cue and sat.

"Lotte has told me all about you," Sternberg said.

Zhenya didn't know what the artist was talking about. He was still surprised that Lotte had even noticed him, and he felt as out of place as a bird that had flown haphazardly in an open window. He had been sleeping on a mattress behind a video arcade, enduring the relentless chatter of machine guns and the whoosh of rockets long into the night. In comparison, the easels were silent and solemn in their drop cloths. Palettes and tables were daubed in colors. He had never noticed before that paint smelled and never seen cloths so mysterious.

"Go ahead, take a look," Sternberg said.

"Which one?"

"Any one."

Zhenya cautiously pulled a cloth from an easel and stepped back to study the painting. Stalin was waving; it wasn't clear at whom or why, only that he was watching out for his people below. Zhenya unveiled a second portrait and a third, each painted with the forceful edge of propaganda. Stalin was a quick-change artist, in army green one moment and summer whites the next, and perpetually waving.

Sternberg said, "I could do five a day."

Zhenya supposed that was "pretty good."

"Good?" Sternberg almost rose from his chair. "That's faster than the school of Rubens. Of course, the market for portraits of Stalin suffered for some time."

Lotte delivered tea to Zhenya and whispered, "Ask my grandfather about his other paintings."

"He's not interested," Sternberg said.

"Whatever," Zhenya said.

"It's not interesting. I painted them privately."

"Look." Lotte unveiled a painting of a village in banks of blue snow.

It was a rustic night scene, and the more Zhenya looked, the more he saw. Rendered in agitated strokes, embers from the fireplaces turned to imps of fire. Frozen shirts flew through the air. Windows lit so late at night suggested gaiety or disaster, and Zhenya crossed his arms for warmth.

The rest of the paintings—half a dozen—were the same and different. Each promised a rural subject and each, on examination, was at the point of explosion. A barn about to be a tinderbox, a skater under the ice, a horse's eye rolling in panic.

"You hid these?" Zhenya asked. "Why?"

"A bold question from a first-time guest, but I like that."

"So?"

"What do you think? To save my head. Lotte, would you bring some cookies too? Thank you, dear. You are too good." To Zhenya, he said, "She loves her grandfather. So, tit for tat, what are you going to do with your chessboard? What are your plans?"

"Nothing in particular."

"Which is nothing at all, of course. Lotte says you're actually quite good at chess, a diamond in the rough. How good are you?"

"I'm okay."

"Just okay? Maybe twenty players in the world make a living at chess. Are you one of the twenty best players in the world?"

"I don't know."

"You aren't even ranked because you don't play in real tournaments. Invisibility might be a shrewd tactic if you're hustling games in a railroad station, my friend, but to the chess world, you don't exist."

Lotte returned with madeleines.

Sternberg produced a smile. "Lotte, I was just telling your friend the good news. The Stalin portraits are beginning to sell again."

Zhenya and Lotte made nice for ten minutes. His glance stole to the paintings of snowbound villages, peasant revels, bear cubs following their mother. Nothing warmed a Russian heart like bears up a tree.

Later, when Zhenya and Lotte were alone in a café, she said, "I love my grandfather. He's a sweet man and a fantastic artist. But to spend your life denying your art? Now no one knows him and it's too late."

Maxim was driving Arkady back to the airport in the rain. The ZIL's windshield wipers slapped back and forth. Foot traffic had become huddled umbrellas. Boots made an appearance. At sidewalk stalls, shopkeepers stretched tarpaulins over boxes of fruit, a table of Prada knockoffs, a row of bicycles.

"Pull over," Arkady said.

"What now? You're going to miss your flight," Maxim said.

"I'll be right back."

He stepped over a gutter and slipped between the water that drained from either end of an awning that read KOENIG BICYCLES. A repairman in a plastic bag repositioned bikes. Another, in the dark of the shop, fine-tuned a wheel, spinning it until the spokes blurred and hummed. The more Maxim gestured for Arkady to hurry, the more Arkady was the picture of someone in a mood to browse among pennants, key chains, calipers, bright biking gear and brighter helmets.

Posters of the Tour de France, Giro d'Italia, Tour St. Petersburg streamed on the walls in one endless, continuous race. A bulletin board announced local races from Kaliningrad to Chkalovsk, to Zelenogradsk, to the Curonian Spit.

"It's an obsession, isn't it?" Arkady ran his hand over a rack of glossy helmets.

The man with the wheel murmured, "It becomes your fucking life. You can't let it take over."

"Well put," Arkady said. "You do a lot of rides?"

His friend said, "We have a club that rents bikes and tents. We're very sociable. I would suggest a nice local tour from Kaliningrad to Zelenogradsk or Baltijsk. We go overnight, build a campfire, have a dip in the lake. It's kind of an adult tour."

Arkady studied the array of pennants. "It looks like you do races too. Do you use your own bikes?"

"Of course. I mean, we're showing off the goods, aren't we?"

"Do you ever fly with them?"

"Sure."

"Do they go as cargo?"

The man at the wheel stopped it short. "Fuck no. I'm going to put a thousand-dollar bike in the hands of those apes in cargo? We buy a seat for the bike and stow it in the vestibule."

"Your name is . . .?"

"Kurt. I'm Kurt, he's Karl."

"A thousand dollars? Is that the limit?"

"There is no limit."

"Ten thousand dollars?"

"We can do that," said Karl.

"Ten thousand dollars? You're wearing a plastic bag and you've got bikes selling for ten thousand dollars?"

"Not in the shop. Not at the moment."

"But we can get whatever you want," said Kurt.

"I want an Ercolo Pantera."

This was the point at which they should have tried to steer him to another "top of the line" bike in the shop. Instead, they asked, "What would a Pantera be doing in Kaliningrad?"

That was the question, wasn't it? Arkady thought.

Chapter Twenty

"Whose place is this?" Lotte asked.

"A guy I know." Zhenya looked into the refrigerator, where a husk of cheese kept a lonely vigil.

"He lets you have a key? He must be a good friend."

"Sort of. He's an investigator."

"Really." Arkady had allowed Anya to hang photographs of convicts and their tattoos, with an accent on dragons, Madonnas and spiderwebs, and they caught the girl's eye. "I saw these in a magazine."

"Would you like a beer?" Zhenya popped two bottles.

"Is your friend a little strange?"

"Arkady? They don't come more ordinary."

Lotte walked along the bookcases. "He really likes to read."

"Your beer. I'm afraid it's warm."

Offhand she said, "It's British. Warm beer is British, cold is American."

"Okay, here's your British beer." He was feeling socially inept. He knew it was a mistake to bring her to Arkady's apartment. It was all too rushed, but he had no other place to take her. He had expected her to beg off with some excuse about a lecture or a previous engagement. In the official chess world he was a bottom-feeder. Fortunately, he did know how to move the pieces. Chess was alive with traps, gambits, the shepherding of a passed pawn or the menace of rooks aligned like cannon. It was drama. The Sicilian Defense smacked of black deeds in back alleys. Each notation read like a story. No matter how lowly, every player brushed shoulders with the game's immortals. Morphy and his shoe fetish. Fischer the genius and Fischer the crank. The serene Capablanca and Alekhine, a glutton who ate with his fingers and choked to death on beefsteak.

Besides chess, they had zero in common, Zhenya thought. A little adventure with a hustler was how she'd remember the day. He figured she was probably nineteen, which made her more than a year older, and most likely had her life mapped out: a year of rebellion, followed by a few minor chess trophies, marriage to a millionaire, children, a series of affairs with oligarchs, finally tossed overboard in Monte Carlo.

"What are your plans?" she asked.

"Plans? Join the army and have my brains kicked in."

"Seriously, what do you want?"

"To be rich, I guess. Have a nice car."

"What about a home?"

"I suppose," Zhenya said, although he couldn't picture what a home would look like.

"You're so evasive."

So she said, but he knew if he told her the truth, she would bolt.

"It's complicated."

"It's simple. I heard you shot somebody."

"Who says that?"

"Everybody. That's why they're afraid to play chess with you."

"You're not afraid."

"Because I'm a redhead. Everyone knows that redheads are crazy." In a sterner voice, she added, "Don't become my grandfather. Don't be a coward."

"What should I become?"

"Somebody."

"I get by."

"Is that so?"

"I live freely, on my own."

"Except when you're in the cold."

"Everyone should have to live out of a backpack. They'd find out what's essential."

"Like an outlaw? What are your essentials? Show me."

He was backed into a corner and it dawned on Zhenya that arguing with Lotte was like chess, and, once again, he was losing.

"Okay." He dug into his backpack and, one by one, placed on the table a folded chessboard, a velvet pouch of chess pieces, a chess clock, a notebook and pencil, a paperback of *Beyond Bobby Fischer* and plastic bags containing a toothbrush, a tube of toothpaste and soap.

"How many games of chess have you won? More than a thousand. And this is all you have to show for it? Some outlaw."

"I can beat you."

"But you didn't." She picked up the notebook and opened it to savor her victory a second time. " 'Bd5 to Rd5, Qe2 to Rd1.' That was your blunder."

He followed her around the table. "I'll play you again, right now."

"The match is over."

"Then if I'm such a waste of time, why are you still here?"

"I never said you were a waste of time." She turned and gave him a kiss full on the lips. "I never said that."

Maxim's apartment was essentially a tunnel bored through pizza crusts, half-empty bottles of beer, totally empty bottles of vodka, and books, newspapers and poetry reviews everywhere, spilling off shelves, stacked on the floor, sliding underfoot. A fine volcanic ash of cigarettes hung in the air.

"It's more comfortable than it looks." Maxim swept a pizza box and manuscripts off the couch. "What made you decide to stay in Kaliningrad?"

"Its charm. Maybe I should just go to a hotel," Arkady said.

"And pay their prices? Nonsense." Maxim batted cushions. "I know there's a bottle here somewhere."

They danced around each other to get from one side of the room to the other.

Arkady said, "I can't help but feel I'm in the way."

"Not a bit. Of course if I'd known I was going to have a guest, I would have ..."

Ordered up an earthmover, Arkady thought. "The life of a poet," he said. "Where would you like me to hang my coat?"

"Anywhere will do. There's only one rule."

"Yes?" Arkady was eager to hear it.

"Don't light a cigarette until you have located an ashtray."

"Very wise."

"We've had some trouble in the past."

"With other poets, no doubt."

"Now that you mention it. Sit, please."

Arkady picked a sheaf of papers off the floor. "For Review Only" was written on the front page.

"The author is a talentless hack consigned to well-deserved obscurity," Maxim said, and added an aside: "He's after the same fellowship in the States that I'm after."

"You know he just died."

"He did? In that case, Russia has lost a singular voice ... struck down too early ... leaves a void. I mean, why not be generous?"

"You never told me."

"Never told you what?"

"The name of the fellowship."

"Didn't I? I don't think they have a name yet. They're just starting. Hush-hush until they make their choice."

"Amazing. You really would do anything to get out of Kaliningrad?"

"There is no Kaliningrad." Starting at the front door, Maxim pantomimed a man entering the apartment, maneuvering to a coffee table, visiting the bedroom and returning with a pillow, from which he pulled a bottle of vodka as shiny as chrome. "It's only a matter of reenacting what you last did."

"Why the pillow?"

"That I don't remember. Are you hungry?" In a cabinet Maxim scouted out glasses, blood sausage and a baguette as stiff as a cane. He had to shout over his sawing. "I'm not a Slav. No offense intended, but a Slav drinks to get drunk."

"I've noticed."

"Whereas a civilized person in a normal country drinks with cordial company, hearty food and a decent interval between toasts."

Which compared nicely with Victor's weakness for eau de cologne, Arkady had to admit.

They started solemnly.

"To Tatiana."

"To Tatiana."

Followed by the first beads of sweat across the forehead.

Arkady asked, "What do you mean, there's no Kaliningrad?"

"Just what I said. No past, no people, no name."

Maxim explained that Kaliningrad had been Koenigsberg, the seat of German kings. But the British bombed it flat during the war, and after the war, Joseph Stalin forced the entire German population to leave. All the people, their homes and memories, were erased. In their place, Stalin trucked in a new population of Russians and gave it a new name, Kaliningrad, after his lickspittle president, Kalinin.

"Kalinin was a little shit, you know. There he was, the head of state, and Stalin sent his wife to a prison camp. Stalin had her brought from her cell to dance on the table. I suppose when you've broken a man that way, you've broken him for good. My God, my mouth is dry." Maxim refilled the vodka. "And here's the joke. No one admits to being a Kaliningrader. They call themselves Koenigs. But it has the worst crime rate in Europe. So you know it's Russian."

The visitor had a bruise under his eye the size of a fist. Otherwise, he looked to Zhenya like the sort of overdressed and overconfident New Russian who had already scored his first million dollars. Before Zhenya could steer him out the door, the man was into the apartment.

"Excuse me, my name is Alexi. I thought this was the home of Investigator Renko."

"It is. I live here too," Zhenya said.

"And ..." Alexi turned to Lotte, who sat at the chessboard and returned his stare.

"A friend," Zhenya said.

"Is anyone else here?"

"No."

"You're having a private party."

"We were in the middle of a game."

"Look at this place. It's like a museum." Alexi took in the heavy Soviet drapes, parquet floor, mahogany table and wardrobe big enough to go to sea on. He fixed on Lotte.

"When the cat's away the mice will play. Is that what you

are? Two little mousies? I don't mean to spoil the fun, only to pick up a notebook like this. In fact, a notebook just like this." He tapped the notebook that lay open by the board. "What are you writing?"

Zhenya said, "When you play chess, you write down the moves to study later."

"Sounds exciting." Alexi dropped down on the couch next to Lotte. When she moved to get up he clamped his hand around her arm. "I'll wait for Renko."

"Arkady is in Kaliningrad," Zhenya said.

"Kaliningrad? Isn't that ironic? In that case, we'll have to start without him." He let go of Lotte and placed a gun in the middle of the chessboard, toppling pieces black and white. "New game."

The bruise on his face was raw. Zhenya wanted to believe that Arkady had administered the punch but couldn't picture it.

"How can I help you?" Zhenya said.

"That's more like it. I'm looking for an ordinary spiral notebook of no value and no use to anyone. Like this one, only the language is a little different. I'm pretty sure it's of a meeting. When you see it, you'll know. I'll give you fifty dollars for its return."

"No."

"One hundred dollars. You look like you could use the money."

"No, thanks."

"A thousand dollars."

"No."

Alexi asked Lotte, "Is your boyfriend serious?"

"Totally."

She was fearless, Zhenya thought.

"He's turning down a thousand dollars for a notebook he claims to know nothing about? I'm sorry, I just don't believe him." He picked up his gun. "This is my X ray machine. It can tell if someone is lying or not. What kind of gun is it?" he asked Zhenya.

"I think it's a Makarov."

"A what Makarov?"

"A 9mm Makarov."

Alexi ran his fingers lightly over the crosshatching of the grip. "That's right. And if you put a gun like this in front of most people, they act as if you put a snake on their lap. How many can stay cool? I hear rumors." Alexi turned to Lotte. "Honestly, did you think he was some ordinary boy? He's like Renko, a time bomb."

"What do you want?" Zhenya said.

"I want the notebook. Find the notebook."

"I don't know what it looks like."

"You'll know."

"Look for yourself." Zhenya moved to the wardrobe and opened it up. Shoe boxes poured out, and from every box notebooks spilled onto the floor. "I have hundreds and hundreds of chess games, openings, situations. What do you like? Ruy Lopez, Sicilian, Queen's Gambit Accepted, Queen's Gambit Declined? I like the Sicilian, myself."

"What are you talking about?" Alexi said.

"We don't have your fucking notebook." Zhenya reached into the wardrobe and threw more boxes onto the floor. He knew he should have been intimidated. But for the moment, he was brave and saw the world through Lotte's green eyes.

The power had gone out in Maxim's building and he recited by candlelight.

> Horses are aristocrats.
> Heads high and dressed in silk,
> Kicked, whipped, ears pricked
> For fear of leopards
> While their true enemies at the Ministry of Light
> Industry call out, "More glue!"

"Lovely," Arkady said.

"Thank you," Maxim said. "I used to do an animal for each letter of the alphabet. Remember? I need a fresh wind."

Arkady opened a window. "You need a fresh liver."

He helped Maxim off the floor and steered him toward the bedroom. Although the vodka bottle was half-full, Arkady declared it the winner and kicked it under the sofa.

"How did you like the blood sausage?" Maxim asked.

"I'm trying not to think about it."

"How are we doing?" Maxim groped his way toward the dark hallway.

"Making progress."

"Missed your plane. Sorry about that."

"That's all right. This way you can keep an eye on me. That's what you're doing, isn't it?"

If Maxim's living room was a tunnel, his bedroom was a pit of male funk, a heady blend of drawn shades, sour beer and aftershave. He was a big man and doubled in weight as he passed out. Arkady searched the blackness for someplace to deposit him, finally tipping him onto the outline of a bed.

Arkady dug a hole for himself on the couch, getting comfortable after he swept aside books, loose change and dog biscuits.

Zhenya gathered notebooks and Lotte sorted. An hour after Alexi had left the apartment their hands still shook. There was more to cleaning up than merely stuffing notebooks into the proper box, but the task was in itself a healing process. The chess pieces seemed comforted to return to their velvet sack.

The one notebook untouched was the one on the chessboard, where it had lain open all evening. When Lotte closed the notebook she found herself looking at the back cover and it took her a moment to understand that the notebook had been flipped and reversed. Front was back, up was down and, read in the right direction, the pages were full of circles, arrows, stick figures with elements of hieroglyphics, maps and traffic signs in an apparently meaningless jumble of shorthand and code.

Chapter Twenty-One

His pea jacket buttoned tight against the wind, Arkady took giant steps down the face of a dune to the beach. Maxim slogged behind, lurching through a morning fog as thick as cotton batting.

"You're indecently happy," Maxim said.

The beach was a mix of pebbles and sand strewn with driftwood and seaweed. In tide pools miniature crustaceans danced on pinpoints back and forth. The *kree* of gulls rose above the sound of the surf. What was not to like?

Arkady asked, "Don't you like the beach? Didn't your father ever take you?"

"My father was rarely caught outdoors. This is the kind of fog he called 'pea soup.' 'Pea soup' is what this is. Why did you insist on coming here?"

"Just trying to get an idea of the place."

"It's all the same. Sand, water, more sand."

"You said there's a border on the spit?"

"Of sorts."

"How long a drive?"

"Ten, fifteen minutes. The northern half of the spit is Lithuanian, the southern half is Russian. They say there are elk. I've never seen any. Fog, yes. Elk, no." Maxim stamped his feet. "You were just going to talk to Tatiana's sister and return to Moscow. Instead, here we are stranded on a spit of sand with a one-lane road. During the summer, there are sunbathers, children with kites, nudists with volleyballs. But at this time of year it's empty and miserable. Why are we here?"

"We're here because both Joseph Bonnafos and Tatiana came here. They weren't in Moscow."

"So?"

"So if you drop your house keys at the back door, do you search for them at the front door because the light is better? Besides, I just like to see."

"You look more like a hunting dog sniffing the wind."

Arkady took that as a compliment. "Why don't you go back to the car?"

"You'll get lost."

"It's hard to get lost on a sand spit. Why did you volunteer to be my guide?"

"I was drunk at the time. Take my word for it, nobody comes here at this time of year."

"So it's a good place to meet somebody."

"Meet who? Meet for what? I don't know if I can take so much speculation on an empty stomach."

They were good questions, Arkady had to admit. Lieutenant Stasov of the Kaliningrad police had never sent photographs of the body or site as he had promised. Hopefully, he didn't know that Arkady was in Kaliningrad.

Maxim said, "The Curonian Spit is narrow but it's long. You can hide anything in the sand. In fact, the sand will do the job for you."

"What do you mean?"

"These are called wandering dunes. They wipe out roads, invade houses and hide evidence."

The idea of a shifting landscape was intriguing. The only structure Arkady saw on the beach was a shuttered kiosk plastered with posters for rock bands and discos, but who knew what had been claimed by nature? Besides Maxim the only other person in sight was a beachcomber so wrapped in scarves he could have been a pilgrim from the Middle Ages. He dragged a sledge with a haul of driftwood, bottles and cans.

The shoreline lured Arkady on. He couldn't tell whether fog was collecting or burning off and whether he imagined or saw movement in the pines that bordered the dunes. An elusive elk? With a blink, binoculars trained on him. The glasses shifted and aimed down the beach to lacy seaweed left by an ebb tide. Two young girls oblivious to the approach of Arkady and Maxim stood ankle-deep in the water and combed the sand with rakes. Barefoot, with sun-bleached hair and skimpy dresses, they looked like survivors of a shipwreck, and, although they shivered from the cold, they examined pebbles by candlelight.

"Amber," Maxim said.

A boy emerged from the pines and crossed the beach, waving binoculars in one hand and a flare gun in the other. He ignored Maxim and Arkady and called for the girls to hurry.

Arkady intercepted him. "Can we talk?"

The boy raised the flare gun. Flare guns were not designed for accuracy but red phosphorus in a flare cartridge burned at 2,500 degrees, which made it weapon enough.

"Vova!" one of the girls shouted.

"Coming!" the boy shouted. His attention turned to the kiosk and, passing by it, a van with an illuminated pig that seemed to float on its roof. It was a pink and happy piggy. Arkady couldn't see the driver but it was someone who had let enough air out of the tires to roll softly on sand.

As the girls ran, the van followed, tipping like a small boat over the uneven surface of the beach. When the van turned on its headlights and cast their shadows, the girls spilled their tools. The boy pushed them toward the pines but the van herded them to the water's edge until Arkady and Maxim stepped into the headlights. The van came to a halt, pausing thoughtfully as fog drifted by.

The driver would have to make up his mind, Arkady thought. Time and tide waited for no man. Every second spent at the water's edge, the van was settling in wet sand.

Maxim said, "*'To market, to market, to buy a fat pig. Home again, home again, jiggety jig.'*"

Cold water crept into Arkady's shoes. Soon enough, it would

reach the exhaust pipe and kill the engine. Before that, the sand would give way and provide no traction at all. The boy called Vova and the pair of girls slipped away while the van concentrated on Arkady and Maxim. Arkady wondered how many options the driver was considering. Then, without a hint of a problem, the van backed up to more solid footing and left in the direction of the kiosk as the pig rolled with the undulations of the beach, slowly to begin with, then at a trot.

Arkady gathered the tools left by the girls in their escape. Their lamp was ingenious: a biking shoe stuffed with a candle and sand. Arkady added a calling card with his cell phone number and a twenty-ruble note.

Maxim was steaming. As soon as they were in the car, he said, "A joke. A man is reading a book, and there's a knock at the door. He answers it, and there's a snail at his doorstep. The man just wants to read his book, so he kicks the snail out into the dark and goes back to reading. Two years pass. There's a knock at the door. He opens it and it's the snail, and the snail asks, 'What the fuck was that about?' So I'm asking you, what the fuck was that about?"

"I don't know."

"It seemed personal. We're chased by a lunatic in a butcher's van and you don't seem particularly surprised. My shoes are wet, my socks are wet and you're putting money in a shoe that's going to go out to sea with the tide. Do you think anybody's going to see it?"

"The kids will. They're pretty bold. As soon as they think the coast is clear, they'll come back."

"What does this have to do with Tatiana?"

"Tatiana bought the notebook from kids on this beach, maybe from these kids. We wanted to make contact and I think we did."

"So it was a great success?"

"Absolutely."

"It felt like getting my feet wet."

"I can understand that. Sorry about your shoes."

Despite the apology Maxim was offended. "Now what?"

"You said there was a border station on the spit?"

"Of sorts."

"I'd like to see that."

"Of sorts" overstated the station. A typical Russian checkpoint was staffed by armed Frontier Guards trained to view every document with suspicion. On any pretext, travelers could be led into waiting rooms where the contents of their backpacks would be spilled and poked.

But the Russian-Lithuanian border on the Curonian Spit was no more than a metal shack beside a spindly communications tower perhaps ten meters high. The station and tower were guarded by whitewashed tires half-buried in the ground and an ancient floodlight that looked as if it hadn't been activated since the siege of Leningrad. Telephone lines hung on the wire fence and disappeared into a spotty screen of birches. A Frontier Guard in ordinary camos roused himself enough to make a circling motion with his arm and shout, "Go back! You can't go any further with a car!"

"This is it?" Arkady asked.

"This is the border," Maxim said. "This time of year they get birders. Otherwise it's pretty minimal. Do you want to report the maniac in the butcher's van?"

"What would we report?"

"We saw a man menacing children."

"Only he's gone and so are the kids."

"They could search."

"Guards are not allowed to leave their posts."

"They could call."

"Let's hope not," Arkady said. "From here on, let's be invisible."

On the way back the fog was so thick that Maxim pressed his face against the windshield. He glanced at Arkady every few seconds. "You have a very high opinion of yourself, Renko. In two days, you think you're getting a grasp on Kaliningrad. You know everything there is to know."

"Hardly."

"But apparently enough to spontaneously wade into the sea. What else do you know?"

"Not much."

"Inform me."

"I know that Tatiana Petrovna thought it was worth risking her life to come to Kaliningrad for a notebook that no one can read. That she fell off a balcony the day she returned to Moscow. That honest journalists have enemies and Tatiana had more than most."

"I suppose experts and computers have been brought in to decipher the code."

"Maybe. That won't help," Arkady said.

"You don't think so?"

"I don't think it's a code. You can no more read it than read someone else's mind."

"Do you have enemies too?"

"Could you be more specific?"

"People who would push you off a balcony."

"Well, I haven't been in Kaliningrad very long," Arkady said. "Give me time."

Without warning, Maxim turned the ZIL onto a road riddled with potholes. A truck boomed by like a rhino, spilling sand and water.

"Where are we?" Arkady asked.

The words had barely left Arkady's mouth when the horizon rose. The steering wheel of the ZIL twisted over ruts as hard as cement and the car came to a precipitous stop looking down at the spectacle of a strip mine and giant machinery at work.

"Gold? Coal?" Arkady asked.

"Amber," said Maxim.

It didn't take a large crew to operate a strip mine. One man to control a front-end loader, another in a bulldozer that pushed the earth this way and that. The maestro was a man on foot aiming a high-pressure hose with the aid of a tiller driven into the ground. Loose soil was hunchbacked; black slag rose in peaks. Meanwhile, an earthmover maintained a pattern of roads that descended six levels from top to bottom. Between the grinding of engines and jet of water, a meteor could have hit the mine and no one would have noticed.

Maxim said, "Ninety percent of the world's amber comes from Kaliningrad. Control Kaliningrad and you control the world's production of amber. That's worth some degree of fuss."

"Who controls it?"

"Grisha Grigorenko did, until somebody shot him. Who knows, maybe there's a new war? Or maybe a man with your talents can start one."

Chapter Twenty-Two

Drawn in the first panel of the first page was = and the words *blah blah*. In the second panel, ⏚: and ☽. In the third, an insect, ✿, and ⊂⊃. In the fourth, ⌒ and 2B. In the first panel of the second page was ⊟⁚ and ☆. In the second panel, ✿, ☼ and ◌. In the third panel, ⏚:, ? and ✕. In the fourth, ⊂⊃ and ⌣. In the first panel of the third page was ☾:, ↓ and ✿. In the second panel, ☽ and =. In the third panel, ◍, ◌ and RR. In the fourth panel, ☆:, ↓, ⧻, RR and └. In the first panel of the fourth page was ⊞:. In the second panel, $ and ✿. In the third panel, ⊟, and in the fourth, ☣. In the first panel of the fifth page, ☡:, in the second panel, ☾, in the third, ♌ and ⊟, and in the fourth, ⊛. And on and on in that inscrutable vein— ☽:, ⫲⫲, ∿, ⚥, ☡:, ℰ —until the name *Natalya Goncharova* and a drawing of a woman wearing a pearl necklace, 👤. Even as a hasty sketch it was clear she was meant to be strong willed and beautiful.

She was followed by blank pages all the way to the notebook's back inside cover, which had five identical sketches of a cat, the word *Ercolo*, and a short list of numbers.

60 cm
56.5 cm
1990 g

Zhenya found the challenge irresistible.

Lotte shook her head. "The sample is too small. I studied linguistics at the university. We can't possibly translate this with so few symbols, not in a million years."

"Don't think of it as a translation, think of it as a game. We have to win a game. Don't go by grammar, go by your gut."

"What makes you think that we can do that?"

"Because I'm a gambler. What are the first symbols?"

"An equals sign, 'blah blah,' and what could be a cannon or a man in a top hat with a colon or dots and a line under it."

"That's a start. If we get a couple of symbols we can triangulate and build a context. Like building a ladder rung by rung."

"I don't think that's possible."

"Sure it is. Like in the rest of the second panel there's an ear or half a heart."

"Third?"

"Some kind of bug and two rings interlocked, which could signify agreement, marriage or handcuffs."

"Fourth?"

"A fish—"

"Or an early Christian symbol of a fish—"

"Or tongs, a rocket or a plane," said Zhenya.

"Two B?"

"An address, a room, 'To be or not to be.'"

"First panel of the second page?"

"A box with a stick through it, maybe carrying something hot, or high explosives."

"Or a box kite?" Lotte said.

"Maybe. Next, a star or a starfish or a Western sheriff's badge."

"Okay."

"The bug; sunrise, sunset, Humpty Dumpty, a sleepy eye, a hedgehog? And a triangle, pylon or nose. In the third panel, the man in the top hat with colon again but without a line beneath, a question mark and crossed swords. In the fourth, interlocked rings and the fish symbol again."

"But this time under a wave," Lotte said.

"Right. Then on the third page, the crescent moon or slice of apple or a fingernail. Then arrow down and bug. In the second panel, the ear and equals sign. The third panel, black and white figs or teardrops, and RR for 'railroad.' In the fourth, star followed by arrow down, and a fence, RR and capital L. On the fourth page, building blocks, dollar sign and the bug. See, it helps to get a rhythm going." Zhenya tried to be breezy.

"Really?"

"In the third panel, the box kite. In the fourth, the symbol for radioactivity. Then on the next page, the man in a top hat with colon—"

"With no line under it."

"With no line. And a spiral, whirlpool or hypnosis. And the third symbol is the ear again, the fourth, the box with a line through it, and an oval shape with an X inside. Then it goes on and on: ending in a crescent moon, fence, wave, arrow pointing down with a loop at the top, the man in the top hat with a line, and the bug, until we get to the drawing of a woman and her name, Natalya Goncharova, the greatest tramp in Russian history, tsarinas excluded, of course."

"We never hear her side of the story," Lotte said.

"She marries Pushkin, Russia's greatest poet, sleeps around and gets him killed in a duel. What that has to do with the Mafia beats me. So, what do you think?"

"Maybe we're not as smart as we think we are. This isn't a secret code, not even language, it's just pictures. The person who wrote it must have had an incredible memory. It's probably one percent of what was actually said."

Zhenya sank back in his chair. "So you think it's impossible."

"I didn't say that. These are notes of a meeting, right? A

colon tells you who is speaking. Six symbols—Top Hat with a Line, Top Hat Without, Box Kite, Blocks, Crescent Moon and Star—have colons. These are the participants and this is their conversation."

"Then why did the guy taking notes divide the pages into panels?"

"Why does a chessboard have sixty-four squares? To keep the pieces from running in all directions. The symbols are personal cues. We'll see where they run."

Now that Zhenya thought about it there were similarities to chess. Its symbols were as definite as pieces—only a player had to figure out what moves each symbol made, and there was a gun at the endgame.

Maxim knew a restaurant that served its guests in a plastic version of the Amber Room, the "Eighth Wonder of the World."

The room was paneled with artificial amber and gold into the likenesses of cherubs and Peter the Great. Waitresses were costumed à la Marie Antoinette, with gold dust sprinkled in their hair and a beauty spot carefully placed on their décolletage. In a gilded cage in the center of the room, a mechanical nightingale opened its beak and spewed birdsong.

"This almost makes up for my wet feet," Maxim said. "Maybe a little foie gras and a duck à l'orange will help."

"And maybe you can tell me why children would be chased by a van with a pig."

"Amber."

"You're not serious."

"Very. When the Teutonic knights ruled here they chopped off the hands of anyone who poached amber. The van was probably just trying to scare off the kids."

"It felt like more than that. I'm fairly sensitive to whatever is chasing me."

"In your profession I suppose that's a gift. Are you treating? I find I'm more talkative when I'm well fed and dry."

"Stuff yourself."

"Excellent. Here's our waitress."

Maxim ordered the feast he had promised himself. Arkady had vodka, black bread and butter.

"Was it?" he asked.

"What?"

"The Eighth Wonder of the World?"

"I should think so. Imagine walls of glowing amber, gold leaf, Venetian mirrors and mosaics of semiprecious stones. People said that when the sun poured in the windows of the palace, the Amber Room appeared to burst into flame. It was the favorite room of Catherine the Great. Unfortunately, it was also the favorite war prize of the Nazis. It was dismantled and hidden in a bunker, in a well, in the Black Forest, or taken away in an icebreaker, or maybe in a submarine. Imagine the Amber Room resting in the dark on the bottom of the sea. Like a seed."

Watching Maxim shovel food around his plate reminded Arkady of the earthmovers at the strip mine. Maxim, in turn, said he found it painful to watch Arkady eat so little.

"There are two kinds of poets. The starving poet and the

randy, dissolute poet. I prefer the latter." He summoned the sommelier.

"Like a seed," Arkady said. "What did you mean by that?"

"A commonplace metaphor. What distinguishes amber from diamonds, sapphires and rubies is that amber was alive. Fifty million years ago, it was resin dripping from a pine tree, capturing a bee here, a sow bug there. Think of a diamond with a mosquito in the center. Doesn't exist. That's why, when other Mafias tried to muscle in on the amber trade, Grisha pushed back."

"Out of scientific interest?"

"Not quite. There was a push and pull called the Amber Wars."

"That sounds quaint."

"Quite bloody, actually. Would you like a charlotte russe? The custards here are very good."

"Is the Amber War over?"

"We'll have the petits fours and the custards," Maxim told the waitress, and sighed when she curtsied and her bosom nearly tumbled free. He cocked an eye on Arkady. "What is the war to you? I thought you were just examining the circumstances of Tatiana Petrovna's death."

"Her death gets stranger and stranger and is as involved with Kaliningrad as it is with Moscow."

"In what way?"

"The interpreter's notebook."

"Which is being decoded by experts even as we speak?"

"I would assume so."

"Why do I have the feeling that great heaping piles of horse-shit are being stacked around me?"

"Because you're a poet."

Zhenya and Lotte were learning the depth of the Russian language. Each interpretation spawned two more, which only multiplied again. They were following streams of words as imagined by someone else's lifetime of experience, anything that would relate to any other symbol or all the unknowns of the interpreter's background: a scuffed knee, a ripe fig, a bedtime story.

They were looking for mnemonic cues, one man's message to himself with a world of symbols and words to choose from. God forbid, the words could have come from another language, and a professional interpreter spoke at least five.

Even a simple arrow could be a child's top, a fallen tree, "exit" or "this way to Estonia." Or a missile. Each interpretation turned the text upside down.

"You should go home," Zhenya told Lotte.

"I'm not going to leave when we're halfway done."

"I wish we were. I think we've gone in reverse." Which was true, he thought. They had learned nothing and they were exhausted. "Your family must be worried."

"It's Tuesday."

"So?"

"On Tuesdays my father meets his lover, an oboist in the symphony, and my mother meets her lover, a baritone in the chorus. They live six-day weeks. They won't notice I'm gone for another twenty-four hours."

"What about your grandfather?"

"He has a new model. He won't notice anything either."

Zhenya's cell phone rang. He made the "quiet" sign to Lotte before answering with a hypercasual "Hello."

"This is Arkady. Are you at the apartment?"

"No."

"Are you alone?"

Arkady had to repeat the question because Maxim's ZIL was outside Kaliningrad and cell coverage was spotty.

"Yes."

"Have you still got the notebook of Tatiana Petrovna?"

"No." Three lies in a row. A good start, Zhenya thought. If cell phone coverage was patchy, that was fine with him. "Have you thought about our deal?"

"How far have you gotten on the translation?" Arkady asked.

"We're working on it."

A pause. "*We?*"

"My friend Lotte."

"A girlfriend?"

"A friend."

There were a number of reasons for Arkady to be furious. The girl's safety for a start.

"If she's a friend, send her home. Any sign of Anya?"

"No."

"What about Alexi Grigorenko?"

The reception broke up again.

Arkady said, "You know the safe you took Tatiana's notebook from? Is my gun still there?"

"I can't hear you."

"The ammunition is in the bookcase . . ."

"Yes?"

"Can you hear me now?"

"Where?"

But the connection was gone.

Lotte had pressed her ear close to the phone. When coverage broke up completely, she asked, "What deal?"

"The army. I needed his permission for early enlistment."

"Now you're scaring me."

"Do you want to go home now?"

"Let's finish the puzzle."

The road back into the city took Maxim and Arkady by housing blocks as stained as pissoirs and storefronts that were little more than shipping containers decorated with posters. Maxim decided to show off what he called the Ninth Wonder of the World, the ugliest building of the Soviet era.

"A Frankenstein's monster of a building. A zombie."

"You sound proud."

"I don't mean merely the ugliest building west of the Urals. I mean from here to the Pacific. From the silver herring of the Baltic Sea to the red salmon of Kamchatka."

"An ambitious scope."

"I speak as a Koenig, a native son."

"How is the cell coverage at the ugliest building?"

"As a matter of fact, excellent."

Streetlamps gave Maxim's ZIL such a translucent quality

that it seemed to float through the city. Heads turned from the cheap goods offered at sidewalk stalls and clothing racks to follow the one-car procession.

Arkady needed space to phone Victor, drunk or not, and send him around to the apartment. There was a new tone to the boy's voice. Not alarm, but definitely anxiety.

"During the war, the British bombed the city of Koenigsberg to dust. Their special target was Koenigsberg Castle, which stood on a hill overlooking the city. When the war was over there was no castle anymore, and Stalin rebuilt where the castle had stood."

Maxim rolled across a dark lot and drew the car to a stop.

At first, Arkady did not see anything odd. It took time to see that half the night sky was blocked out.

"The last Communist Party headquarters," Maxim said. "Koenigs call it the Monster."

Dogs barked hysterically on the other side of a chain-link fence, waiting for Maxim or Arkady to do something as foolish as offer a finger through the links. Arkady suspected that they were fed infrequently. Bottles and trash had accumulated where winds had blown them.

Arkady craned his neck to take in the size of the Monster. Twenty stories high, the building loomed over him.

"It's the largest building in the city and it's never been used," Maxim said. "Not for a day."

Most windows were broken out. The Monster had four legs, and more than anything it put Arkady in mind of a headless elephant.

"What is the problem?"

"History. Before they even finished the top of the building, the bottom started to flood from old tunnels underneath the castle. Now the entire building is sinking and too expensive to demolish. The Party borrowed from the banks and would have had to pay them back. They're all sinking together. It's wonderful."

"They can't go on forever."

"Why not? When Putin visited, they merely painted the building blue and pretended it wasn't here. It was the world's greatest mass hallucination."

At least the cell phone coverage was good. Maxim made himself scarce while Arkady called Victor, who assumed a righteous tone.

"Where the devil are you?"

"Kaliningrad."

"I thought you were only going to be there overnight."

"I thought so too. Things got complicated."

"That will be on your tombstone, '*Things Got Complicated.*'"

"Have you seen Alexi Grigorenko?"

"As a matter of fact, I was doing surveillance at the Den when Alexi came in. He had a hell of a shiner."

"We had an encounter at the marina."

"So he didn't run into a door. Abdul gave him the horse laugh."

"Abdul?"

"That snake wanted the manager to play his video in the restaurant. It's an insult to every Russian soldier who served in Chechnya. I couldn't abide it."

Arkady watched Maxim buff the fender of the ZIL.

"What did you do?"

"I told Abdul I would stuff my gun down his pants and blow his balls off."

"See, this is why I can't leave you alone."

"Well, you'd better hurry back. Anya and Alexi are getting very close."

"Anya's doing research."

"Is that what you call it?" Victor asked. "The sooner you're back here, the better. Just look out for the so called poet Maxim Dal. He's a slippery character."

"I'm doing my best."

Arkady heard a whistling sound from on high and looked up in time to see a windowpane sail through the air and explode on impact. A monster at play, he thought.

Zhenya said, "According to Arkady, there's an old navy saying, 'First speed, then direction.'"

"Meaning what?" asked Lotte.

"Going anywhere is better than going nowhere."

They pitched in words together, listening for a more solid echo, writing them down on index cards by speaker as they went.

Man in the Top Hat with Line: ear, bug in a circle, two rings, fish and 2B.

Box Kite: star, bug, sunrise, triangle.

Man in Top Hat No Line: question mark, crossed knives, two rings, fish under wave.

Crescent Moon: arrow down, bug, ear, equals sign, black teardrop, white teardrop and RR.

Star: arrow down, railroad tracks, RR and the letter L.

Building Blocks: dollar sign, bug, box kite, radioactive.

Top Hat No Line: spiral, ear, box kite, face with X for mouth, or a bug in a circle.

Zhenya said, "What kind of bug, anyway?"

Lotte leaned forward to show him the pendant that hung around her neck. Trapped in amber was a wasp.

They tried themes. Railroads, as in RR and train track.

Naval, as in fish and wave. An underwater fish had to be submarines or torpedoes. L could be Lenin; that was always safe. An arrow could mean direction, exit or consequence. Or Diana the Huntress or William Tell. The teardrops could be agony, oil, blood, apple seeds, figs or pears. The fence could be a zipper, a railroad track or stitches. The waves could mean the sea, the navy, the Baltic Fleet.

"Sometimes you play the player, not the board," Zhenya said.

"Meaning what?"

"I can see some of these players. There's the interpreter himself. He's relaxed, confident, writes down 'blah blah' for the formalities. Maybe acts a little superior. Then there are the others, mainly the first Man in a Hat. The first thing he tells everybody is that they are all equal. Everyone's going to get a fair hearing. Classic Soviet-time etiquette. He opens the meeting and he closes it. There's no confusing him with any other player. He has a line under him, like the braid on an admiral.

The second Man in a Hat, the one without a line underneath, is enforcement. He carries the knives. We can learn a lot from little details."

"That reminds me," Lotte said.

"Yes?"

"I was at a tournament in Warsaw, playing a Chinese girl. It's amazing how many good players they're producing."

"And?"

"Her name was on a plaque that had the box kite symbol. Actually, it stands for China."

"Oh." So to keep things in perspective, while he had been hustling in railway stations, Lotte had been traveling the international chess tournament circuit. "That's a pretty big detail. How did you do?"

"Second place."

"That's great. Do you remember anything else?"

"One of the sponsors of the tournament was a Chinese bank, the Red Dawn Bank of Shanghai."

"Not Sunrise or Sunset?"

"No, in China, the dawn is always red."

"Probably because of all the pollution there. So, we're making progress. What do you think Natalya Goncharova stands for?"

"Beauty," said Lotte.

"Or adultery." He spread index cards across the kitchen table. "Everything is open to interpretation. It could be, 'Due to a Chinese spy ring, a torpedo sank a damaged nuclear submarine and left the victims in a vast oil slick, for which the

Russian defense minister awarded himself the Order of Lenin.'"

"Or?" Lotte asked.

Zhenya rearranged the cards. "'The great Russian poet Pushkin and his unfaithful wife, Natalya, were sailing off the coast of China when she was fatally stung by a wasp. The music at her funeral brought tears. Fish and figs were served after the ceremony.'"

They drove around the parks and lantern-lit paths in the center of the city, to what purpose, Arkady did not know. To escape the Monster? To impress a tourist?

"Here's the future," Maxim said. "The so called Fishing Village, a facsimile of old Koenigsberg."

"It looks like a theme park," Arkady said.

"The future will be a theme park."

The village's half-timbered buildings and lighthouse were a disguise for expensive shops and upper-class housing. Where were the bustling of fishmongers, barrows of herring, nets hung to dry and glistening like a bright arras of silver scales? Not even a single true fishing boat, only a pair of dinghies kept for maintenance and only one of them with an outboard engine.

"Sometimes, to complete the scene, a friend and I take out one of the boats and fish for perch. It's relaxing."

"Did Tatiana go with you?"

"Tatiana? No. She never relaxed. She knew she was in danger every time she left her door. Even in her own home.

But she welcomed danger. Her life was a waltz with danger. Only Kaliningrad could have bred a woman like her. She told me once that she preferred a short life, a dash across the sky."

"A dash or a waltz?" Arkady asked.

"Somehow both, my dear Renko."

"As long as she could take her dog with her? That's what Obolensky told me. A little pug, isn't it?"

"You've seen it?"

"I'm not sure. What was its name?"

"Polo."

"When was the last time you saw her?" Arkady asked. "Tatiana, I mean."

"The day she died."

"You were over her by then?"

"I was still fond of her. We respected each other, but we were long past the white-hot stage of a relationship."

"She confided in you?"

"To a degree. I'd say she was closer to her sister, Ludmila, and Obolensky."

"Did she mention any Mafia?"

"No one in particular."

"What about Abdul? The Shagelmans? Ape Beledon? They each had a grievance, as they saw it."

"Criminals always have a grievance," Maxim said. "The fact is they want Kaliningrad. There's much more here than amber. Auto plants, shipping, the Baltic Fleet and soon, maybe, casinos. Under the rough surface, a handsome principality."

"All of which Alexi Grigorenko wants as his inheritance."

A Mercedes slowed out of respect, it seemed, to let the ZIL go by. BMWs built in Kaliningrad seemed to jump directly to Moscow; Nissans and Isuzus made the reverse trek from Pacific ports and had the look of secondhand shoes.

"Are you looking for somebody?" Arkady asked. Maxim kept glancing at his wing mirrors.

"Acquaintances."

"Maybe your old fishing companion? There's nothing like old friends to keep you on your toes."

A bridge led to a small island and the sharp spire of a cathedral.

"Tatiana will have a statue here one day when we are long forgotten. People will ask why we did nothing while she was murdered. You carry the weight for all of us."

"I wouldn't count much on that," Arkady said.

"Then we're in trouble."

The church spire stood in its own bed of lights. Maxim approached at a crawl.

"Our cathedral." Maxim pointed at a tomb that was tucked into a corner. "Our philosopher."

The tomb was rough stone surrounded by a portico and a wrought iron gate. The headlights of the ZIL brushed along a plaque that read IMMANUEL KANT.

"Is this a midnight cultural tour?" Arkady asked. "Or are we simply adrift?"

"Come, come, you must have studied Kant at the university," Maxim said. "The greatest mind of his age? Perhaps the most famous philosopher of any age? 'Rational beings.' 'Categorical imperative.'"

Maxim kept the car moving slowly, weaving between trees, making a turn at the narrow end of the island.

"I'll take your word for it," Arkady said.

"Or 'the inquiring murderer.' Even if a murderer asks the whereabouts of someone he intends to kill, honesty requires you to tell the truth."

"I'm afraid that went over my head."

"But the old boy may have been sick," Maxim added. "Now doctors think it's possible Kant had a brain tumor. He displayed all the signs. Loss of vision, loss of social inhibition, fainting spells. We may have been taking our moral cues from a man who was going crazy."

"It wouldn't be the last time."

A bright light was followed by a shove. Arkady twisted around to see a black Mercedes SUV ride the ZIL's rear bumper. The ZIL leapt forward and plowed through a flower bed to a walkway by the river. As the SUV pulled alongside, Arkady saw one man at the wheel and two in back. Maxim shouted and pointed at the glove compartment. Arkady pulled on it, punched and kicked it, but the compartment stuck. The SUV inched ahead, gaining enough angle to steer the ZIL off the walkway and toward the water. Maxim had no choice but to stop. Two men emerged from the Mercedes, each with a semiautomatic pistol. They stood side by side along the ZIL, illuminating the car with muzzle flashes, punching holes in its doors, planting star patterns on its windshield and windows and shouting, "You want to fuck with me? Say hello to my little friend."

The work was over in a matter of seconds. Their pistol clips were empty. They shared a moment of satisfaction until the ZIL came back to life. No rounds had penetrated the bullet-proof interior of the car. The windows were starred but not shattered. Heavy as a tank, the ZIL backed onto the path and broadsided the other car even as the would-be assassins piled into it. While it could, the Mercedes sped off past the philosopher's tomb.

Chapter Twenty-Three

Zhenya and Lotte awoke on the couch to find Alexi sitting at the table and studying their notes.

"This is progress. Especially since you didn't even know what notebook I was talking about, especially since you lied."

"I found it after you left," Zhenya said.

"And you're still lying."

"I found it," Lotte said.

"Now you're lying for each other, a sign of true love."

Zhenya sat up and made the small adjustments of embarrassment. "How did you get in?"

"With a key, how else?"

"Where is Anya?"

Alexi said nothing but lit a cigarette and observed the burning tip as if it were a poker on a hearth. It occurred to Zhenya that although Alexi's black eye still looked tender, he was freshly dressed and shaved and back in command.

"Do you have a gun?" Alexi asked.

"No."

"I heard that Investigator Renko was given an engraved gun for his good services. I can't imagine Renko getting an award for anything, but that's what people say."

"I wouldn't know."

"Lotte?"

She said, "I've never met him."

"It's important that I find out where in Kaliningrad the investigator is. He didn't call?"

Zhenya said, "No."

Alexi smiled. "He didn't ask you to translate the notebook?"

"No."

"Of course he did." Alexi flipped through pages of symbols and lists of possible meanings. "The question is, where exactly is Renko now? You don't know and Anya won't say. He operates with a Detective Victor Orlov."

"Orlov is a drunk."

"That's what I hear. So it's just the two of you, and as of now, you're translating the notebook for me. I want you to stay right here until you're done. We're on the same team now."

Zhenya said, "I haven't succeeded in translating anything so far."

"But you and your friend have an idea, a general sense of what it's about. You're onto something."

"It's a private language. It could take weeks, if ever."

"Well, let's give you an incentive. The temperature at the core of a burning cigarette is seven hundred degrees."

"So?"

"And your girlfriend has tender, virginal skin."

"What do you mean?"

"Two plus two. A couple of geniuses ought to be able to work out who's most vulnerable. The slowest zebra. The tenderest girl." Alexi collected their cell phones.

Zhenya's heart pounded. Lotte shivered so hard her teeth chattered.

"I'll give you ten hours," Alexi said.

"That's not reasonable."

"Do I look like a reasonable man?"

"But it's impossible," Zhenya said.

"I'll give you ten hours. I'm leaving a man at the door."

"Who is Anya?" Lotte asked.

Alexi said, "If I were you, I wouldn't worry about another woman. Where are the scissors?" Zhenya found a pair in the desk and was still as a statue as Alexi cut the cord of the apartment phone.

In a fairy tale Zhenya might have surprised and overpowered Alexi. It wasn't so in reality. It wasn't the convenient appearance of ashtrays and blunt instruments that won the day for heroes, it was willpower and nerve. How did he propose to be a soldier for Mother Russia if he couldn't defend himself? He knew where Arkady's gun was. Where were the bullets? Another puzzle.

Lotte watched Alexi leave and whispered to Zhenya, "You did shoot somebody, didn't you?"

Zhenya nodded, afraid of horrifying her sensibilities, but she seemed to find it a comfort.

"The bullets are in the bookcase," Lotte said.

"Yes." He wondered where she was going with this.

"We just have to find the right book. Something appropriate."

"Renko has thousands of books. He's mental about books."

"What kind of books?"

"His father's war books. Fairy tales. *Alice in Wonderland, Ruslan and Ludmila, Oz*. He used to read them to me."

"Then he'd choose the right book carefully." She walked along the shelves of fiction and scanned the authors—Bulgakov, Chekhov, Pushkin—sliding each volume forward to search the space behind.

"That must be it." She pointed to a title too high for her to reach. "Hemingway. *A Farewell to Arms*."

"Are you feeling clever?"

"Very."

But when Zhenya pulled the book off the shelf all he found was a single lonely cartridge.

Arkady waited until the other car was out of sight before sitting up. He felt a sting on his forehead from a sliver of glass but the car's inner shell of armor plate had not been breached and the bulletproof windows were cracked but not shattered.

He reached across to unbuckle Maxim and push him out the door. With a pocketknife blade he popped the lid of the glove compartment that Maxim had been so desperate to open. Inside were two ferry tickets and a gun.

Maxim shook from outrage. "They tried to kill us."

"That's right. You have to choose your friends more carefully." Arkady climbed out and dragged Maxim down a pathway.

"My beautiful ZIL."

"Well, it was an armored car built for Kremlin duty and I have to say that for an antique, it held up very well."

"What about the car rally?"

"You have a way with words. I'm sure you'll think up something."

"And what do you mean by 'choose my friends more carefully'?"

"I mean you agreed to be at this spot at this time. How else could they find us in an entire city?"

"I thought they wanted to talk to you."

"Instead they tried to shoot us."

"I thought—"

"And you have two one-way tickets for tomorrow's ferry for Riga. Who was the other ticket for?"

"I know it seems that way—"

"Shut up." Arkady walked around Maxim as if he were a specimen. "Alexi saw your disappearing act at the marina when he tried to flatten me under a barge. When he needed you to help him, you ran. That's the sort of thing that a killer takes personally."

"You're spinning this out of whole cloth."

"There was a dog at the marina, a heroic pug named Polo. There aren't that many pugs in Moscow."

"Pure fantasy."

"Did Alexi offer you money? What about the wonderful American fellowship and the fifty-thousand-dollar prize?"

Maxim was deflated. "It's over. They chose someone else."

Arkady gave the big man a push to get him moving.

"Why didn't you tell me?"

"I wanted to know what was in the notebook."

"Why?"

"For Alexi."

"Why help him?"

"I was afraid."

Arkady wondered if that was the truth, half truth or poetic license.

Zhenya and Lotte didn't know if the man that Alexi had stationed outside the apartment was big or short, dressed to the nines or covered in cigarette ash. They heard him shuffle back and forth like a bear in the zoo.

Zhenya had loaded Arkady's pistol and tucked it into the back of his belt. Lotte had found skiing gear in a closet; she removed discs from the poles and had herself a pair of flimsy spears.

Meanwhile, Zhenya had found a theme.

"If you align them right, the waves are the ocean, the fish are ships or submarines and the star is Russian authority, most likely the navy."

"Could be."

"Since there is a dollar sign, RR could be Russian rubles, not railroad. In which case 'two B' wouldn't be Shakespeare but two billion. Even in rubles that's a lot of money. What do you think?"

"What does this have to do with Natalya Goncharova?"

"This is the cute part," Zhenya said. "There's no mention of where or when the meeting in the notebook took place. None. I think it might be Grisha's yacht, the *Natalya Goncharova*, which would be a brilliant stroke. It would have established for everyone that Grisha was in charge."

"Does it matter? It's in the past, isn't it?"

"Not from the way Alexi acts. He acts like it's a matter of life and death. He takes it personally."

"Name something that isn't," Lotte said.

"Chess."

"You've obviously never had a male opponent stare at your breasts for an entire game. Anyway, I hope this was in the past. What worries me is on the fifth page, a face with nothing but an 'X' for a mouth. That means nobody talks. I think that includes us."

It wasn't a matter of most trust as least distrust. Now that Alexi had tried to have him assassinated, Maxim seemed willing to cooperate. Until they came to the next bend in the road. Besides, where else would Arkady stay but Maxim's apartment? Kaliningrad felt more and more an island, with hotels and terminals watched by the Mafia and police. And Arkady had not slept, it seemed, for days. He closed his eyes and dreamed that a bottle of vodka rolled back and forth beneath the couch, that a worm of lead ate into his brain, that a small monkey-faced dog licked his face until he woke to the sunrise chirps of sparrows and found Anya sitting opposite him in a chair.

She said, "You have a cut."

Arkady touched his scalp.

"Ow."

"Maybe next time, you'd like to try an ice pick."

"Where's Maxim?"

"He left to rent a car."

"What are you doing here?"

"What a lovely welcome."

Arkady ignored the cup of tea she offered him. Her face was scrubbed clean, although she still was dressed in the tight party gear of red sequins.

He asked, "Where is Alexi?"

"In Moscow, in Kaliningrad, I don't know. He zips back and forth in Grisha's company jet. At the moment, I think he's hiding his face, but maybe you know that better than anyone. You've made a very bad enemy in Alexi."

"I never found him charming. He brought you to Kaliningrad, didn't he?"

"Yes, but now we've gone our separate ways."

"Is this a recent tiff? You became tired of each other?"

"He dropped me."

"You? That's hard to believe. The two of you seemed to be getting on."

"Arkady, you can be such a son of a bitch sometimes."

"How is the research going for your article on Tatiana?" he asked.

"Moving ahead."

"Glad to hear it."

"And your investigation?" Anya asked.

"Coming along."

"Yes, well, any time I see you with broken glass in your hair, I know your investigation is making progress."

Arkady shifted and a stack of records slid off the end of the couch to the floor. He didn't know what she was waiting for. For Alexi to return and sweep her off her feet again? Arkady realized that he had experienced one other dream, or not so much a dream as the memory of sharing his bed with Anya, of her sleeping in his shirt, of his breath caught in her hair. Strange to see that same woman through another man's eyes. An eerie displacement.

"Have you heard from Zhenya?" Arkady asked.

"No. Sometimes he goes into hiding, like you."

"You don't happen to know if he still has the notebook?"

"Maybe. It's useless."

"Then why does Alexi want it?"

She shrugged.

Alexi probably dropped her when he discovered she no longer had the notebook, Arkady thought. Well, here she was, no worse for wear after her nights with the rich and dangerous.

Anya asked, "Are you going back to Moscow?"

"After I take care of some loose ends."

"Such as?"

"Did Alexi ever have access to the keys for my apartment?"

"I never gave them to him."

Arkady said, "That's not what I asked. Was there ever a situation when he could have gotten into your handbag?"

"It's possible. You don't trust me?"

"I don't know. I don't know who you are. Am I talking to you or am I talking to Alexi's dancing partner?"

Arkady's cell phone rang. It was Vova, the boy from the beach. Arkady listened for a minute before hanging up.

"I have to go."

"No one is stopping you."

"May I have the keys?"

"Certainly." She dug into her handbag and slapped them into his hand.

"Thank you." Arkady edged past her and headed for the door.

Anya dropped into the chair. What had she expected from Arkady? You could push him only so far. She listened to flies browse on the windowpane, stared in an unfocused way at the jazz albums littering the floor, opened a pillbox for a handful of aspirin that she chewed and swallowed. She pulled up a hem of red sequins to look at a cigarette burn applied on her inner thigh.

Chapter Twenty-Four

Arkady rented a Lada, a tin can compared to the ZIL, and drove to the sand spit where he had first seen Vova and his sisters searching for amber. Vova was waiting, barefoot again, ready to wade or run for his life. When Arkady asked where he lived, Vova pointed to a shack half-engulfed by a dune.

"It moans at night. We have beams holding it up. Someday it's just going to cave in but until then, it's all ours." He gave Arkady a sideways look. "You ran into Piggy."

"The man with the butcher's van? He's pretty frightening."

"Yeah. But nobody will believe me."

"Try me."

Vova continually scanned the beach, a lookout's habit. He had found the business card that Arkady left in the biking shoe of Joseph Bonnafos and had something to tell. Or sell, would be more likely, Arkady thought.

"Are you the police?"

"In Moscow, not here."

"Because the police will just steal whatever I've got."

They were known for that, Arkady thought. He watched air holes appear in the sand as water retreated, evidence of an unseen world.

"Vova, so far as I'm concerned this is a private affair."

"Me too."

"What are your sisters' names?"

"Lyuba and Lena. Lyuba's ten. Lena's eight."

"On the phone you said you had a bike."

"A special bike. Black with a red cat."

A constant wind sculpted sand and whipped Vova's hair around his brow. Arkady had to wonder what it would be like to live in such a relentless element.

Arkady asked, "Have you shown the bike to anyone else?"

"I told the guys at the bike shop."

"How much did they offer you?"

"Fifty dollars."

"That's a lot." Maybe a six-hundredth the value of a Pantera, Arkady thought. "Sight unseen?"

"I know these guys, they'd keep the money and the bike."

"That's true."

Vova walked in a tight circle.

"Is there something else?" Arkady asked.

"Piggy."

"What about him?"

"We saw Piggy kill the biker. We watched from the trees."

Most eyewitnesses, young or old, tried to recreate the intensity

and horror of a murder, like crayoning over the lines of a col-
oring book. Vova was cool and matter-of-fact. The biker was
still alive when Piggy threw him into the butcher's van. There
was a brief sound like feet drumming on the side of the van
and then a gunshot. Piggy emerged and went through the
biker's jersey, seeming to become more frustrated as he went
and finally tossing it aside.

"Did he see you?"

"I don't think so."

"Then why is he after you?"

"We took the bike."

That altered the situation. "You stole the bicycle from
Piggy?"

"Yes."

"Does he know?"

"Kind of."

"Kind of?"

"He saw Lyuba wearing the helmet and tried to run her
down, but he couldn't drive up the dunes."

"Where are your parents?"

"They're coming back." It sounded less a boast than a
wish.

"What about you? Who takes care of you and your sisters?"

"Our grandmother. She lives back toward town."

"Does she feed you?"

"We get by."

"What's your full name?" Vova was short for Vladimir.

Vova shut his mouth. No parents, no last name.

231

"Okay," Arkady said. "Besides the bike and the helmet, what else did you take?"

"Just a notebook I found in the grass. It was full of gibberish."

"Then why take it?"

"We found a card too with a cell phone number. When people put a cell phone number on something, they want it back, right?"

"That's smart."

"And the lady who answered was nice. She came right away."

"What did she look like?"

"She looked brainy."

"Did she say her name?"

"No. She had a little dog."

"What kind?"

"It had buggy eyes."

"Buggy eyes? What about the tail?"

"Short and twisty. She was pretty."

"The dog?"

"The woman." Vova added man to man, "And she had nice legs."

"You noticed that?"

"You asked."

"How much did she give you for the notebook?"

"Fifty dollars. What I really need is a gun."

What kind of world was this, Arkady wondered, where children lived in holes in the ground and casually asked for a gun?

Arkady said, "I tell you what. I'll give you fifty dollars if you and your sisters stay off the beach."

"You're serious?"

Arkady opened his billfold. "Stay off the beach for a week, can you do that?"

"No problem." Vova cheered up. "I wish you were here during the Amber War. Bodies washed up on the beach every day."

"You'll be rich after you sell the bike."

"There's a problem. Lena took the bike out and forgot where she left it. The sand shifted and now it's disappeared."

Zhenya and Lotte had a plan that, much like a chess game, depended on the opponent's moves, on whether the man in the hall would call them out onto the landing or step into the apartment, be alone or have accomplices. Zhenya would take the gun and if he missed, Lotte could follow through with the ski poles, assuming the man obliged and came within reach. Four hours of Alexi's deadline had already passed and fear and exhaustion were wearing them down.

In Zhenya's hands the gun was a leaden question mark, a loss of control rather than control, a sense of doom instead of decision. Lotte couldn't help staring at the door as if blood were already seeping over the threshold. One idea about a symbol was haltingly followed by another and sometimes minutes would pass without a word being spoken.

Lotte tried. "Two interlocked rings could mean cooperation."

"Or two eyes, two eggs, two cymbals, two wheels," Zhenya said.

"So you think it's a bad idea."

"No, but we don't have time to be an encyclopedia."

"It goes with the equals signs, the ears for a fair hearing and the 'blah blah' of the opening."

Zhenya said nothing.

"So you think this is possible?" Lotte asked.

"Tricky," he conceded.

"Except for a chess hustler, I suppose."

"Yes." Zhenya wasn't a psychiatrist, but he felt that he could read the character and skill level of anyone who sat across from him at a chessboard. What he saw in the notes of the interpreter suggested vanity. What he saw in Lotte was that she was scared but game.

He said, "Money, China, banks, rubles, dollars, submarines. What does it all add up to?"

"What does 'L' stand for?"

"I don't know."

"Black figs?"

"Teardrops?"

"Oil," Lotte said. "When Russia can't pay in cash, it pays in oil."

"And natural gas, the white teardrop."

"For what?"

Zhenya asked, "What if the fence isn't a fence at all, but stitches? What if they're repairs?"

"What about Natalya Goncharova? She has no connection to anything."

"She's an anomaly," Zhenya conceded.

"An anomaly is something you don't know how to deal with. Isn't the best clue what doesn't seem to fit?" Lotte asked.

Scandals of the imperial court had never been Zhenya's strong point. He said, "As I remember, Natalya Goncharova dragged her husband into a duel and he was killed. That's about it. The stuff of romance novels."

"Or murder," Lotte said. "Her husband happened to be Pushkin, Russia's greatest poet. The other duelist wore a coat studded with silver buttons. Pushkin's bullet bounced off. Three days later he was dead and Natalya Goncharova found solace in the arms of the tsar. So, adultery, conspiracy, murder. Where do you want to begin?"

Chapter Twenty-Five

Since his first visit to Ludmila Petrovna's garden, her sunflowers had become slightly blowsy, her tomatoes had grown heavy on the vine and her zucchini had gone rogue. Her weeds, on the other hand, were thriving.

A pug ran out of the cottage door in chase of a rubber ball. The dog seized the ball, shook it furiously and began to race back to a woman who leaned against the doorway with her arms crossed.

"Polo!" Arkady said.

The woman looked up. The dog stopped and tried to look in two directions at the same time, then, with an eye to a new playmate, carried the ball to Arkady.

"You're back," she said.

"I'm afraid so." Arkady extracted the ball from the dog's mouth. "I'm sorry to say your friend has no sense of loyalty."

She didn't smile but he had the sense that in some grim

way, she was amused. "Every time I try to garden, Polo wants to play."

"Maybe that's the price of friendship." He looked around the garden. "Your vegetables look ready to burst."

"Perhaps I haven't been paying them enough attention."

"I couldn't tell you," Arkady said. "I'm not a gardener."

"It's supposed to be pretty simple. Plant them and water them."

"And keep the dogs out. A lot of your vegetables look ready to pick. I could help you."

"What about your investigation?"

"It can wait," Arkady said.

"What makes you think I need help?"

"When I was here with Maxim, you wore dark glasses because you were sensitive to light."

"Maxim is always looking out for me."

"That was my impression. And you haven't weeded since then. Ludmila was the gardener."

"How did you know?"

Besides the dog, the derelict garden and the absence of dark glasses? He had listened to Tatiana's voice on tape for hours. He'd have known her anywhere.

She turned and walked into the cottage and although there had been no invitation, Arkady followed. The pug followed Arkady, dropping the ball as a suggestion, letting it roll and retrieving it. While she heated water for tea, Arkady looked at knickknacks that occupied kitchen shelves and cabinets.

Family photos of Ludmila Petrovna holding babies and small children of varying ages. Postcards from all over the world. Framed photographs of the same two girls with bright smiles and golden hair biking, kayaking, running down a sand dune with arms outstretched as if they could fly.

"Who was older?"

"She was. We were only ten months apart."

"Are these pictures of her children?"

"No. Cousins, friends, children of friends. In spite of her poor eyesight, Ludmila was an avid amateur photographer." She placed two cups of tea on the table and sat. "Sugar?"

"No thank you."

"All the men I know have their tea plain. Why is that?"

"I don't know. Why do all the women I know suck tea through a sugar cube?" He caught her in the act.

"I told Ludmila not to come to Moscow, but she always had to be the big sister. She hated to worry and I'm afraid I made her life miserable. How did you know? Oh, yes, the dark glasses."

"You seemed to have been miraculously cured."

"It was as simple as that?"

"More or less."

"Do you think I'm going to get out of here alive?"

"I doubt it. You could take your chances as Ludmila, but my guess is that they're suspicious."

"Why do you think they're suspicious?"

"I noticed on the way in there's a man in a car watching your door."

"That's Lieutenant Stasov. He's made me his personal project. He pushed his way in and searched the house. Now he lingers on the street."

For a second Arkady had the impulse to touch her and see if she was real and wondered how often she had that effect on men, the creation of a faint vibration.

He pressed ahead. "Let's assume the person who killed Ludmila was waiting in your apartment. Where were you?"

"I was working late at the magazine with Obolensky. Maxim swooped in and said I had been reported dead, that I had jumped from my balcony and we had to get out of Moscow as quickly as possible. Because once you're officially dead you soon will be. It's a matter of bookkeeping. We drove all night to Kaliningrad. I didn't know Ludmila was going to my apartment."

"The question is who pushed her. She would have rung the bell when she got to your apartment."

"I wasn't there."

"But Ludmila had a key of her own, didn't she?"

Her voice hollowed out. "Yes. My sister was mistaken for me and she died. Now I'm alive pretending to be her." Although she clearly despised tears, she wiped her eyes before she changed the subject. "Maxim told me about your adventure on the beach. So you met the boy called Vova."

"He drives a hard bargain."

"I know. I paid fifty dollars for the notebook."

"What's in it?"

She said, "I confess, I don't know."

Arkady almost laughed. "You don't know? People are being

shot and thrown off balconies for this notebook, and you don't know why?"

"Joseph, the interpreter, was going to translate it for me."

"And this was going to be a big story, as big as a war in Chechnya or a bomb in Moscow?"

"That's what Joseph said. And the proof was in the notebook."

"He didn't give you any idea?"

"Only that it couldn't be understood by anyone but him."

"Why was he willing to help you? Why was he willing to put his life in danger?"

"He wanted to be somebody. He wanted to be something besides an echo, which is what he had been all his life. Besides, he thought that keeping everything in notes that only he could read would keep him safe."

"Instead it's poison passed from hand to hand."

"Have you got the notebook?" she asked.

"It's with a friend."

"An interpreter?"

"You could say that."

The tea had gotten cold. Tatiana stared out the screen door at a row of watermelons that had swollen and split open.

"It's my fault," Arkady said. "If I had just kept my nose out of it and not questioned the identification of Ludmila's body, you might be safe."

"Now you have to follow through. You're the investigator."

Arkady heard a noise. The pug had nudged open a cabinet and spilled the box of dog biscuits.

Tatiana swept them up. "What a little pig."

"That reminds me, how did Polo get here?"

"Maxim brought him later."

"That's a long drive. You have to go through Lithuanian and Polish customs and all. Maxim was happy going back and forth?"

"He seemed to be."

Arkady wondered what they would do to her, those censors who follow journalists with a pistol or a club. Just as she must have been wondering.

"Do you know Stasov?" Tatiana asked.

"We've talked on the phone."

The gate was open. Arkady pulled a window shade aside to see a man in a weathered Audi parked across the street at a travel agency that promised romance in Croatia. He didn't look like someone planning a holiday.

"Do you have a gun?" Arkady asked.

"Do you?" She read his pause. "What a helpless pair of human beings."

Arkady shrugged. So it seemed.

He went to the other rooms. The house was small and snug, feeding off one narrow hallway. The furniture was prewar oak. Ancestors looked out from oval frames. The back room had been made into a photography darkroom with a back door that did not open.

"You're not going to find anything. Stasov took my laptop."

"But he still thinks you're Ludmila?"

"So far. I erased everything."

On the bed was a backpack stuffed to the gills. It wasn't the sign of someone resigned to being trapped.

"Where is your canary? She seems to have taken her cage with her."

"With a friend."

"Then you're ready to go."

She took a second to say, "I suppose so."

"Where?"

She fixed Arkady with a look that told him he was asking for more trust than he had earned. After all, how long had she known him? Fifteen minutes? And what could he do for her while she was trapped?

Arkady went first with Polo and rolled the pug's rubber ball underneath the detective's car. The dog set in yapping hysterically enough that Arkady had to shout, "Don't move."

Stasov rolled down his passenger window. "What? What are you talking about?"

"My dog is under your car. If you move, you'll run over him."

"Then get him out."

"I'll try if you don't move."

"I'm not moving, for God's sake."

"He was chasing a ball."

"Just get the fucking dog. What an idiot."

"Do you have the emergency brake on?"

"Hurry up or I'll run you both the fuck over."

"He's only a puppy."

MARTIN CRUZ SMITH

"He's roadkill if you don't get him out."

"Can you reach his leash from your side?"

"No, I can't reach his fucking leash."

"Oh good, we have more people to help."

"We don't need more people."

"You can't blame a puppy."

"I will fucking shoot you if you don't get away from the car."

"Well, he seems to have disappeared."

"Disappeared?"

"Oh, I see him. It's all right, thank God." Arkady pulled Polo out by the leash and picked him up. By then Tatiana had slipped out the garden gate and joined the shoppers in the stalls.

"Six letters, a breed of dog, starting with the letters Af."

"I don't believe this," Zhenya said.

"Come on, don't be such a stick. You're doing a puzzle, I'm doing a puzzle. We can help each other. Okay, favorite television show, two words, starting with Da. It's not like you're going anywhere. Okay, have it your way."

Half an hour passed before the man in the hall pressed his mouth to the door again. "Don't be such a hard-ass. Two words, starting with Da."

"*Dating Game*," Lotte said.

"It fits. See, that wasn't so bad. Now you can ask me one."

"Ask you?"

"Fair is fair."

Zhenya wondered what the man on the other side of the

door looked like. Tall or short? Thin or fat? In between murdering people did he bounce a baby on his knee? Zhenya and Lotte waited with one shot from Arkady's gun and ski poles under the table.

"It's a different kind of puzzle," Zhenya said.

"You have a very superior air. I'm only trying to help."

"Do you have children?" Lotte asked.

"No, no. Nothing personal. Personal is verboten. I shouldn't even be talking to you."

"Then don't," Zhenya said.

"Suit yourself. You've got about an hour, according to my watch. Look, I'll just talk to the girl. She doesn't even have to say anything. Write it on a piece of paper, slide it under the door."

"This is a total waste of time," Zhenya said. "The man is a killer. He's just torturing us."

"I'm only talking to her."

Lotte took a piece of stationery from the desk and wrote the letter L. She slid it under the door.

"That's it?" the man asked.

"This should be beautiful," Zhenya said. "He wouldn't know an Afghan dog if it bit him."

The page came back. The man on the other side of the door said, "The Roman numeral for fifty. It's only in every fucking crossword puzzle ever written."

Lotte went down the list of interpretations for the letter L and looked at Zhenya. "We missed that one."

"It could be fifty thousand, fifty million, fifty percent."

"For what? And what about the face with an X—or is it a wasp?"

Zhenya found himself looking at her breasts. "The wasp," he said. "If it's a wasp caught in amber, then amber is the clue, not the wasp."

A cell phone rang in the hall. The puzzle man took it and sounded unhappy.

Zhenya asked, "Everything okay?"

There was silence on the other side of the door.

"Is Alexi coming back? We still have half an hour," Zhenya said.

Again, nothing.

"You just told us we had almost an hour," Lotte said.

Nothing.

"You can't kill somebody ahead of time," Zhenya said, even as he knew how ridiculous he sounded. "Is he still on the phone? Let me talk to him." He opened the door a chain's length and the puzzle man held the phone up to the crack. "Alexi, we're making progress."

"What have you got?"

"It's not like the usual notebook or minutes of a meeting. There's no date. I just know that a submarine will be repaired and that considerable Russian rubles will change hands."

Alexi said nothing, but the silence was significant. This was the point in a chess match when a player had no choice but to bring his king out from the protection of the back row and plunge it into the center of the board.

"There is going to be another meeting," Zhenya said.

"On board the *Natalya Goncharova?*"

"Yes." What else could he say?

"Thank you, that's all I needed to hear. Give the phone back to my man."

Zhenya returned the phone and closed the door.

Lotte asked, "Did it work?"

"I don't know."

All he got from the other side of the door was silence. No "You did it, kid!" Only a clammy feeling and a dry mouth.

He and Lotte no longer looked at each other. It wasn't fair. If anyone should hew to a schedule, it should be an executioner. They took in the sounds of the street, the emptiness of the building, the sound of a silencer being screwed onto the muzzle of a gun. He was only seventeen. Chess, he found, was no longer that important to him. He had fantasized about having a chess opening named for him. Now all games seemed trivial. He had other ambitions. This was unjust. Oddly enough, he thought it wouldn't be so bad to be an investigator like Arkady.

Lotte decided to give up chess for music. Her family had always been artistic. She heard a bow drawn across the strings of a double bass. Something grim from Wagner. *Götterdämmerung*. The Twilight of the Gods.

Zhenya brought out the gun from the back of his belt but Lotte was in his way, trying to hold the door shut. He reached for her hand and they leaned together against the door.

The puzzle man heaved into it at full force. The chain snapped and Zhenya glimpsed a thin man with a vein-lined beak of a nose trying to insert a gun. The door slammed shut and was opened by an elderly man in a bathrobe and slippers.

"Lotte! I found you!" Lotte's grandfather, the coward, struggled for the gun. "You must run!" The puzzle man swiped him away.

The door shut. Zhenya heard a head being cracked against the doorjamb. The door opened again like a reshuffled deck of cards as Victor Orlov rammed the puzzle man two more times against the doorjamb and threw him down the stairs.

Chapter Twenty-Six

White lights in front, red in back, a line of bikers wound through the early evening chasing streetlights, swerving in and out of streets and parks.

Arkady and Tatiana had signed on for one of the bike shop's overnight excursions and left Polo in a neighbor's care.

Joining the group had been Tatiana's idea. She had batted down every means of escape he suggested. He merely mentioned the bike shop excursion and she seized on it. She rented a bike and gear. Arkady's pea jacket counted as unusual attire and Karl, the shop owner, asked him when he last rode.

"It's been a while. I suppose I could use a pants clip."

Karl looked him up and down. "As long as you have money for a taxi."

The bikers were not a political crowd. Half were female. Most carried a bedroll and tent and although the route was only fifty kilometers, hardly a tour at all, there was an air of anticipation, especially once the bikers cleared the city.

Arkady wobbled at first, but traffic was light and he regained his sense of balance. Tatiana bit into the wind and plainly enjoyed herself. Military trucks went by, but that was to be expected so close to the home port of the Baltic Fleet.

Karl was in the lead. At a signal from him, the bikes peeled onto a nearly invisible path between spindly birches and pushed through waist-high ferns to a black palisade of firs. Finally the group came to a stop at a charred circle of stones. At once women gathered wood and men set up tents. Arkady was given a flimsy two-person affair of nylon and plastic hoops. By the time a campfire was flaming, a feast of vodka, wine, sausages, fatback and bread was spread out on newspapers.

All the other bikers seemed to know each other. Karl leaned across the campfire to tell Arkady, "Your friend should take her helmet off. We're all friends here."

Tatiana removed her helmet. No one gave a hint of recognizing the famous journalist from Moscow.

"Much better," Karl said, as if a threshold of friendship had been crossed.

Appetites set in. The bikers were in their thirties and forties, attractive mainly because they were fit. Klim was an accountant, Tolya a fireman, Ina a schoolteacher, Katya a beautician. Arkady couldn't keep track of all their names, especially as their faces danced in the light of the campfire.

Ina passed a glass of vodka to Arkady. "What do you do?"

"I'm an investigator."

"And this lady, I suppose, is a *femme fatale*?"

"Exactly," said Tatiana.

Karl said, "Well, there is a campfire tradition of tall tales, but there is also a tradition of songs." From out of the dark, he produced a guitar.

They sang about women with dark eyes, wolves with yellow eyes, Gypsies, sailors, tearful mothers, train tracks that stretched far into the horizon, each song accompanied by a round of vodka. Cheeks grew flushed and as the fire mellowed, Arkady became aware that Ina, the schoolteacher, had stripped to the waist.

Karl said, "The naturist movement has a long tradition in the Baltic states."

"I can see that," Arkady said.

"Some do, some don't."

Karl had also brought a balalaika, always an invitation for someone to kick his heels like a Cossack. Halfway through a squat, Klim went down like a wounded deer, a cue for the club members to bank the fire and retire. But not for long. Arkady heard bodies slipping in and out of tents.

Tatiana zipped the tent shut. "This is crazy."

"You wanted to get out of the city."

"Not at the cost of all dignity."

"You are welcome to mine. It's battered but you can have it."

Arkady unrolled a foam pad that softened a ground cover of needles. Darkness magnified a background of crickets and cicadas.

Tatiana said, "I have to confess, there was a nudist beach on the spit. When we were girls, Ludmila and I used to sneak in and gape. It's probably still there."

Feet padded by the tent and stubbed a toe. Arkady waited for the visitor to move on.

"It's like a badly organized orgy," Arkady said.

She almost laughed.

"And tomorrow?" he asked. "Kaliningrad is dangerous for you and Moscow is no better."

"I'll think about it. Maybe things will calm down."

"You've already been murdered once. I'd say things have gone far enough."

"Not for you. You can return to Moscow."

"No," he said, even though he recognized how seduced he had been and how small his role was. This was her drama and it struck him that she wasn't interested in escaping. Perhaps escape was the last thing on her mind.

They slept as far apart as possible within the tent, but the night was cool and he woke to find her curled against his back. The other tents were silent, the campfire reduced to the ping of embers.

The assassin's name was Fedorov. He was smaller and older than Zhenya expected and had the full suit and pencil mustache of an actor from the silent screen, and although Victor had hand-cuffed him to a radiator, the man maintained a professional air.

"I didn't like the job. Killing kids didn't sit well with me. I was just supposed to babysit. Alexi said don't let them get away or start a ruckus or anything. They seemed nice enough."

"But you would have shot them?"

"I would've done what I was told. What are you going to do?" He shrugged at Lotte. "Sorry."

"That's the difference between you and us." She gathered her grandfather to take him to the elevator. The artist's act of courage had left him a wreck.

"Maybe." That was the man's statement, this assassin who did crossword puzzles to while away the time. Zhenya looked for tells, the marks and blinks that gave away a gambit before it was played. Fedorov was going to cozy up to Victor because that was where the power lay.

"A smart girl, but unrealistic," Fedorov said. He managed to free a pack of cigarettes and a disposable lighter. "Like one?" he asked Victor. "No? Could I have an ashtray? Don't you love these old apartments? High ceilings, fireplaces, parquet floor. Frankly, I'm glad nobody got hurt. I'm the injured party, right? This can all be settled. Do you think you can loosen these cuffs?"

"I don't think the cuffs are your problem," Victor said. "Your problem is whether you're alive ten minutes from now."

"Well, to be blunt, you're a notorious drunk and the kid is a hustler. I think you two are just now realizing what trouble you're in. Just my opinion."

Victor took his time opening a bottle of Fanta; in interrogations, as in comedy, timing was everything.

He asked, "What is Alexi after?"

"Revenge, I suppose. Trying to find Grisha's killer. That's his filial duty."

"What has that got to do with the notebook that the kids are working on?"

"Beats me. Could I have some ice? I have a terrific headache. You put my head through the fucking wall. I probably should go to the hospital."

"What were Alexi's exact words?"

"To wait until he got back. Then he calls and says he wants the kids taken care of right away. No loose ends, that sort of thing."

"Did he mention Investigator Renko?" Zhenya asked.

"Who's Investigator Renko?" Fedorov asked Victor.

"Answer the kid," Victor said.

"You I'll talk to, not the kid."

"Is Renko okay?" Zhenya asked with enough heat that even Victor was surprised.

"Fuck knows. You know, it occurs to me that since I didn't actually do anything, you have no legal reason to hold me. Maybe I should charge you with assault and kidnapping. You're lucky if I call it even."

"Talk to the kid," Victor said.

Fedorov noticed the Makarov resting on Zhenya's lap and he hiked himself on his elbow the better to ask, "Is that my gun? Zhenya, is that your name? Zhenya, have you ever handled a real gun before?"

Zhenya broke the pistol down to its slide, spring, carriage and clip, as Arkady had taught him.

"Huh." From Fedorov, a mild surprise.

Zhenya reassembled the pistol and aimed at Fedorov. "Where is Alexi?"

"This is stupid. I made it clear, I don't answer questions from a kid."

Victor said, "Don't tell me, tell him."

"Who knows? Alexi's got his own jet. He's here, he's there . . ."

"Don't be flustered," Victor said.

"I am not fucking flustered."

"Don't tell me, tell him."

"In Kaliningrad?" Zhenya asked.

Fedorov smiled. "Maybe he can strip a gun. That doesn't mean he can pull the trigger."

"You forgot the silencer." Victor handed Zhenya a matte black tube.

Fedorov said, "Believe me, I've had guns waved in my direction a hundred times. With kids, it's always bravado."

Zhenya screwed the silencer onto the barrel.

Fedorov's smile ran out of air. "I'm just warning you, little boys shouldn't play with loaded guns."

Victor said, "Zhenya is not a boy."

The gun popped and the parquet floor next to Fedorov exploded. He was covered with splinters.

"Where is Alexi?" Zhenya asked.

"You're crazy!"

Zhenya's second shot splintered the floor on Fedorov's other side. Fedorov's complexion turned to suet gray and he grimaced in anticipation.

"Where is Alexi?" Zhenya asked again.

"I don't know!"

Zhenya let the silencer rest on Fedorov's forehead and squeezed the trigger slowly enough for him to hear the firing mechanism of the gun glide into place.

"Kaliningrad," Fedorov said. "They're all there. Alexi, Abdul, Beledon, everyone."

"I found a ride for my grandfather," Lotte said as she came back in the door. She halted and took in Zhenya, the gun and the smell of carbon in the air. In an instant, she disappeared back into the elevator.

Zhenya pounded down the stairs after her, caroming off the walls. He caught up at the lobby, but she wrested from his grasp.

"You're no better than him," Lotte said. "You just need a better excuse."

"It's not what you think."

"Then what is it?"

"A game." Zhenya put the gun to his head and pulled the trigger. The hammer clicked on an empty chamber. "A shell game. I unloaded the clip and only reloaded two rounds. I'm not a killer, just a hustler."

Victor found babysitters.

Detectives Slovo and Blok should have been in Sochi, but two days after retirement they had returned. In Moscow they were men of authority. In Sochi they were paunchy, middle-aged nobodies in sandals joining other nobodies in sandals filling supermarket carts with bargains on Australian wine, hoping for a smile from the cashier, slathering imitation caviar on sodden crackers, passing out on the sofa with a glass in their hand. They were happy to keep Fedorov handcuffed to a bunk at Victor's favorite drunk tank.

Communicating with Arkady was not so easy.

"You know what would make me happy?" Victor asked. "If he bothered to call us. Where is he? Is he in a hole or out to sea? Because his friends from Moscow, they're all headed his way."

Chapter Twenty-Seven

Arkady and Tatiana stole away from the slumbering bikers before dawn and picked up the road with their headlights. The air carried the taste of salt and made the birches bow and sigh. She led and he followed.

As the sun rose the resort town of Zelenogradsk began materializing out of the dark with an array of fish-and-chips stands, video arcades and, along a promenade, the silhouettes of prewar hotels with spiked German roofs. On the beach a few early risers watched waves march in and die on the sand.

"It's out of season now," Tatiana said as they rode. "The only ones who come are birders. It's a flyway for hawks and eagles. Ludmila and I used to come here all the time."

Zelenogradsk dwindled down. Arkady recognized the kiosk and tattoo posters he had seen with Maxim. The same beachcomber dragged his sledge along the shoulder of the road. Headed north, the road itself became a single lane. Cottages turned to fishing shacks and became fewer and fewer, while the beach narrowed to a spit of sand with a lagoon on one side and ocean on the other. Not a single car. Only the sound of surf.

"It's still magic." Tatiana sounded refreshed in spite of herself.

When the cottages were truly far apart, she stopped at one with weathered paint and gingerbread trim, like the home of an indigent witch. Arkady recognized it from a photo he had seen in Ludmila's kitchen.

"Sometimes nobody comes out here for months at a time. Ludmila had the only key."

She searched under an array of gnomes, starfish and abalone shells. Arkady watched for a minute, then found a beachcombing rake and jimmied open a window.

"This is your cabin, isn't it?" he said.

The cabin had a living room with a fireplace, a kitchen with a wood-burning stove, a water closet, two bedrooms and a screened sleeping porch. Water for bathing came from a pump. Board games filled a chest, paperback novels overflowed a bookshelf and the pantry was down to canned sausages and pickled herring. A ring with more keys than seemed necessary hung on the wall.

"There is a storage shed too," Tatiana said.

She led him outside and unlocked a wooden structure not much larger than a sauna. Bicycles hung from a central rack. Security cables ran through their wheels. The bikes were serviceable, nothing special, an intelligent choice, Arkady thought, considering the cottage was unoccupied for months at a time.

Shelves were stocked with everyday hammers and saws, jars of nails and screws arranged by size, hand-labeled cans of caulking and paint and the sort of esoteric hardware that only a handyman could appreciate. Outdoor furniture tied together by cable gathered dust in the corner. There wasn't much in the way of fishing gear.

When they returned to the cabin, Arkady dropped into a wicker chair. His legs told him it had been years since he had bicycled.

Tatiana ducked from room to room.

"My father loved this place."

"What was he like?"

"He was a historian. He used to say, 'Sometimes, the less you know the better.'"

"What kind of historian is that?"

"A Russian historian. He said that in a normal country, history moves forward. History evolves. But in Russia it can go in any direction or disappear completely, which makes us the envy of the world. Imagine a Kaliningrad anywhere else."

"Was your father depressed?"

"Totally." She returned and dropped into a rocking chair. "That was all he wanted Russia to be. Not perfect, just normal. What about your father?"

"More murderous than depressed. You could say that the war allowed him to vent."

Light framed her. Arkady thought she wasn't beautiful in a conventional way. Her forehead was too broad, her eyes too gray and her attitude far too provocative.

He said, "Maxim claims you would rather be a bright meteor than a steady little moon."

"Maxim says a lot of stupid things."

"Does he know about this place?"

"I brought him here once."

"Perfect."

"He wants to do something grandiose."

"He's still in love with you, isn't he?"

"I don't know."

"Yes you do. He was willing to watch Alexi crush me under a ton of ballast at the marina in Moscow."

"You're lying."

Arkady described the scene. "I have a witness. Polo. He saved my life. Maxim probably thought they were just going to throw a scare into me and he could call Alexi off. Old poets lose their timing. I suppose that goes first, like the legs of a fighter. Anyway, I don't think Maxim was doing it to get at me. He was trying to protect you, to prevent me from finding out you were alive."

"Now he wants to risk his life. I told him that at his age it no longer matters."

"If you don't mind my saying so, you are a difficult person to be in love with."

"And you?" Tatiana asked. He didn't know what she meant by that, and she changed the subject as if she sensed they were approaching an abyss. "Ludmila and I used to run up and down the dunes. Every day they were different. Different place, different shape. And, of course, our father taught us how to search for amber. He thought the only real history was geology; everything else was opinion. Did you know that the youngest ocean in the world is the Baltic Sea?"

"Is that why we're here, to watch the sea grow old?"

"Not quite." She rocked forward to offer him a cigarette.

"No thanks."

"Are you sure?"

She tapped the pack and caught a computer memory stick as it dropped out. It was plastic, about the size of a restaurant matchbook.

"What's on there?" Arkady asked.

"What do you want? The murder of journalists, the beating of protesters, corruption at the top, the rape of natural resources by a circle of cronies, a fraudulent democracy, the erection of palaces, a hollow military. If you had been a source, the mention of any of this could earn you or someone close to you a bullet in the head. It's all here in single-spaced articles."

"But they've all been published, haven't they? There's nothing new?"

"The notebook. The notebook is new. Only I don't have it. I have all this data leading to the top of a pyramid but I can't reach it without knowing what Grisha was doing, and that's in the notebook. I know who but I don't know what. Your experts may know what but they won't know who. Tell me about the people working on it. They're linguistic experts or military analysts?"

"They're two kids who play chess."

She sat back. "That's it?"

"That's it. They're good at games."

"They're children?"

Arkady nodded.

"Joseph . . ." She had to laugh, stunned. "Joseph was sure the notebook would be impossible to decipher because you would have to live his life to understand his personal vocabulary. His sophisticated music, books, films and so on."

"To be a middle-aged Swiss male who probably doted on Mozart? No. He's lucky to have these two."

"Poor Joseph. He got in over his head."

"Where you led him."

"Yes, that's true," she said after a moment. "Do you think I have led you in over your head?"

"Without a doubt."

Victor maneuvered an easy chair to face the front door of Arkady's apartment. Anyone coming in would have to go through him. Every few minutes he checked his cell phone in case Arkady had texted or left a message. Victor hated the Internet.

"Tell him," Lotte said.

"There's a nautical theme," Zhenya said. "Navy, ship, submarine, torpedo, water, sea."

"I'll tell you what's a theme," Victor said. "A lot of money changing hands and every crook watching every other crook. Nobody trusts anybody else. That's why they're meeting."

"Explain it to him," Lotte said.

"Please," said Victor.

"This is what I think the notebook says: 'The Red Dawn Shipyard in China agrees to pay Russia two billion to repair and refit a submarine to seaworthiness. Maybe fifty percent to the Russian Ministry of Defense and fifty percent to certain anonymous partners of . . .'"

"Amber something," Lotte said. "It has to be."

Zhenya was disconcerted but he continued. "And there will be no public accounting. The parties will meet on the *Natalya Goncharova*."

"You mean Grisha's yacht."

"I guess so."

"Only Grisha is dead and the notes are two weeks old."

"Then they're meeting again, everyone but Grisha," Zhenya said.

"Who is meeting?" Victor asked.

"We don't know," Lotte admitted.

Victor opened a fresh bottle of Fanta. "Amateurs."

Chapter Twenty-Eight

Arkady and Tatiana sat on the porch and watched waves rip and roll as foam up the beach. In the eaves, cobwebs billowed with each blast of wind. Tatiana wrote nonstop on a yellow pad. She looked so slight, a moth in lamplight, it was hard to believe she inspired anger and fear among armed men.

"Do you mind if I ask what you're writing?"

"It's an *opus horribilis*. Or a chronicle of corruption, whatever you want to call it. There's so much corruption to choose from it's hard to know where to begin. Imagine a defense contractor embezzling three billion rubles out of its budget for building docks for nuclear submarines. That's a hundred million dollars in real money that was invested into real estate. The police say when they raided the apartment of one of the alleged embezzlers they found art, jewelry and, guess what, the defense minister himself with his mistress.

"But that's nothing compared to the siphoning of seven

billion rubles from our satellite navigation system, which might account for all our failed satellite launchings. The list goes on and on. The Defense Ministry admits that a fifth of the military budget is stolen. One can only imagine what an independent investigation would find."

She wrote effortlessly, but it struck him that there was something guarded, omitted, incomplete.

"That's it?"

"In a nutshell, yes."

"Do you have a tape recorder?"

"A journalist always has a tape recorder." She reached into her backpack and handed the recorder to him. "Why?"

From his pea jacket he took a cassette. "I've been carrying this around for days for no good reason except that I found it in your apartment and, in very small letters, the label says 'Again.' Again what?"

He pushed "Play." The tape was tinny but distinctive, a continuous metallic tap, tap, tap, scrape, scrape, scrape until Tatiana turned it off.

"An SOS from the submarine *Kursk*," she said. She could as easily have said hell.

"Why should you care about an accident at sea that took place a dozen years ago?"

"Nothing has changed," she said.

Arkady waited.

She said, "When the torpedoes on the *Kursk* exploded, our navy press office reported that the submarine had encountered 'minor technical difficulties.' By that time it had plunged to the

268

ocean floor. Altogether, we made fourteen futile attempts to rescue the men inside before Norwegian help was accepted. The entire crew of one hundred eighteen men died. How could this happen to a submarine in the Red Navy? What did we learn? That the torpedoes were volatile and the hatches refused to close and, most important, when reporters revealed the truth they could be threatened with criminal libel. That's what we learned."

"That's the past."

"No, that's the future. We have a new nuclear submarine, with much the same problems as the *Kursk*."

"What is it called?"

"The *Kaliningrad*."

"Of course."

"Only there's a problem. The *Kaliningrad* didn't pass muster. They don't dare let it operate. It has to be refitted from top to bottom. The original construction costs were a hundred billion rubles and the refit will cost just as much, yet the Kremlin and the Ministry of Defense are happy."

"How is that possible?"

"It's all in the notebook. All I know is that we don't have a government anymore, just thieves."

"Is that what you're writing about? The *Kaliningrad* is just one more example?"

"No, this is not the same. The *Kursk* was an example of incompetence. The *Kaliningrad* is an example of incompetence and greed. It carries a blood curse. It's a black mark that can never be erased."

"Maybe the submarine's problems can be reengineered or remedied, at least?"

"Maybe. My experience is that it's easier to put reporters into the ground. The interpreter Joseph knew and he's dead."

"Who knew about your connection to Joseph?"

"No one aside from my editor."

Arkady's impression of Sergei Obolensky was that he was a gossip, but no one needed to have talked. The interpreter Joseph Bonnafos had served his purpose. Once the meeting was over, he was a loose string fated to be clipped.

She said, "You're playing investigator again."

"I make a stab at it from time to time."

"What does it matter? You have no authority here."

"I have no authority anywhere, but I like to understand things."

"That sounds like a perverse pleasure."

"I'm afraid so. What do you know about Grisha?"

"Personally? He was rich, he was feared and he had fun. A full life, you could say."

"As a businessman?"

"A businessman, public benefactor and Mafia boss."

"In both Kaliningrad and Moscow."

"Well, he was a man of ambition. A leader."

"And how would you describe Alexi?"

"Crazy."

The word had a razor's edge.

"You'll stay away from him, won't you?" Arkady said.

"He killed my sister."

"I think so too, but don't dismiss Ape Beledon or the rest of Grisha's pallbearers. They are all capable of killing anyone who gets in their way. For them it's like swatting a fly."

"You can be a monster," Tatiana said evenly.

"From a line of monsters." He handed back the tape recorder. As Tatiana reached for it, her backpack tipped over and a pistol spilled out. It was a small pistol, the sort of firearm that women carried more for reassurance than protection. "So you did bring a gun." He picked it up and let a loaded magazine spring out of the grip. "Very well. There's one thing worse than carrying a gun, and that's carrying an empty gun, but you would have to get close to do any damage with this."

"I just want to hear Alexi confess to murdering Ludmila."

"And if he does?"

"I'll shoot him. I'll write my final chapter from the grave and then I'll happily disappear."

Arkady thought of Tatiana's father, a man who didn't want to know too much. He looked out at a band of darkening clouds that stretched across the horizon and seemed to suck up the sea.

On the computer, Zhenya found images of the yacht *Natalya Goncharova*. Its specifications were daunting: one hundred meters from stem to stern, with a seven-thousand-horsepower engine and a top cruising speed of twenty-eight knots. It was a slap in the face of the working class. At the same time he had never seen a boat as luminous and sleek.

Lotte asked, "Why would criminals from Moscow meet in Kaliningrad? Why sneak into there?"

Victor said, "You can't sneak through Kaliningrad airport. It's too small. Besides, part of the roof might fall on your head."

Zhenya called Kaliningrad airport security and was given the stiff-arm.

Victor took over. "You stinking pile of shit, who are you to ask questions of the Moscow police? You're going to cooperate or I will pull your entrails out your asshole. Understood?"

The operator's attitude improved. There was heavier-than-usual traffic of private or chartered planes moving in or out, he said. "You should have been here a couple of hours ago. We had that rap artist Abdul arrive. The Chechen? We took measures. A private plane and a car waiting out on the tarmac. Didn't help. Once the women spotted him they were hysterical. They had him sign everything, and I mean everything. Could you live like that?"

"Was he with anyone?"

"No entourage. A couple of businessmen. I was a little disappointed by that. I expected a supermodel or two."

"When is Abdul scheduled to leave Kaliningrad?"

"In his private plane? He's a billionaire. He can leave any time he wants."

"Wait, I have some other names for you. Call me if any of them arrive or go." Victor gave the operator the names and his cell phone number before disconnecting.

"So maybe the second meeting didn't take place already. But why else would Abdul be in Kaliningrad?" Zhenya said.

Lotte asked, "What about the bullet in Arkady's head?"

Conversation ceased.

She said, "Zhenya told me a doctor warned Arkady a bullet in his brain could move a millimeter either way and he'd drop dead. He isn't supposed to do anything strenuous. Shouldn't he be quiet and stay at home? You're his friend—is he suicidal?"

Victor considered the point. "No, but he isn't a ray of sunshine."

Tatiana had brought a change of clothing and a stack of papers in her backpack. By lamplight, Arkady flipped through papers of incorporation for Curonian Investments, the Curonian Bank, Curonian Renaissance, Curonian Investment Fund, all of them subsidiaries of Curonian Amber. Altogether, pretty serious work for a spit of sand, he thought.

"Everything refers to Curonian Amber but I didn't see much activity at the amber pit."

"High-pressure hosing is dirty but excellent for laundering money."

"So everything here is owned by a virtually nonexistent amber mine. Except, the way they use it, it's a gold mine."

"It was Grisha's invention," Tatiana said. "I still haven't figured it out. Everybody has a grand dream. Every criminal wants to drive a BMW and every politician needs to live in a palace. Only our sailors are willing to accept a modest burial at sea."

"The moment you started gathering these papers, you targeted yourself."

"But I don't have the hard facts or names, which is maddening."

The beam of a spotlight swept across the screen of the cabin porch.

"Get down," Arkady said.

A speedboat headed in, trying not to get broadsided in the surf.

"Is this Maxim?" Tatiana asked. "He should know better."

"It's not Maxim."

Arkady made out Alexi at the wheel of a sleek wooden runabout, a classic emblem of motorboat bravado and the worst possible choice for landing on a beach. He inched closer without swinging sideways and rolling but he should have come in an inflatable boat designed for landing in rough seas.

"Tatiana Petrovna! I want to talk to you! Come out and show yourself!" Alexi shouted.

"He's stuck. He can't come in any further," Arkady said.

The searchlight probed the screen and the corners of the porch.

"If you come out, I'll tell you what happened to your sister. You're a journalist, don't you want the details?"

The wind batted his words away. He jockeyed the boat back and forth, letting the inboard engine cough and rumble.

"Renko, don't you want to know what happened to your boy, Zhenya? Don't you care?"

"What boy?" she whispered. "You have a son?"

"In a way."

Alexi called, "Doesn't either one of you care about anyone?"

The spotlight found Tatiana as she opened the porch door and moved down the stairs to the sand. Alexi motioned her closer. The sky cracked open and in the white glare of lightning, Alexi raised a gun and fired.

The shot went wide. Alexi was a good sailor, but the work he was doing demanded hands on the wheel and the gun while the deck under his feet moved in all directions. One shot went into the water, the next into the air.

She didn't duck. To her, the shots seemed irrelevant, contemptible, no worse than rain. Arkady caught up to her and felt a hot pluck on his ear. Waves rushed up, fanned and slid away. Alexi fired until he was left squeezing the trigger of an empty gun, like the last strike of a serpent.

Then the boat backed up, seesawing through waves, and retreated to the dark.

"Hold still." Tatiana patted Arkady's earlobe dry. "We're lucky. My father overstocked everything. We have bandages and antiseptics until the next millennium. Hold still, please. For a detective, you're very squeamish."

"How did Alexi know we were here?"

"I don't know, but it will be a while before he returns. There's no place on the spit to tie up a big motorboat. He'd have to go to Zelenogradsk. Then he'd have to get a car and return. That will take hours."

"It makes no sense. Why did he even come here in a boat like that?"

"He was in a rush. People who are in a rush make bad decisions."

"Now we can't wait. We have to leave right away."

"Right away," she said.

She brushed his hair away from his ear. The Band-Aid would do. He felt her breath on his neck. That and the pain made a strange combination. Her hand stayed longer than need be. He felt her body lean against him. Then her mouth was against his and his hands were inside her shirt, against the curve of her back, against the heat and coolness of her body. Standing with her on the beach, he had been invulnerable despite being nicked. How could she impart so much power and, at the same time, hold on to him as if she might drown without him?

Her depth was astonishing. Endless. And in her eyes he saw a better man than he had been before.

"Afterward" was an overused word, Arkady thought. It meant so much. A shifting of the planets. A million years. A new sea.

"Alexi will be back," Tatiana said, although without urgency. "Tell me about Zhenya."

"There's not much to say."

"Tell me anything."

"He's seventeen, quiet, scrawny, very bright, unbeatable at chess, brave, honest, deceitful, an excellent shot, and right now he wants to join the army. Both of his parents are dead."

"Did you know them?"

"I never met his mother. His father shot me."

"The father was a criminal?"

"Yes."

"Does Zhenya feel guilty about that?"

"Not that I've noticed. Anyway, he shouldn't. We have, I suppose you could say, a complicated relationship."

"Do you love him?"

"Yes, but I'm afraid it hasn't done him much good. Every time we're together, we clash. We just rub each other the wrong way. On the other hand, if I had a son, I would want him to be like Zhenya. As I said, it's complicated."

"I think you're being hard on yourself. Let's enjoy the moment."

"Is that allowed?"

Tatiana found a mattress, luxury itself. She rolled toward him and said, "Definitely not allowed."

"You think we're going to pay for this?"

"A thousand times."

"Why?" Arkady asked.

"Because God is such a bastard, He will take you away from me."

Chapter Twenty-Nine

Arkady and Tatiana dressed in the dark and carried their bikes to the road.

There was only one way to go. It might take Alexi three hours to rid himself of the motorboat and return by car from the south. The northern half of the spit was Lithuania and from what Arkady remembered of his earlier trip with Maxim, the Frontier Guards at the border station were probably snug in their beds. A person could practically walk through.

Which was a fantasy, he knew. Alexi had chased them from the cabin. They were mice on the run. The batteries for their headlights were running low and the light they cast was growing feeble. The sound of the ocean rolled on one side and trees murmured on the other. Arkady had no idea how far they had gone. He thought if they could just keep riding, they would be swallowed up by the dark like Jonah and the whale and never be seen again.

Tatiana's headlight died first and she drew almost even with him to stay in contact.

How did the heart measure distance? How many revolutions of the pedals? How many revolutions of the wheels? He more imagined than saw waves lap the beach and trees sway above the dunes.

As his headlight faded, Arkady halted Tatiana and they came to a standstill in the dark, going nowhere as sand swirled at their feet. He heard breathing dead ahead. Tentative. Waiting.

A blinding light filled the road. The beam was white tinged with blue and emanated from the border station's ancient searchlight, searching not for high-altitude bombers but targets approaching on foot. Even shielding his eyes, Arkady couldn't see more than the fire flash of automatic weapons and he couldn't tell if they were Frontier Guards or Alexi's men. Between Arkady and the station, figures poured over the road, a carousel of shadows in midair. Silhouettes with antlers milled in confusion, took cover in trees and ran again, while over and around them, branches snapped and bullets ripped the air.

Carrying their bikes, Arkady and Tatiana retreated along the edge of the searchlight's beam. It seemed to stretch forever, finally faded to a glow and then grew stronger again as the headlights of a car approached.

Arkady knocked Tatiana to the ground. "Stay down."

The car passed them and stopped. The station searchlight shut down, replaced by flashlight beams that swung back and forth.

Arkady heard the opening of car doors and recognized Alexi's voice.

"Did you get them?"

"Not yet, but we know they're here."

"Then let the dogs out."

"We let them out, but there's all these fucking deer."

"Elk, you idiot."

"Whatever. The dogs are going crazy."

"But you did see them?"

"I thought we did."

"Then find them."

"What about birders?"

"We'll get fair warning. I have eyes on the road."

After Alexi drove away, Arkady and Tatiana struggled through branches. Occasional shots rang out. Finally other car lights left the station, burrowed through the dark, and the night was still.

Dawn didn't break so much as slowly reveal dunes on one side of the road and sea on the other. Arkady and Tatiana rode silently, saying nothing. Ahead, a figure emerged from the mist dragging his sledge full of trash. The beachcomber, although he could have been a pilgrim or mendicant priest or a Volga boatman heaving on his rope. In any case, he was part of the background, someone seen without being noticed. At the sight of Arkady and Tatiana he hesitated, as a man will when confronted by ghosts. Arkady coasted by before abruptly reversing direction. Tatiana did the same on the other side. It took a moment for the beachcomber to move and when he did, he overturned the sledge, spilling its cargo. Unburdened, he sprinted past Tatiana, knees high, tripped and regained his balance even as he lost his scarf and sack. As Arkady weaved through rolling cans and bottles, the beachcomber plunged like a hare up a dune. Arkady abandoned his bike and climbed after, slipping in a treadmill of sand. At the crest of the dune Arkady caught him by the ankle and dragged him down. He was a small man with a raw, half-starved quality and eyes that seemed to start from their sockets.

"You were watching us," Arkady said.

"Just watching. No harm in that."

"And reporting to Alexi."

"I was doing nothing. I was walking down the road and you attacked me. I've got my rights."

"Forget Alexi. Where's the butcher? The man in the van with the pig on top. Who is he and where can I find him?"

"No. No way."

Terror lent strength. The beachcomber wrested one hand free enough to throw sand in Arkady's face. By the time Arkady cleared his eyes, the man had vanished in the pines.

When Arkady returned, Tatiana was examining the litter of soda cans and bottles, twists of driftwood, shells, scarf and sack. In the sack were a sandwich and a cell phone.

"He's gone," Arkady said.

"That's okay, he won't be communicating with anyone soon." Tatiana handed him the cell phone.

He punched up the cell phone's recent calls. The last was a call to a Kaliningrad number only minutes before. He pressed "Contacts." The name that popped up was Alexi.

"Are you all right?" she asked.

"Sure, I'm just sorry he got away."

"He didn't say anything?"

"Nothing."

There were different ways to be on the run. One was to flee, the other was to blend in. In the tourist town of Zelenogradsk, they bought hooded ponchos and binoculars to join the birders who tracked migrating flocks as they streamed overhead. What was it like to be ordinary people? With a baby and grandmother waiting at home, a pan of water on the radiator, a cat with a whimsical name, no fear that a neighbor might put a gun to your head. When a black car cruised by, Arkady and Tatiana played newlyweds and ducked into a souvenir shop to price amber jewelry. Amber was on sale everywhere as pendants, bracelets and necklaces that were honey colored or dark as molasses, with apple seeds or the wings of a primordial fly that had buzzed its last as resin started to encase it.

"You're enjoying this," Arkady said. "You like the hunt even if you're the hunted."

"When I was growing up, I never understood why, when games began, girls sat down while the boys had all the fun."

"You haven't changed."

"I'm a woman who doesn't like to be left behind, if that's what you mean."

She was the one who found an Internet café, a basement dive soaked in screen glow. Fluorescent decals blossomed on the walls. A counter served espresso and herbal tea. Globs rose and sank in lava lamps. There were only two other patrons. Tucked into their separate headphones and carrels, between the cigarette haze and fruity exhalation of hookahs, the denizens of the café were oblivious to each other.

Arkady called Victor on the café phone. It was Zhenya who answered.

"Is it you, Arkady? You're alive?"

"I'm afraid so."

"Me too."

A sign on the wall said, NO BLOGGING, NO FLAMING, NO SKYPING. However, the waitress, a girl with a shaved head and blue tattoos, said the warning was meant for tourists, not Koenigs, the native sons of Kaliningrad.

Once the visual connection was made, Zhenya, Victor and a pretty girl with red hair appeared on the screen.

Arkady said, "This, I take it, is Lotte. She must be a good friend."

During introductions, Lotte regarded Arkady with undisguised curiosity. What a sight he must have made, Arkady thought. A knackered horse next to the beautiful Tatiana. Tatiana studied Zhenya much the same way. Victor maintained a straight face and kept his eyes on the café stairs.

There was no sign of Alexi's men; it wasn't their scene, Arkady thought. Alexi was not Grisha. He was calculating but he didn't command the same loyalty or respect. He was perverse, and even in the underworld that wore thin. Men who should have relentlessly pounded the pavement, foul weather or no, would stop in a hotel lounge for a drink to drive the cold out of their bones.

Zhenya held the notebook up for Tatiana to read. She had seen it before. All the same, the speed at which she scanned the pages was impressive.

He said, "Lotte figured that the symbols with colons were people speaking at the meeting. They were partners."

"First among partners would have been Grisha Grigorenko."

"The man with a top hat with the line underneath."

"Next," she said, "the man without the line underneath would be Ape Beledon. Old and deadly. The crescent moon could be Abdul. Abdul makes a fortune out of videos and makes even more protecting gas lines that cross Chechnya."

"I have no idea about the symbol of the blocks," Zhenya confessed.

"Building blocks," Tatiana said. "The Shagelmans, Isaac and Valentina, have a construction company. They build high-ways, high-rises, shopping malls. In fact, they wanted to tear down my apartment house. As for the last two partners, I can't be so definite. The star stands for official power, someone high up in the Defense Ministry or a strongman in the Kremlin. One of those perpetual thugs. And China. Joseph Bonnafos spoke Chinese, but he also spoke Russian, French, German, English and Thai."

"Why the wasp?" Victor asked.

"Amber," Lotte said.

Zhenya proudly said, "We think it's an agreement between the Chinese government and a company close to the Kremlin."

Arkady asked, "Would it be Curonian Renaissance? Curonian Bank? Curonian Investments?"

"No."

"Curonian Amber," Tatiana said.

There was a long pause at the other end. Lotte said, "That's it."

Tatiana said, "I've been studying this strange entity for years. On the face of it, Curonian Amber is a virtually dead amber mine on the spit. Dig a little deeper and it's also the holding company for the Curonian Bank, Curonian Investments, Curonian Renaissance and all the rest. It's Grisha's brainchild, a way to move money in any direction. Who would stop him? He was a billionaire with allies everywhere. So far, remarkable but not unique. Moscow has a dozen more Grishas. What Joseph Bonnafos was hinting at would have been a coup that set Grisha apart. It was also potentially another *Kursk* disaster."

"I think that Curonian Amber plans to repair a Chinese nuclear submarine here," Zhenya said. "There's a price tag of two billion dollars mentioned. Wouldn't that put Grisha in a league of his own?"

That wasn't the only possible interpretation, Arkady thought. Tatiana thought so too; he saw it in her face. But a sum that magnificent inspired respect. Even Arkady felt it momentarily.

"It doesn't change the fact that Grisha was nothing but a thief. They're all thieves," Victor said. "Somehow the repair was a scheme to steal money. A lot of money."

Arkady asked, "Was there any mention of Alexi in the notebook? Doesn't he feel that he is the heir apparent and that whatever was Grisha's is now his? Alexi has been trying to cut in from the start. Zhenya, when he had you and Lotte translate the notebook, was there anything in particular that he was after?"

"Everything."

"What was the last thing he asked?"

"Where the meeting was going to be. I told him on Grisha's yacht, the *Natalya Goncharova*."

"Abdul is in Kaliningrad," Victor said. "His concert is over. He's sticking around for something."

"I'll keep working on it," Zhenya promised. "Nuclear submarines, that's pretty wild. Maybe I got it all wrong. Maybe it's about rubber duckies in a tub."

"Come home," Victor said to Arkady.

"Good night," said Tatiana.

The screen returned to a home page of the Milky Way. Arkady noticed that Tatiana had not mentioned the submarine *Kaliningrad* and its failure in sea trials, rather than feed Zhenya's assumption. She saw the big picture; anything less was a distraction. Tatiana thought in terms of nations and history, just as Arkady focused on the small picture of three children and a man in a butcher's van.

Chapter Thirty

All the cars in Zelenogradsk had gone to bed, except for black sedans that continued to cruise the streets. Arkady and Tatiana had not slept for days and took their chances on a motel that featured plastic swans and called itself the Bird Haus. The front desk was stocked with wildlife guides and offered wake-up calls for early birders.

They set out their shoes and her gun beside the bed, she laid her head on his shoulder and almost instantly, before he even turned off the nightstand light, she was asleep.

It occurred to Arkady that he and Tatiana were too cynical. As mature Russians, their dials, so to speak, were set by experience at "the Worst," at disaster, not success. For example, Zhenya had it backward. That Curonian Amber would repair a nuclear submarine for China was bad enough. The worst, however, was the possibility that Curonian Amber would outsource a Russian nuclear submarine to be repaired in China.

Arkady remembered the name of the faulty submarine. The *Kaliningrad*. That didn't sound Chinese at all.

He drifted off listening to the hull of a submarine being crushed and bent, the sound of the ice maker in the hall.

Morning traffic backed up on the road to Kaliningrad as police in yellow vests sorted out cars, trucks and bikes.

Arkady said, "We have to separate now. They'll be looking for couples on bikes. I'll go first. If there's no problem, wait ten minutes and see if you can hitch a ride."

"I know how to do that."

"Be careful." Although he saw that he was preaching to the joyously deaf.

For the driver of the delivery van it was another day of miserable weather, slippery cobblestones, "Bony Moronie" on the radio and a breakfast of glutinous peach pie. He had picked up the woman because she looked good from the back and not so bad from the front either, trying to hitch a ride on the highway. Police were waving all the traffic to the side of the road, like maneuvering a herd of elephants. She threw her bike in the back of the rig, hopped in the cab and said, "If anyone asks, I'm your sister." Pretty nervy. They were checking papers but it was the driver's regular route and he got through with a wink. Sailed along.

He expected some reciprocation and a kilometer down the road they pulled into an empty fruit stand. She said she wanted privacy. She said she'd do it in the back of the truck.

But there was no room because of her bike. He courteously climbed up and handed the bike down. She jumped up, pulled down the gate and locked him in. It turned out she could drive a rig. And she picked up her boyfriend on the way.

They didn't stop until they reached a zone of eerie quiet and when people finally heard him pound on the side of the truck he found himself in a lot of windblown trash beside the empty colossus of Party headquarters.

"Where are you now?" Victor asked.

Arkady said, "We're having coffee in Victory Square in Kaliningrad. Tatiana is with me."

"Have you made contact with Maxim?"

"Not yet." Why not? Arkady asked himself. He and Tatiana had been in Kaliningrad for two hours and hadn't tried to connect with anyone. She kept her backpack. Otherwise, they ditched their bikes and traveled light. It was intoxicating to be a tourist, to climb the stairway of a pastry shop and take in a view of the city's central square with its bubbling fountain, a requisite victory column, skateboarders clicking over tiles and a new church that looked snapped together from plastic parts.

In the pastry shop, vitrines of glass and chrome offered strawberry tarts, Sacher tortes, cream puffs, and figures of Grover and Elmo sculpted in marzipan. The shop was also a display case for trophy wives dressed in Prada and Dior. Upstairs, Arkady and Tatiana were on a level with a street banner that announced in stark black and white letters a hip-hop concert by Abdul, larger than life-size, scowling, with the pallor of a healthy vampire. The concert had taken place the night before. Arkady imagined Abdul sleeping in a closet upside down.

An Audi rolled into the shadow of the church. The driver emerged to tuck in his shirtfront and comb his fingers through his hair. Detective Lieutenant Stasov, surveying his domain.

"I'm coming out there," Victor said.

"No," Arkady said. "You're needed in Moscow. If you come here, Zhenya will follow and then Lotte."

Victor asked, "What about Maxim?"

"We'll get in touch with him."

Lieutenant Stasov started across the square. Whether he had spotted Arkady and Tatiana or had a fondness for pastries didn't matter. In a minute he would be walking through the door, strutting with the lopsided swing of a man wearing a gun, and if he climbed the stairs, Arkady and Tatiana would be in full view.

The lieutenant changed his mind and retreated to his car, to release a pug with a monkey face. The little dog dragged Stasov by the leash, eyes rolling like marbles, tongue flapping from side to side.

The shop's glass door was directly below the table that Tatiana and Arkady shared. For the dog the shop was a blend of irresistible aromas and he balanced on his hind legs to view each display case in turn.

Stasov played the indulgent pet owner. "There's no stopping him any time we're near sweets."

A woman asked, "What's his name?"

"Polo. That's what it said on his dog tag. I rescued him from a criminal. Can you imagine?"

Did the lieutenant carry the dog as a social icebreaker wherever lonely women congregated? Arkady wondered.

"How old is he?" another woman asked.

People always asked certain questions, Arkady thought. How old is your dog? Your baby? Your grandmother? Another constant was, is your gun loaded? Tatiana's pistol rested on her lap.

"I swear, he's as curious as a cat. Come on, Polo. Don't bother the nice people, Polo. Good boy. Oh, now he's going up the stairs."

Arkady heard the dog scamper up. He was halfway to the balcony before Stasov snagged the leash. Arkady got a glimpse of the lieutenant's bald spot when he scooped up the dog.

"Excuse me," he told the ladies. "Excuse me, please. Such a rascal. Ah, well, here comes his treat."

"A bonbon!"

"He'll gobble this down in two bites. See?"

"What a character."

"Well, ladies, duty calls. My friend and I must go fight crime."

Polo made a final bolt for the stairs but Stasov stepped on the leash and reeled him in like a fish.

"*Au revoir*."

"*Au revoir*."

Stasov retreated to his car and held high an extra bonbon. Polo was enraptured.

"I told you that dog had no loyalty," Arkady said.

Chapter Thirty-One

Maxim knew. He knew as soon as Arkady and Tatiana walked into his apartment that the situation had changed. He had gone from suitor to also-ran. All the risks he had taken were worthless chips. He was a poet without words.

"I'm sorry," Tatiana said, although she didn't mean it. Not really, Maxim thought.

"They've been here already, Alexi's men and the police."

"Good, maybe they won't be back so soon," Arkady said.

"How is your boy, Zhenya?" Maxim asked. "Has he deciphered the notebook yet?"

"Most of it. The 'what' and the 'where.' But not exactly 'when.' We think there will be another meeting."

"All this sound and fury for a notebook of incomprehensible symbols. This calls for a drink, only I haven't got a bottle in the house." Maxim poked around in an empty liquor cabinet. "And they'll hold the meeting without Grisha?"

"It's still a good plan," Tatiana said. "The Defense Ministry provides two billion dollars for a submarine refit. Half will actually go to the shipyard that does the work. Curonian Amber will take the other half and carve it up like a wedding cake. Everybody gets a piece. Friends in the Kremlin, the Defense Ministry, the banks and the Mafia. That was Grisha's genius. He was generous as well as inventive."

Maxim said, "So it's one more rip-off. What's so unusual about that?"

"Actually, it's a Chinese refit of a practically new Russian nuclear submarine, the *Kaliningrad*," Tatiana said. "It's new but in such poor condition it's never actually gone into service. So now they're going to fix it on the cheap in China."

Maxim shrugged. "'Made in China.' What isn't these days?"

"This is different. Hold back that much money and the *Kaliningrad* could be a disaster on the scale of the *Kursk*. If so, the public won't stand for it. If anything could bring down these crooks, this is it."

"Sit, please," Maxim said. "I apologize about the heaps of clothes. Creative people are messy. I must have something to drink here. I should be a better host. Tea? Coffee?" Maxim wandered in and out of the kitchen searching for clean cups. In the living room, some bookshelves were bare, not carefully removed but swept aside. Shakespeare, Neruda, Mandelstam commingled on the floor, and it occurred to Arkady that Maxim probably had not left the apartment for days.

Tatiana saw that she was not penetrating. "Are you okay?"

"Not really." Maxim slapped his hands together and studied

them. "So, the two of you have been on the run. That's always romantic."

"Do you want us to go?"

"No, no. You're my guests. I told myself not to be bitter or vituperative. I should have known better than to have set you up with someone as long-suffering as Investigator Renko. Tell me, Renko, have you noticed that our Tatiana likes the sound of bullets? Has she done anything you would consider a little reckless, like stand in front of a moving train? Does she inoculate herself with fear on a regular basis? I see you have a mark on your ear. Has it occurred to you that it's not safe to stand next to a martyr? Unlike Anya. Have you been in touch with her?"

"We talked," Arkady said. Days ago, he realized.

"She was one of the also-rans, like me," Maxim said.

"I don't think she cared one way or the other."

"Surprise."

It occurred to Arkady that Anya may not have betrayed him. She had delivered the notebook to him, not to Alexi, and had not told him where Arkady was. What else could he have misread?

"Where is she?"

"Moscow, I suppose. Moscow suddenly seems sane. Ah, here we are." Maxim pulled out a half-empty bottle of vodka from under the couch. "And where is this meeting going to take place?"

"The *Natalya Goncharova*, Grisha's yacht."

"Pushkin's whore," Maxim said. "As a literary man, I can appreciate that. When?"

"Tonight, we think."

"How do you know that?"

"Last night Abdul gave a concert of hate here in Kaliningrad. Tomorrow night he'll be in Riga, but tonight he's still here, as are Ape Beledon and the Shagelmans."

"There's not much you can do about it, is there?"

"I think there is, but we need your help."

Maxim transferred his gaze from Arkady to Tatiana. "This is rich. Help you ascend to martyrdom? First, your friend is going to get himself killed. Second, I'm not a fucking Sancho Panza. Not even a Pushkin. Now I really do need a drink."

Tatiana said, "It's simple. Arkady will go to the meeting with a cell phone. You will be waiting on the other end here, listening with a tape recorder."

"And where will you be?"

"We'll need a witness."

"What does that mean?"

"I'll be with Arkady."

A wolfish grin spread on Maxim's face. "You two. You two are too much. Every time I think I've got you topped, you come up with something better. A witness? You mean a floating body. Two floating bodies, and I'm supposed to be on the other end with a phone up my ass. This is fucking moral blackmail."

"You should be safe," Arkady said.

"Exactly, and that's all people will remember me for, staying safe while you get your throats cut."

"You don't have to do it."

"Right." Maxim took a long pull on the bottle and exhaled a cold cloud of vodka. "What makes you so sure the partners of Curonian Amber will be there?"

"Because these are the sort of partners that keep an eye on each other. We don't want to get into a violent confrontation. We just want to threaten to take their plans public."

"Will Alexi be there?"

"Apparently Grisha didn't tell him about the first meeting, but he knows where this one is."

"No, no, no, no. I won't do it."

"I understand," Arkady said.

"No you don't. I'm going with you." He pointed at Tatiana. "She can stay with the tape recorder."

"That's not what we're asking," Tatiana said.

"It's that or nothing. I'm not going to be a butt of contempt and derision the rest of my life. Besides, you don't know anything about the harbor. The *Natalya Goncharova* doesn't mix with lesser craft. She's anchored in deeper water and you'll need a boat to get to her. I happen to know where one can be found."

"We'll find another," Tatiana said.

Maxim said, "I doubt it. Kaliningrad harbor is closed to personal craft. Soon it will be evening and you'll be searching in the dark in an active harbor of ships moving back and forth. Not to mention, it's the port of the Baltic Fleet. They'll shoot us dead and our bodies will be swept out to sea."

"Then I'm going too," Tatiana said.

"You're staying here," Maxim said. "That's the deal."

"Do you know what to look for?" Arkady asked.

Maxim had the smile of a poet whose words had finally fallen into place. "Of course: the most beautiful boat in the harbor. A true Natalya Goncharova."

There were two boats at the dock of the Fishing Village, only one with an outboard engine. While Maxim drew it alongside the dock, Tatiana pressed her face against Arkady's and whispered, "As soon as I have everything on tape, I'll catch up."

"Don't. It will be confusing enough."

"Maxim is acting very strange."

"What is he going to do? He's not a killer even if he thinks he is."

"You're sure of that?"

"Positive."

Maxim pulled a cord and jerked the engine to life. "Are you coming or not?"

"Coming." Arkady kissed Tatiana lightly on the cheek as if he were going on an evening cruise.

The dinghy was a tin tub with an outboard engine that rattled and spewed fumes. Before leaving, Maxim leaned into the other boat and slipped its oars into the water. Arkady watched their outlines float away.

"Why did you do that?" Arkady asked.

"So nobody gets any ideas. I'm the captain now."

There was nothing Arkady could do about it. It was done. He kept his eyes on Tatiana until she faded into the evening's haze.

The harbor was a different world. A mirror of itself. A black avenue that reverberated with the passage of larger boats. The far-off lights of harbor cranes. Plan A was that Arkady and Maxim would search for no more than two hours and go nowhere near the naval yard. It was a feather in the air, the sort of promise that absolved everyone of responsibility.

Maxim tooled along like a man in command, one hand on the tiller. A chill clung to the air. Arkady bailed a week's accumulation of rain from the bottom of the boat and the water that remained shivered from the vibration of the engine.

They were running dark, no green light for starboard or red for port. No conversation; voices carried on open water. Engine noise was, at least, mechanical, though there was little river traffic, mainly the rising sounds and lights of the surrounding city and reflections that cupped the surface of the water.

Arkady thought of Pushkin as he set out to defend the honor of his coquettish wife. How tired the poet must have been. With her taste for costume balls and life at court, Natalya Goncharova had spent him nearly into penury. Forced him to borrow. To spin out inferior poems for dubious occasions. To let the tsar himself cuckold the poet and pretend to be his patron. Finally, to lower himself to a duel with pistols with a soldier of fortune. When Pushkin saw his adversary's vest of silver buttons, why didn't he object? Was complaint beneath him, or was he simply tired of beauty and its demands?

Maxim said that watchmen were not required on the harbor

and that police preferred to stay inside on damp nights, but Arkady wasn't sure that his plans and Maxim's were the same.

The *Natalya Goncharova* had moved down the river in the direction of the fleet. Traced by lanterns, she was an apparition floating on black water. As Maxim circled the yacht at quarter speed, Arkady expected that at any second Alexi would appear on deck.

However, the interior stayed dark. Nobody showed at the bridge. There was no sound of a crew rushing to their stations. Maxim went four times around the *Natalya Goncharova* before giving in; no one was aboard.

Maxim opened the throttle and swung the boat toward deeper water. From east to west the city gave way to the river and the red warning lights of giant cranes stood against the sky. When the banks receded enough, Maxim killed the engine and let the dinghy drift. It was a restful moment, the water lapping against the sides of the boat as it rolled slowly in the wake of a ship they couldn't even see.

"Just as I thought," Maxim said.

"What did you think?" Arkady asked.

"There is no meeting."

"I'm a little disappointed myself."

"That's not why we came."

"There's another reason?"

"To kill me."

Arkady wasn't sure he'd heard right. "Kill you?"

"Lure me out here with some fantastic story, shoot me and dump me in the water."

In some spots oil lay on the water like marbled paper. Arkady tasted it on his lips.

"You insisted on coming," Arkady said.

"I was manipulated. Tatiana manipulated both of us. That's what martyrs do."

"Why would she?"

"Martyrs don't share the glory."

"Even if they die?"

"It's win-win for them."

"I don't have a gun."

"Fortunately, I do. Face me."

When Arkady turned he found that Maxim had brought an undersized pistol, probably Spanish or Brazilian, common as coins. All he needed do was shoot Arkady, strip him of any ID and push him overboard. Granted, Maxim should have brought along some cinder blocks to weigh Arkady down, but a man couldn't think of everything.

"Did you bring any vodka?" Arkady asked.

"Ran out."

"Too bad. For this sort of work, vodka is usually essential."

Maxim looked miserable but determined. "I wrote a poem for Tatiana years ago," he said. "My best poem, people say. I was a professor and she was the student. There wasn't that much difference in age, but everyone described me as the seducer and her as the innocent. Lately I've come to think it was the other way around."

"How does the poem go?" Arkady asked.

"What poem?"

"The poem about Tatiana."

"You don't deserve to hear it."

"*'Shall I compare thee to a summer's day?'*"

"I'm warning you."

"This is the third time you've tried to kill me. A warning seems superfluous."

"I could shake your head until I hear a bullet rattle."

"Tell me about your poem."

"You're stalling."

"I've got all night. Do you mind?" Arkady took out a cigarette and lit it. "You? No? Well, you only have so many hands. Did you forget your poem? Recite anything. *'You are my song, my dark blue dream of winter's drowsy drone, and sleighs that slow and golden go through gray blue shadows on the snow.'*"

"That's not mine."

"I know, but it's lovely, isn't it?"

"Stand up."

"You're not a murderer."

"I can kill you all the same."

Arkady stood. He flipped his cigarette into the water and braced himself to dive when he heard a hum in the pocket of his jacket. While Maxim hesitated, Arkady took out his cell phone and put it on speaker.

Zhenya sounded triumphant. He said, "You're looking for the wrong boat. There's another *Natalya Goncharova.*"

Chapter Thirty-Two

Grisha's *Natalya Goncharova* was a yacht with a Cayman Islands registry. The *Natalya Goncharova* they needed to find was an oil tanker out of Kaliningrad.

The port handled grain and coal, but mainly it handled oil, a viscous sludge for domestic use and diesel for export. Every ship was enormous compared to the dinghy, every sound produced an echo, every rope that rode slack with the tide had reason to creak.

Arkady read by flashlight the name of each ship they passed. Some were nearly derelict, others ready to sail. He understood that for Maxim this was only a pause and unless they found the meeting of Ape Beledon and his partners, Maxim would resume where he'd left off.

Finally there were lights on a ship ahead and the *Natalya Goncharova* appeared through the mist. Whoever named her had a sense of humor. Instead of Grisha's elegant yacht, this

Natalya was a tramp, a stubby coastal tanker ringed with tire bumpers. A mood of mutual congratulation hung in the air. Although Arkady couldn't make out what was being said, Alexi's laugh was unmistakable. Arkady looked back at Maxim, who followed Arkady up a rusty ladder and over the side.

The tanker's deck was an intricate maze of valves painted red. Squeezed against the deckhouse was a table and ice buckets of Champagne.

Arkady recognized Abdul, the Shagelmans, Ape and his two sons. Abdul was dressed in black Chechen chic, as if he might drive a Porsche during the week and a tank on weekends. The Shagelmans looked like old folks staying up late. Arkady couldn't put names to the coterie of deputy ministers and naval officers gathered around the table but he knew their types. A pair of Chinese businessmen in stovepipe suits played at being invisible. They all froze as Arkady and Maxim stepped into the open.

Alexi recovered nimbly, as cool as a croupier. "I guess this means your friends figured out the notebook. It doesn't matter. As you can see, everything is going ahead."

Bodyguards who had been stationed at a respectful distance on the dock came running. Ape motioned for them to slow down. In the notebook, Grisha had been the first among equals, the Man in the Hat with a Line Underneath. That title would have gone to Ape by seniority now.

Arkady could see that Alexi wished for nothing more than to have him and Maxim shot where they stood. However, for the moment at least, it might have seemed a breach of good manners. A little pushy. Premature. With his hairy wrists and single brow, Ape might have seemed primitive and bent by age but he was a stickler for manners. Waiting for a cue, the navy brass held their Champagne glasses at half-mast, ready to be raised as soon as this hiccup was over. It was a simple ceremony. No caviar. More like a first shovel breaking ground for a new enterprise.

"Welcome," Ape said. He skipped introductions except to add, "And this must be the famous poet Maxim Dal." Maxim was flattered. What greater recognition than a nod from a legendary criminal? "Do you think you could write a poem about this? Obviously, you can't write with a gun in your hand. See, this is an amicable meeting of friends from far and wide. Give me that. It's a pop gun, anyway. Please." Ape took the pistol.

"Let me handle them," Alexi said.

"Why? We're not doing anything illegal," Ape said.

"They know about Curonian Amber," Alexi said in a stage whisper to help the old man along.

"Let them."

Arkady said, "The notebook left behind by your interpreter wasn't as impossible to decode as people thought. We know that a Russian nuclear submarine that failed its sea tests is going to be refitted in China."

"Yes. It's called outsourcing," Ape said.

"And we know that half the money for the refit will be raked off the top by you and your cronies in the Defense Ministry and the Kremlin. It's criminal."

"Business costs. Totally normal. Administration of a task of this magnitude is often fifty percent of a budget. Anything else?" Ape asked.

"Murder."

Signs of anxiety started to appear among the guests. No introductions had been made, but Arkady had seen them and their species in newspaper photos standing at attention or adorned by military caps. The two Chinese gentlemen traded significant glances.

Alexi said, "That's a lie."

Arkady shook his head and said, "The correct response is 'Who?'"

"That's true," Ape said. "But, Investigator Renko, you're playing a dangerous game. My partners in Curonian Amber have already invested time and money."

"You have great expectations?"

"You could say that."

That was good but not enough, Arkady thought. He needed a clear admission of a crime recorded on tape.

"What if the *Kaliningrad* becomes another *Kursk*? That would be a disaster for you and the Kremlin."

"Accidents happen."

"But you're loading the odds when a nuclear submarine is built by thieves at a cut rate. The downside, as they say, would be enormous."

"There's a risk."

"Would Grisha have taken it?"

"Grisha was a risk taker," Abdul said.

"Now he's dead." Arkady turned to Ape. "Didn't you once advise me to ask, 'Whose ox is gored?'"

"Circumstances are different. In Moscow you were a man with authority. Now you're away from home."

Again, good to have on tape, but not enough.

Alexi said, "I'm not going to listen to this bullshit anymore. What are we waiting for?"

"We want to hear more," one of the Chinese said.

Doubt had been raised. In the eyes of the visitors from the Red Dawn Shipyard, Arkady could practically see the beads of an abacus sliding on a rack calculating the risks one way and the other. Isaac Shagelman looked toward his wife, Valentina, for a decision, as if the question were about putting down a dog. She looked at the ship's ladder and gasped.

Tatiana appeared from nowhere, shining from the water that dripped off her. She climbed onto the deck but she could as well have landed like a Valkyrie. She had come in the second dinghy and must have swum to collect its oars. Arkady thought he should have anticipated this. She had warned him that she was not the sort of woman to miss the fun.

"It's not so simple," she said.

Ape said to Alexi, "You led us to believe that Tatiana Petrovna was dead."

"It was my sister that Alexi killed," Tatiana said.

"And your sons killed Maxim's ZIL," Arkady added. "Maxim and I happened to be inside it at the time. They like to play *Scarface*. Did they do that on your orders or are they taking orders from somebody else?"

Ape shook his head. "A classic car. I would never do that."

"It doesn't matter who ordered it," Alexi said. "Our plan is still good."

Arkady said, "You weren't even in the plan while your father was alive."

"I've been watching you for years," Tatiana said to Ape. "I've been following your corruption of the state."

"And I've read your articles," Ape said. "They're very good but they're all in the past."

"Not Curonian Amber. Not building a deathtrap of a nuclear submarine. We'll print it, and if you try to stop us we will see you in court."

Alexi said, "So what? We'll buy the court. We'll buy the Kremlin if need be."

"Aren't you forgetting something?" Arkady asked. "Who killed Grisha?"

The deck was like a chessboard, Arkady thought, except that all the pieces were moving at the same time. The partners from the ministry set down their glasses and rose to their toes. The Chinese were no longer playing invisible; they were gone.

Ape turned to Maxim. "I liked your poem."

"What?"

"That poem. It was years ago. 'F Is for Fool.'"

"Yeah." Maxim had to laugh.

"I don't remember all of it. Something like, 'F is for fool, the man who returns home early and finds himself replaced. Another man is in his bed, folded like a jackknife around his wife.' Is that it?"

"Close enough."

"I could never get over the image of the jackknife. Would you say the poem is about betrayal?"

"I was inspired."

"I can believe it. We're all betrayed at one time or another and we never forget." Ape asked Arkady, "*Scarface*, huh?"

"I'm afraid so."

The old man said, "Renko, remember how we talked about Grisha? We couldn't understand how he let his killer get so close. There's a word for it. It's a big one."

"Patricide."

Ape whispered and nodded to his sons. "Let one boy get away with it and you encourage the others."

Tatiana was on her own tangent. She aimed a pistol at Alexi and asked, "Remember my sister?"

It was her moment, but the trigger pull of a cheaply manufactured pistol could be stiff and hard to gauge. So Alexi shot first. Maxim, who had seemed adrift, stepped in between and took a bullet in the shoulder. Ape fired. Alexi's head rang like a cracked bell. He dropped facedown and Ape stood over him and shot him twice more in the back.

"You crazy Russians," said Abdul. The Wolf of the Caucasus bolted to the gangway ramp and the Shagelmans hustled after him.

Ape turned the gun on Arkady. "Why shouldn't I shoot you too?"

"Because we're still recording." With elaborate care, Arkady brought out his cell phone.

"Are you? Well, maybe you are and maybe you aren't." After consideration, Ape let his gun hang. "As it is, all you can charge us with is saving your miserable lives. Get out of here. Next time, you may not be so lucky. Sometimes it's more important to teach my boys a lesson than to make another hundred million dollars. We'll pack away the Champagne for another day."

As Maxim struggled to his elbows Ape pressed his gun into Maxim's hands. "Congratulations. By the evidence, you just killed your first man. Now that's something to write about."

Chapter Thirty-Three

Sand.

Arkady let it pour from his fist to the valley of her back and when she turned over Arkady let it run off her stomach to the hollow of her hip, scattering over her skin like grains of salt. It got in every crevice, into her hair and into the corners of his mouth.

Wind.

Constant breezes played like spirits on the cabin's steps. There were dead dunes and live dunes, according to Tatiana.

Time.

A live dune remade itself and changed from day to day. The entire spit moved like the sweep hand on a watch.

"Have you ever looked at sand through a magnifying glass?" Tatiana asked. "It's many different things. Quartz, seashells, miniature worm tubes, spines."

The cabin had its small discomforts—the thin mattress and

rough wooden floor—but they lent a sharpness to the senses. The heat within her made up for a cold stove. The cabin creaked agreeably like an ancient ship.

A few birders came their way. All in all, however, the beach belonged to Arkady and Tatiana. Their sand castle.

Insomnia arrived in the middle of the night like a tardy guest. Arkady saw a lantern moving through the trees. He chased the light to the road, where it moved too fast to follow. In the morning he found a pair of footprints circling the cabin. The wind had erased them by the time Tatiana woke.

Arkady watched Tatiana walk down the road trying to get a cell phone signal. It was like ice fishing, he thought, not a sport for the impatient, but a hundred meters away, she waved her arm, and when she returned it was with a flush of excitement.

"I talked to Obolensky. He's coming to Kaliningrad to do a special edition of the magazine about Russia's most corrupt city."

"Well, that's a kind of honor." Arkady paused in the task of hammering a plank in the cabin's porch. "Written by you?"

"The main article, yes."

"I would think so. It's not every day his favorite journalist comes back from the dead. When?"

"It's a rush job. I'll be gone one day, maybe two. What do you think?"

It was the first anxious note he'd heard in her voice.

"I think you've got to do it."

"I told Obolensky I would."

"You did the right thing."

"Can you come with me?"

"I'll find things to do around the cabin." Arkady tried to sound like a handyman.

He wondered what they looked like from a distance: a man and woman seesawing over something as innocent as a day apart. In fact, Obolensky had done him a great favor. Ever since Arkady had felt Piggy's presence, he had wanted to remove her from the scene.

"You don't mind, then," she said.

"I'll stay busy."

The spit was famous for birding. It was home to mergansers and swans and was on a flight path for migrant eagles and kites. Cormorants with crooked necks perched on driftwood, gray herons stalked the lagoon and devout birders with cameras sat for hours to capture the image of a sodden duck.

Arkady dressed for the weather in a poncho and rainproof cap. He walked the beach and climbed the dunes, trying to stay a moving target. His only weapon was Tatiana's Spanish pistol, as useful as a peashooter in the wind.

The problem was the conviviality of birders, who pursued each other to verify whether their sighting was a grebe, an eider or a goose, or to compare life lists of birds they had spotted.

He didn't know what he hoped to see. He didn't know how he would identify a murderer. They had met at this same beach but it was at night, Arkady had been staring into the headlights of a van and the driver had never said a word.

As the wind picked up birders trudged home. Arkady found a group sharing a flask of brandy under the eaves of Tatiana's cabin. Ivan, Nikita, Wanda, Boris, Lena. All of the birders boasted over a thousand species on their life lists, fifty from the spit alone.

"But these conditions are impossible," said Nikita. "Between the headwind and the sand . . ."

Wanda agreed. "It makes your teeth rattle. If you're not having fun, what's the point?"

A notebook dropped from Arkady's hand. As Ivan snatched it up the wind flipped through the pages. "Your list seems to be blank."

"I'm just getting started. So you're all friends or colleagues? You came to the spit together?"

"Most of us," Lena said.

"Misery likes company." Boris slapped his hands together. They were thick hands, slabs of meat.

"Are you looking for any bird in particular?" Nikita asked Arkady.

"I can't say."

Boris said, "I can tell you from experience that sometimes when you concentrate on one bird, you miss a better one. I remember in Mexico, I was looking for a particular bird and I almost missed a quetzal, which you know is a rare bird with spectacular plumage sacred to the Aztecs. The Aztecs, you know? Human sacrifice raised to its greatest heights? They would cut out a heart or skin a man alive. At the same time, they were a civilization of great beauty."

Arkady thought they were getting a little far afield from bird-ing.

"I'll know what I'm after when I see it," Arkady said.

"You must be after a special kind of bird."

"Or a pig," Arkady said.

Boris's eyes went as flat as a dead fish.

For the rest of the day, Arkady watched terns fight the wind, twist and plunge headfirst into the water. That was him, only not into water but cement.

At night, pines swayed and sea grass flattened in the wind. Finally, the storm that had been building in expectation all week arrived and waves seethed up to the cabin stairs, sound-ing like the columns of a temple falling. At the same time, the lagoon flooded the road behind the cabin. Water plowed through the beach and revealed nuggets of golden amber.

Arkady woke and sat up, and although his teeth chattered from the cold, he staggered to the front door and opened it to find that the wind had, in fact, died down and the waves had retreated to the sea.

He wondered how anyone dared sleep. Tatiana hadn't returned. Just as well, he thought.

The sea grew still. Clouds parted and revealed a moon bal-anced on the water. The off-season was soon to be the season; birders would be leaving and tourists would be pouring in.

Arkady boiled some instant coffee and took the key ring and lamp to the shed. What was it that Tatiana's father wanted? A normal country? This little space with its simple tools must have been a refuge for the man.

The security cables that ran through the bikes were vinyl-coated steel with heavy-duty eyelets connected by padlocks, each cable about five meters long. Not long enough. Arkady sorted out the collapsible chairs in the corner of the shed and disentangled them from two more cables. He rummaged through overstocked shelves and found cables still in their plastic cases. Maybe not as many as he wished, but they would have to do.

Because he would have to get close. His only weapon was Tatiana's pistol. Anything that Piggy carried would be bigger. It helped that Piggy was a conversationalist; that would draw him in. And he craved recognition, something for his own life list.

When Arkady was ready, he put on his poncho, blew out the lamp, slipped out the back door and circled to a patch of sea grass and waited. In summertime, music would be drifting from cabin to cabin. People would exclaim at shooting stars. Now the world was as black as a tunnel and the only sound was the idle lapping of water.

From a distance, he saw an ember that became a bouncing ball, which turned into a glowing pig dancing on the beach. Headlights off, the van rolled to a stop directly in front of the cabin and Piggy swung out to open the back door of the van. One by one, he tossed out Vova and his sisters like freshly caught fish. They were trussed hands and feet and crying hysterically, appealing to be saved.

There was a touch of the ham actor in Piggy; his hair was long and topped by a bowler and his gestures with a gun were exaggerated as he stood over Vova and shot into the sand. The sound mingled with the waves.

He called out, "Did that get your attention?"

The children were stunned into silence. Arkady cradled the Spanish pistol under his poncho.

"Don't be shy," Piggy said. "Come on out or I really will put a bullet in boychik's brain. That's better," he said as Arkady stood.

"Let them go. You want me, not them."

"Such egotism. How do you know what I want?"

"I don't. What do you want?"

"Horror."

Arkady did not have an answer for that but didn't particularly care. From here on it was logistics. He was about twenty paces from Piggy. He hoped to cut that to five.

"What about the biker? Was he on your list?"

"I would say he was on Alexi's list."

"How did you know to target him?"

"I watch people in hotels. Butchers go in and out. No one sees us."

"That's clever. Your name's not Boris, is it? And you've never been to Mexico, have you?" Arkady started to approach. "I wouldn't even say you were a bird person."

"They're idiots. Get up at five in the morning to see a fucking sandpiper?"

"People do crazy things."

"Well, you're the craziest."

"Did you know I have a bullet in my brain? Do you know

what that does to you? Can you imagine? Like a second hand on a watch, just waiting to make one last tick. One tick and everything goes black. That's how I live my life. Moment to moment."

Arkady continued moving forward. It was unnerving; a man about to die should retreat, not approach.

"The strange thing is that having a bullet in the brain makes me feel invulnerable," Arkady said.

"Stay where you are." Piggy raised his gun.

Arkady took another quick two paces, even forcing Piggy back a step.

"Try it."

Piggy fired. The shot knocked Arkady to the ground. It felt like being hit with a spike but he rose and Piggy fired a second time, dropping Arkady again. For a second time, Arkady got to his feet. Hesitation showed in Piggy's eyes and in that moment, Arkady pulled his poncho aside, revealing an armature of steel cables that were coiled in double layers around his chest. In two places the cables were mangled. In his free hand he held the Spanish pistol and at a distance of four paces he couldn't miss.

Chapter Thirty-Four

Seawater and sand were a bicycle's worst enemies. Arkady and Zhenya disassembled the Pantera and spread the parts like a puzzle on a plastic sheet that covered Arkady's living room floor. The steel frame and aluminum gears had not been damaged, but the drivetrain had suffered from being thrown around and buried.

It was hard to say whether the bike was salvageable or what it was worth. Lorenzo, on the phone from Bicicletta Ercolo, groaned at the news they were going to attempt to resurrect the bike themselves. He sent instructions and washed his hands of the operation. Arkady went ahead. It mainly demanded patience and a steady stream of obscenities. And rags. He and Zhenya and everything they touched were covered in grease.

Zhenya had asked one question: "Have you ever done this before?"

"No."

Zhenya was impressed.

They washed sand from the crank and the bearings of the derailleurs, adjusted the tension of the cables and wiped every surface with solvent and oil. Arkady tightened the gear screws until the derailleurs shifted smoothly. He thought that perhaps when they were done, the result would look more like a tricycle, but whatever money Arkady could get for it, he intended to give to Vova and his sisters. The bicycle's provenance and pedigree were issues; who ever heard of a Pantera in Kaliningrad? In any case, if he had left the bike it would most likely have been claimed by the police.

Tatiana was in Belgium receiving another prize for journalism. Then to Rome for more honors while Arkady took care of her dog. He considered retiring from the prosecutor's office and taking up golf. The game looked pretty simple.

Zhenya adjusted the brakes, tightening and twisting a holding bolt so the pads made full contact with the rim of the bike, testing the bolt to be sure it wouldn't slip or break.

Lotte was in a women's chess tournament in Cairo. She called Zhenya twice a day. There was no more talk about the army.

Anya covered fashion.

Maxim finally had a poem published.

Svetlana and Snowflake had disappeared.

Zhenya corrected bent spokes, squeezing them like harp strings. He and Arkady cleaned the shifters and brake levers. Pumped the tires, polished the bike's frame until it had the sheen of black satin and the logo of a red panther seemed to leap off the frame. When Arkady spun the wheels, they sang.

Martin Cruz Smith

Gorky Park

*They lay peacefully, even artfully, under their thawing crust
of ice, the centre one on its back, hands folded as if for
a religious funeral, the other two turned, arms out
under the ice like flanking emblems on embossed
writing paper. They were wearing ice skates.*

*Pribluda shouldered Arkady aside. 'When I am satisfied
questions of state security are not involved, then you begin.'*

It did indeed become a triple murder investigation
for Chief Investigator Arkady Renko. Three corpses had
been found in Moscow. But why the horrific mutilations?
And why had they been buried in the snows of Gorky Park?

'Magnificently sustained, rich and mature, it is
a book to read and re-read' *Financial Times*

Paperback ISBN: 978-1-47113-108-0
eBook ISBN: 978-1-84983-822-1

Martin Cruz Smith
Polar Star

Arkady Renko, former Chief Investigator of the
Moscow Town Prosecutor's Office, made too many
enemies and lost the favour of his party.

After a self-imposed exile in Siberia, Renko toils on the
'slime line' of a factory ship in the Bering Sea. But when
an adventurous Georgian woman comes up with the
day's catch, the signs of murder are undeniable.

Up against the Soviet bureaucracy in a complex
international web, Renko must once again become the
obsessed, dedicated investigator he once was. And in doing
so, he discovers much more than he bargained for . . .

'A true storyteller . . . think Joseph Conrad on
amphetamines' *Newsweek*

Paperback ISBN: 978-1-47113-109-7
eBook ISBN: 978-1-84983-824-5

Martin Cruz Smith

Red Square

Arkady Renko has returned to Moscow from his exile in
the darkest reaches of the Soviet Union. He is reinstated
as an Investigator in the Moscow Militsiya, only to find
the home he once knew so well is crumbling under
a new world order – the Russian mafia.

After the brutal murder of a black-market banker, Renko finds
himself wrapped in the rich, ruthless and highly powerful
underworld of the new elite. The case will take Renko on an
international journey that will lead him to someone he thought
was lost to him forever – defector Irina Asanova.

'One of those writers that anyone who is serious about
their craft views with respect bordering on awe'
Val McDermid

Paperback ISBN: 978-1-47113-110-3
eBook ISBN: 978-1-84983-825-2

This book and other **Martin Cruz Smith** titles are available from your local bookshop or can be ordered direct from the publisher.